The Golem of 2020

by
Robin Bailes

The Universal Library Books

@robinbailes

Cover by Books By Design -
www.pikapublications.co.uk/BooksByDesign

Prologue – The Artist and the Astrologer

"Hello, astrology fans and welcome back to another episode of *Your Stars*, with Al the Astrologer. That's me!"

The web-series was shot using a phone on the end of a selfie stick, with audio barely audible in the wind as 'Al the Astrologer' presented from the roof of a tower block, where he had set up a telescope to study the stars.

"Now if you look there, you'll be able to see – can you see? – you'll be able to see Venus in the sixth house. What does this mean? Change is what it means, people. Change is a-coming. I don't know what. Could it be the end of Lockdown? The end of the pandemic? Doesn't look big or friendly enough for that, but something is coming, my friends. Something not big, something not small, but something. And you guys know I hate to be the bearer of bad tidings but I don't think it looks good. Mercury is in retrograde and that's always a bad sign. That said, I don't know that it looks all bad either. Something not good, something not bad; something not big, something not small. It's coming people. You know it, because Al the Astrologer sa…"

The artist paused the video and took a moment to contemplate the enthused (some might say 'insane') expression of London-based YouTuber, Al the Astrologer. His overall message seemed to be, '*Something vague is coming*', which was at least a more honest prediction than most astrologers were willing to make. But, however lacking in fortune-telling chops Al might be, something about him had caught the artist's imagination.

The artist's real name was Benjamin Lowe, but to the art community and the general public he was better known by the pseudonym 'Henrik'. At least, he hoped one day to be better known to the art community and the general public by the pseudonym 'Henrik'. He hoped that the time would come when that name would trip off the tongue as readily as that of Banksy. There weren't many celebrity artists, and while it was, in many ways, a betrayal of his artistic integrity, Henrik dearly wanted to be one. Then he would show all those people who had sneered at his work. And, of course, cash in big time.

It now seemed as if his moment had come.

A week ago, when he realised that the time was right, Henrik set to work. Since then he had lived in his studio, as fired up as he could ever remember being. He felt like one of those athletes who has hit a rare patch of form and can suddenly do no wrong. The clay flowed beneath his hands, his fingers finding features that lay buried within the unsculpted lump, waiting for him to unearth them, features that had lived in his head for almost ten years in anticipation of this moment.

He worked close up to the clay, the smell of it in his nostrils, eyes intently on his task, using his fingernails to score fine detail rather than the wire tools he usually favoured – this was personal and he wanted to feel it. That said, he spent time smoothing away any fingerprints with his palette knife, removing all trace of himself – it was his, but it was also everybody's. That was important; it could not *appear* to be his.

For that week he lived and breathed the clay, sleeping on the battered, slip-stained sofa by the wall, tasting clay as he ate from his unwashed hands. In fact, he ate and slept sparingly, resenting every moment spent away from his work. He needed to get this out now, in the fit of passion, before that lightning strike of creative energy left him. He had spent so long dreaming of this, but it still felt new and exciting. Every moment was a discovery; what might the clay show him next?

The statue's head was finished first, and he used a ball-tipped tool to gouge the eyes, giving it an intense stare. Through its arms and torso he lavished the same care, picking out in clay those specific details he had researched and sweated over through the idea's conception. Down its stocky legs he worked – it would need a strong stance, for it would stand unsupported (that too seemed important to him). Finally, its feet, where he allowed himself a trace of humour, and on the soles of which he inscribed the pattern of interlocking Hebrew characters which he had designed on a November afternoon three years earlier.

After an intensive five days of work, Henrik stood back to

look at what he had created: The Golem.

It was an extraordinary moment, to look upon the gleaming reality of something that lived in his head for so long, now lying on his work bench waiting to be fired.

But while the statue was finished, it was also incomplete.

The Golem, to Henrik at least, was a Gestalt entity; many minds in one body. In the Jewish legends from which it came, it embodied the Ghetto. His version would embody London. And it would do so in the fashion by which the Golem was always given life; by the written word.

In the most famous version of the legend that word was the Hebrew 'emet', meaning 'truth'. But in the modern world, 'Truth' had become eroded by perception, by perspective, by opinion. It was mass-owned, purchased, resprayed and sold on as something else to an unsuspecting buyer who took it on faith without looking closely at what lay beneath the paint. It was press releases and social media gossip, fake news and pub rumour, unsubstantiated, deliberately divisive and tribal. 'Truth' had become complicated, so it could no longer be represented by one word. Henrik's Golem would have its own truth, spoken by the people.

Where that would truth come from was a question that Henrik had struggled to answer, until his online research lighted on a web-series, shot on the top of a tower block in South-East London.

"Hello, astrology fans and welcome back to another episode of *Your Stars*, with Al the Astrologer. That's me!"

Henrik used a cheese wire to slice the Golem into sections, scooping out the clay from within and filling the void with slips of paper, dozens of them, each one bearing a Truth, the truth of an individual, all coming together to make the truth of The People. This was what would elevate a statue into a symbol, and art into Art.

That night, Henrik hunkered by the kiln, the tension making him sweat as much as the roaring heat, the strange alchemy of fire, clay and paper coming together to make something greater than the sum of its parts. Or it could crack irreparably and take his dream with it – he knew that this was not something he could recreate.

The '*ding*' of the timer seemed too prosaic for the solemnity of the occasion.

    Henrik took a deep breath, and opened the door of the kiln…

    "Something not good, something not bad; something not big, something not small. It's coming people. You know it, because Al the Astrologer says so."

Chapter 1 – Harrigan

Former detective inspector, late of the Cambridge City Police and ex-resident of Cambridge, Clive Harrigan sometimes felt that he was defined by things that he no longer was. But that was probably just lockdown-brain.

Lockdown, a concept that had seemed unthinkable not so long ago, was now a month old, a desperate response to a virus called Covid 19 that no one had even heard of six months ago, and which now dominated, and dictated, everyday life.

2020 was a weird year.

The door sounded abnormally loud when Harrigan closed it, not exactly echoing but seeming to expand to fill the empty street. As goldfish are supposed to grow to fit the size of their bowl, so it seemed to Harrigan that small sounds had got louder to fit the silence that was so much bigger than it had used to be. Birdsong, cars going by, even the tick of a clock; it had all got bigger. He was still a relative newcomer to London, but even to him the emptiness of the streets and the silence that muffled them like a blanket was disconcerting.

He checked the door, then walked off down the street, feeling like the last man on earth. The parked cars sat idle, the traffic lights looked bored, the road felt expansively wide while the houses seemed to huddle together for protection. He heard the wind in the distance and waited for the tumbleweed to blow by, completing the ghost town ambience. You were *never* able to hear the wind in London. In the middle of the road, a cat had curled up to sleep, just because it could.

Each footstep sounded like a gunshot, and Harrigan realised that it was not just the oppressive silence that was doing it; it was the sensation that he ought not to be out. His footsteps had a guilty echo, and he felt as if he should be wearing a badge (or possibly carrying a sign) that said '*I have a valid reason for travel*'. This would be his first time *out* out since Lockdown had descended. He had thought he would enjoy the sensation of freedom after weeks of being cooped up, made crazy by the sight of his own walls, but it was just making him nervous and, again, guilty. Even with his legitimate reason, he felt judgement from the windows of the houses to either side of him, and he had a hunch that his sons would not approve.

His mind flashed back to a phone conversation that had been only a few weeks ago and yet seemed to have taken place in another age.

"No, Dad, that's not okay."

Harrigan sighed. "Will, it's just to the shops. It's fifteen minutes there and back. And that's if there's a queue."

"A queue? Do you understand how transmission works?" Will snapped back at his father. "Or do you think infection takes a full half hour? You need to take this seriously."

"I am taking this seriously." Harrigan didn't much like being berated by his son.

"Then why are you going out?"

"I've still got to eat, haven't I?"

"*I* will go shopping for you," Will said firmly. "Or if I can't, then Don will."

"I'm not putting Don to the trouble, he doesn't live anywhere near..."

"He doesn't mind. I don't mind. And even if we did, we would still do it. This is not up for negotiation, Dad."

Harrigan pouted. "So it's okay for you two to go to the shops?"

"No, it's not," Will retorted. "Ideally you would have your shopping delivered – God knows that's what I'd be doing if I could get a slot, but they're like gold dust right now. But Don and I are low risk, while you, like it or not, are older."

"You mean old."

"Fine, if you want to be like that then, yes; old. You've seen the stats on TV, you've seen the death figures..."

"I don't watch those briefings," dismissed Harrigan. "I don't believe a word they say."

"Well tune in ten minutes late and you get to listen to scientists rather than politicians."

"I don't believe a word they say, either."

10

"And what with your degrees in epidemiology and virology I take your opinion very seriously," said Will, sarcastically. "Just because you lived in Cambridge doesn't make you a scientist. Haven't you got friends back home who work at the University?"

In fact, owing to a case he had worked on, Harrigan did have acquaintances in the biochemistry department of Cambridge University, but he had not contacted them because... well, because he could guess what they would say and he didn't want to hear it.

It was all a big fuss over nothing. You couldn't let something like this dictate how you lived your life.

"Dad," Will went on, "you're in a high risk age group and you're not exactly a model of fitness. *You are at risk.*" He paused. "For the love of God, Dad, we've only just started talking again, I don't want that to come to an end."

He might have meant that he didn't want to lose his temper and hang up. He might have, but he didn't.

And Harrigan realised two things. Firstly, that you didn't *have* to let something like this dictate how you lived your life, but if you had a family then it was the responsible thing to do. Secondly, this might actually be a big fuss over something.

"So if I want a paper...?"

"If you want a paper then you can damn well go online and get the news there like a normal person," said Will. "But if you need something important, like milk, then yes, give me a call and I will bring it to you. But I won't be coming in for a cup of tea. I'll be standing a safe distance from the door waving."

There had been a time, not so long ago, when even that was more than Harrigan could have expected from either of his sons. All things being considered, he ought to be touched that they still cared so much about his wellbeing.

"It's for a few weeks, Dad," Will remonstrated. "You just need to keep yourself to yourself for a few weeks. Then we can all meet up again."

After years of distance, a few extra weeks apart ought not to have been such a big deal, and yet Harrigan felt the burn of frustration. More than anything, it seemed unfair.

It was less than a year ago that, following his retirement from the Cambridge Police Force, Harrigan had sold the little flat that had been his home since his marriage had ended, and moved to the big city. London had never held any appeal for him and didn't now, but it was where his sons lived and so it was where Harrigan would now live. He had not been the best father. Even now, it hurt to think it. Perhaps especially now, because now there was no going back, no way to change things and be there when it had mattered, when they were kids. He couldn't fix the past, but the future was still up for grabs. A near-death experience had brought his sons to his bedside and he was determined not to let them go again; so London it was.

And it had worked out better than he had expected. He had got to know his sons again (for the first time really), he had got to know their wives and their children. His grandchildren. He had *four* grandchildren (a fact that still astonished him); John, May, Greta and little Hans (Don's wife was German).

Christmas 2019 had been the best he could remember, as had Will invited him to spend it with the two families, who always got together on the day itself. The children had been a riot; John, the eldest and therefore the ringleader, led the others in a series of ever more manic games, while their parents tried to get them to calm down and be respectful while others were opening presents. Hans, the youngest, was not quite old enough to understand Christmas, but understood that he was being given a bunch of new stuff. Harrigan had spent four and a half hours in one toy shop, pacing the aisles, picking things up and putting them back, trying to make up his mind what to buy kids whom he barely knew. The sight of their eyes lighting up with excitement when they opened the presents was one that he would take to his grave. He had bought May a plush stegosaurus (she was going to be the next Mary Anning) and as soon as she saw what it was, before the paper was fully off, she hugged it and said it was the '*best thing ever*'. Harrigan felt like he'd won Christmas. They'd eaten lunch together and in the afternoon Will's in-laws had arrived, bringing yet more presents. Harrigan had bought them chocolates and wine, which seemed a safe bet, and they had bought him a scarf, which looked more expensive than the chocolates and wine combined. They seemed nice and they clearly loved Will. Into the evening they all played games together until the children, one by one, became too tired to keep their eyes open and were drifted off to bed. Harrigan sat in an armchair which had been positioned in the corner just for him and watched his two sons laughing together; being husbands, being fathers, doing, easily and naturally, what he himself had failed to do. He didn't feel proud (he could take no responsibility for them) he felt lucky. For the first time in a very long time, Clive Harrigan felt part of a family. He resisted requests for him to stay the night, but promised to be back early Boxing Day morning, then he went home and cried for a bit before bed. It had been the best day of his life.

The New Year promised more of such days – maybe not quite like that one, but good days, happy days, days spent together. There was no hurry, the kids were still young and there was lots of time. 2020 was going to be a great year, a fresh start.

If you want to make God laugh then tell him your plans.

"Could you bring the kids along when you deliver my shopping?" asked Harrigan, tentatively. "I know they can't come in, but… Just so they remember what I look like."

"They know who you are." Will's voice had softened now that his Dad seemed to be doing what he was told. "But yes, of course I'll bring them."

"I do appreciate what you're doing."

"It won't be for long," Will reassured him. "But if it seems like it might drag on past three weeks then we might try a video call."

"I've got no idea how that would work," admitted Harrigan, who could only deal with technology by accepting that it was all basically magic and leaving it at that.

"Dead easy. I'll send you a link. I can talk you through on the phone if anything goes wrong."

"That'd be good."

"We can get Don on as well. The whole family."

"The *whole* family?"

"We can chat with Mum separately."

13

"How are the kids managing?"

"They'd rather be at school with their friends but they're not bouncing off the walls yet. I don't know how people in little flats are managing. Must be so difficult."

Harrigan nodded. There were some big families crammed into tiny, box-like apartments in tower blocks that they now could not leave; this would be toughest on them.

"I've got to go. And you'll call me if there is anything – *anything* – you need?"

"I will," Harrigan agreed, adding, "And, likewise; if there's anything I can do for you then let me know."

"What we need you to do is stay put and take care of yourself."

And that was the worst of it. For a parent, even a lapsed one like Harrigan, not being able to help your kids was the worst of it. For a former-policeman, it went deeper. It would be too much to call him a man of action (*way* too much), but a man of *activity*. In times of crisis, Harrigan's first reaction was always; *what can I do?* It was incredibly frustrating when the answer came back; *not a damn thing.* Perhaps that was the underappreciated malaise of the 2020 Lockdown: people wanted to help, and not only were they unable to do so but they were actively dissuaded from trying. The best way to help was to stay put and do nothing, and people did not respond well to that. Harrigan remembered a works party, back in his early years on the force; they had hired a little venue adjacent to Parker's Piece and, afterwards, the man who ran it had asked if everyone could leave swiftly so he could clear up. Naturally, people offered to help, but he knew where everything went so their help would only be a hindrance; they should just go. But that didn't stop them from 'helping', actually making matters worse as the man had to keep moving things that had been put back wrongly. And the helpers kept apologising for messing it up and he kept saying '*Well it's probably best if I do it alone*' but they still kept 'helping'. People find it very difficult to accept that doing nothing is sometimes the best help you can be.

For Harrigan, that situation was exacerbated by the fact that his girlfriend was still working *and* helping. Apparently.

"You can't tell me what you're doing?"

Elsa shook her head, making the corkscrew curls of her red hair bounce. "I can't even tell you where I'm going."

"You're not supposed to travel."

"We sort of have to. It's essential travel. How's your food?"

Harrigan shrugged. "It's good. I got take-out. Been getting it too much, to be honest. You?"

"I cooked. Which may have been an error."

It was their goodbye dinner but, cautiously abiding by the current restrictions, they were having it via video chat (Will had been right, it was dead easy).

Harrigan went back and forth on referring to Elsa as his 'girlfriend'. On the one hand it seemed juvenile and inappropriate for a man in his early 60s and a woman who, while younger than Harrigan, was no spring chicken either. On the other hand, he liked the look on people's faces when he used the word. It made him feel young.

"You know, I've never pressed about what you actually *do*," said Harrigan slowly, aware he was broaching a forbidden subject.

"And I've always appreciated that."

"I even lied to the boys about it."

"How are they doing?" asked Elsa, forbidding the subject once again by changing it.

"They're good."

"And the kids?"

"They're great." She knew that Harrigan couldn't resist talking about his grandchildren. "Full of energy. We video chatted the other night. May was showing me pictures she'd been drawing and there was one of you."

"Really?"

"I'll send you a copy." One thing about Lockdown, it was forcing Harrigan to get more comfortable with technology. "I'll be honest, I wouldn't call it photo-realistic – you're mostly boots and hair – but I do think she's captured something of you."

"A little artist in the making."

Harrigan grinned. That was what he had said.

"So if you can't tell me where you're going or what you'll be doing, then can you tell me when you'll be back?"

"I don't even know that myself," replied Elsa.

Harrigan was quiet a moment. He had met Elsa through work, when they had both been in pursuit of a serial killer who had turned out to be invisible. Pursuing serial killers was his line of work, pursuing invisible people was hers. It was no surprise that such work was secret, and the secrecy did not stop with the job; he did not even know her surname, and was quietly confident 'Elsa' was an alias.

It seemed a pretty shaky basis for a relationship, but somehow it did work. They liked each other. The boys had liked her, the kids had *loved* her. It was the sort of romance that Harrigan had not expected to happen at his time of life, and if the compromise was a certain vagueness about details like what she did, where she went and what her name was, then it was one he was willing to make.

Before Lockdown there had been tentative talk of moving in together. Now she was off on some new mission. And 'mission' was the word – he knew that much.

"It's important, then?"

Elsa paused for a long time, fork halfway to her mouth.

"Are you thinking or has my screen frozen?"

"Thinking. Yeah. I'd say it was important."

"You had to think about it."

"Definitions of 'important' have been in flux recently. I used to think what I did was pretty big, but right now I wouldn't put myself up against a bus driver."

The pandemic had certainly redefined what jobs were 'important'; bus driver, street cleaner, bin-man, delivery person. It seemed to Harrigan that most of those jobs were done by people who had not been born in this country, and he was not wholly comfortable with the impression that Britain had imported a disposable workforce to keep the country moving while everyone else (himself included) sat around in splendid isolation until it was safe to go outside again. It was nice that the importance of what they did was now being recognised, but it was probably too much to hope that society could hang onto those redefinitions once all this was over. In a couple of weeks. The end of Lockdown was always a couple of weeks away, no matter how many it lasted.

"Will you be in danger?" Harrigan asked.

"Damn it all, Harrigan," she had always called him Harrigan – another thing he liked about her as he had never really felt like a 'Clive', "you know the score."

He did. Her job was dangerous. If it wasn't an invisible man then… well, he actually didn't know what else she faced. You couldn't base a career around invisible men so there had to be other things. Nothing good. Nothing safe.

"At least be careful of… You know? Pack masks. Hand sanitiser." Even if he didn't know what other dangers she would be facing, there was always the virus.

"I'm not in such a high risk group as you."

"Indeed." Harrigan dared to raise an eyebrow.

"Are you commenting on a lady's age?"

"All I said was 'indeed'."

"Your eyebrow went up."

"It was acting without my permission."

He would miss this; the back and forth. He would miss her sparky presence, the way she made him feel ten years younger, how good she was with his grandchildren. He would miss her curling up beside him as they watched *His Girl Friday, Bringing Up Baby* or some other fast-talking Howard Hawks film (*The Thing From Another World,* perhaps), his face full of her curly hair – he never minded. He would miss the smell of her shampoo as well. He would miss her alongside him in the little bed that now seemed huge. He had never been to her place (did not even know where her place was), but that was part of the deal. Whatever she did, it put a strain on a relationship, but perhaps they treasured the moments all the more for that. This would not be the first time that she had gone off on a mission for weeks on end. He was always worried, but this time he was *worried*.

He had a vague idea that she was out there keeping the world

17

safe for everyone else, but this time the world wasn't safe to start with.

It had made it difficult – to know that Elsa was out there helping (albeit it in a non-specific and probably quite unusual capacity) while all he could do was stay at home. It had grated as much as all the other strictures of Lockdown. Harrigan was not a man who went out every night or even every day, but he had always known that he *could*. Losing that had affected him more than he had anticipated. What *did* you do? The time hung heavy.

So he had tried to help. He had joined his local neighbourhood support scheme, only to discover that people of his age were expected to be more helped than helping. He had joined the NHS Volunteers, but having sold his car (*'No one needs a car in London, Dad'*) he was only eligible to be a call and check volunteer, which meant calling lonely, elderly people and making sure they were alright. Important work, but after one call Harrigan was reasonably sure that he had made things much worse. He was not someone you spoke to for comfort.

Then the call had gone out for volunteers *in his age bracket* for a vaccine trial.

The empty streets had a curious familiarity and Harrigan realised he was remembering a zombie movie that had been on TV the other night (what were the schedulers thinking?!). It was that emptiness, that silence, that stillness, and then, in the distance, you a saw a figure – the only other person on the street – and your heart clutched in your chest as you wondered if this was going to be the person who killed you.

Back in the day, Harrigan had worked his share of night shifts, walking alone through the nocturnal streets of Cambridge at two or three am, and, outside of the obligatory drunk students, it had been empty. But not like this. It was the quiet more than the emptiness. It was as if the Lockdown restrictions had silenced everyone, and that silence sat heavy on the country's chest, crushing the air from it. Everyone was waiting for what happened next; how long could this last? How bad could it get? Surely it'll be over by summer? And that *not knowing* seemed to have become tangible, so you could taste the tension on the breeze. It was like having suspects pinned down in a house; you had told them to come out but got no response, so now it was a matter of kicking in the door and there was no way this was ending well; that tension in the air beforehand.

Everyone knew, Harrigan realised, that more people were going to die. Every day brought a grim and ever-rising death toll. They all wondered who was next; my neighbour? My friend? Me?

The figure at the end of the street passed on, and Harrigan was ashamed at how relieved he was. The figure hadn't shuffled like the walking dead, but that was how it had felt.

"They're coming to get you, Barbara!"

Harrigan nearly leapt out of skin as the words echoed about the empty street, bouncing from house to house, hiding which window they had been shouted from. Laughter followed.

Trying to not to judge, Harrigan walked on. People were stir crazy and you had to make your own entertainment. At least they had good taste in film.

It was a long walk to the Trial Centre, but Harrigan had decided against the bus, for obvious reasons. Besides, it was a fine day, and it *was* good to be out (although it was embarrassing how much his legs ached – he would have to start walking around his living room or something). During the journey, Harrigan's nerves loosened somewhat. He was out for a walk, it was something he had used to do habitually; no need to be scared. He was also starting to feel good. After weeks of doing nothing, of being a useless drain on his sons and society in general, he was *doing* something. He sort of wanted a badge that said that. What was the badge that Tony Hancock had wanted in *The Blood Donor*? '*He gaveth unto others so that others might live*'. Yeah, something like that.

That said, every passer-by made him tense and he started unconsciously judging every one of them (*I've got a reason valid to be out – do you?*). London was not the friendliest of British cities and, let's be honest, British cities are not that friendly to begin with, because they are full of British people who consider a casual '*Good morning*' to be an outrageous intrusion into their privacy. Even so,

Harrigan was taken with how people no longer even acknowledged each other, as if the dreaded Covid could be passed through eye contact or smiling. Even in good times, Londoners did not smile at each other, but it now felt so much more deliberate.

"Hey! Hey mate!"

He had almost reached the Trial Centre when the sound of someone actually speaking to him made Harrigan's heart do calisthenics and he jerked back a step.

"Yeah mate. Here mate. You wanna buy a roll?"

The voice had come from a man with a handkerchief tied about his mouth that looked more likely to add to the dangers of infection than mitigate them. He was lurking down an alley, as if he had been told that this was what black market vendors did, and was palming a roll of toilet paper from hand to hand like a rugby ball.

"Five pounds a roll."

"No thanks."

"Four fifty then. There's none left in the shops, you know. You don't want to end up crapping into your hand. Three fifty."

"I'm all set, thank you."

Harrigan hurried on towards the Trial Centre. No matter how bad the situation, there were always people who profited.

Chapter 2 – It Rises

It rose…

It gave the impression of having slunk out of a sewer, a cellar or a grave, and perhaps It had. It belonged in the darkness, amongst the rot and the rats, bathed in the stench of decay; unseen, waiting. Where It had first come from, who could say? But It rose up now from the depths where It had lain dormant, drawn up by the scent of disease and the dying. The world had turned while It had slept and eventually arrived at this point again, as it always would. The crises that drew It were the immutable of existence and so It rose to meet them, to take advantage of Its natural prey.

The streets above were empty now, but even had they not been It would have passed quite easily through the tides of humanity, not because It looked like one of them – far from it – but because they did not see It unless they looked. And they never looked. Because such things did not exist.

It lived among them, but they never saw It. And so It thrived.

From the buildings, that lined the empty streets, It smelt – almost felt – the press of humanity, crammed into their homes, sealed away, huddled in sweaty fear. It felt their cramped heat, It tasted their terror on the air. It took no satisfaction in the knowledge that now they had one more thing to be afraid of – that was not in Its nature. It was not a hunter, It was not a killer, It did not revel in the pursuit of Its prey or play cat and mouse games. It was a feeder; It consumed.

People talked about the circle of life, but from the creature's point of view it was more a pyramid than a circle, and it was good to be at the top.

So much to choose from. The trails of smells criss-crossed as It crept soundlessly along the street, moving through the shadows, insinuating Its way between whatever light pierced the night. For a moment, a stray car headlight caught It before It could recede into the shadow, and a person looking at that exact moment might have glimpsed their worst nightmare come to life, eyes wide, mouth open to snarl at the hated light, clawed hands raised in defence. Then they would have shook their head and dismissed it as a delusion, a trick of the light or a terrified cat. After all, there was nothing there now – not that they could see.

Once It had fastened onto a trail It liked, one strong with the tang of infection, It sped up, still moving without a sound, stealthy as a wraith. On and on; following the scent with single-minded purpose. While It had slept for long decades It had had no need of sustenance, but now that It was awake once more, the hunger was on It and seemed to grow with every passing moment. It *had* to feed.

The trail led to a house like any other. The window was open which made things easier, though nothing would have kept It out at this point. Inside the lights were off. It did not stop to observe the photographs on the mantelpiece, the mementos of last year's holiday (to Florida) or the detritus of the evening meal (pasta) abandoned by the sink (the washing up would keep). It ignored the makeshift office set up at the kitchen table – diary and laptop neatly squared – everyone was working from home at the moment. Even had It noticed any of these things It would have understood none of them. It understood only the gnawing from within, and the smell that led up the stairs.

A loud coughing came from one of the doors that led off the landing, and a sympathetic voice spoke in a language It did not understand. The answering voice was in a comforting tone that said, '*I'm fine, it's just a cough*,' in any language. Another cough. Another brief, worried exchange.

During this It remained still in the stairwell, and you did not know what still was until you saw It remaining still. A shaft of moonlight through the window caught one of Its fangs and made it gleam, though those teeth had never been cleaned.

Finally, the noises of wakefulness drifted into those of slumber, though the cough kept on trying, breaking the rhythm of the sleeper's snores. It was the sort of cough you had to worry about at any time, and in the current times every cough made a person's stomach contract in anxiety, and for an instant they wondered; could it be?

The shadow on the stairs did not understand any of that, but

It could have told them what that cough was. Its nose made It the sort diagnostician that health services around the globe would have given their collective right arms for. It knew that this cough was exactly what was feared. It also knew that it didn't matter anymore, because the virus associated with that cough was not what was going to kill the sleeper.

It made no sound as It ascended the stairs, nor as It opened the bedroom door and breathed in the viral scent that had drawn It here. For a moment It experienced something that might be described as satisfaction, as It drew in that smell and knew that It had found Its first prey of this new season.

There were two figures in the bed, but they were like night and day; It saw only one of them, and that one might as well have been outlined in fluorescent yellow. It stole closer and stooped over the bed, over the nearer of the sleeping figures, who coughed again uncomfortably in his sleep.

Then It fed.

Chapter 3 – A Pin Cushion

"Hi, my name is Emily, I'll be looking after you today. What do I call you?"

"Harrigan," Harrigan replied, hastily adding, "Clive Harrigan," because, although he didn't like his first name, he didn't want to come across as a gruff, unfriendly old man. It oughtn't to have made a difference, but the fact that Nurse Emily… (he checked her name badge) …Jennings was black made him still more keen not to come across as unfriendly, in case it was misinterpreted. His generation (and especially men of his generation) did not have the best track record when it came to tolerance.

Nurse Emily smiled. "Pleased to meet you Clive."

Damn it. Now he was stuck as Clive.

"Did you drive yourself here today or did someone else drive you?"

Harrigan shook his head. "I walked." Who was there to drive him? He hadn't even told his sons about this yet, and he could imagine what they were going to say when he did.

"Really?" Nurse Emily smiled again. Was it possible that nurses got special training in smiling? She was very good at it. "That's what we like hear. It's a great way to keep fit."

"Too late for that," Harrigan replied, ruefully.

"Never too late," Nurse Emily insisted. "So, I've got some questions for you, then I'm going to take some blood and do some tests. Assuming all that goes well then you can come back in a couple of days and get your first dose of the trial drug. How does that sound?"

"Sounds great," said Harrigan, politely terrified.

"You're happy with all of that?"

"Absolutely." '*Happy*' was a pretty strong word but… Sure, why not?

"You can pull out at *any* time," Nurse Emily stressed. "Do you understand that?"

"I do."

"Are there any questions you'd like to ask me before we get

started?"

"I don't think so."

"Great." Nurse Emily turned to a laptop. "I, on the other hand, have a whole bunch of questions for you."

She wasn't kidding. They began with the usual '*Who are you and where do you come from?*' questions, that sounded like a game show, then continued into more personal areas.

"You live alone?" Nurse Emily's voice betrayed a shadow of concern.

"Is that a problem?"

"We'd prefer it if you didn't. Is there someone who can check on you?"

"I've got a girlfriend," said Harrigan, which was true but also deliberately misleading as she wasn't in the country. He was also aware that he sounded like a twelve year old boy trying to impress the thirteen year olds.

"But she doesn't live with you?"

"We were talking about it but… You know."

"Got cold feet?" suggested Nurse Emily.

"No. Got a pandemic."

"Oh." Nurse Emily blushed. "Sorry. Didn't mean to… What's her name?"

"Elsa. It asks that on the form?"

"No," Nurse Emily admitted. "I was just trying to move on from the awkwardness of me implying that your girlfriend wouldn't want to live with you. Would you like a different nurse?"

Harrigan shook his head. "No, I think I won that lottery." Was he okay to say that? Did it sound like an inappropriate suggestion? To Harrigan, talking to women in the modern world always seemed a minefield. Thank God for Elsa.

"Thank you," said Nurse Emily, her smile dispelling Harrigan's panic.

"She's younger than me. Elsa is." Why the hell had he told her that?

Nurse Emily laughed. "Way to go, Clive."

"Would you mind calling me Harrigan?" They seemed to be

getting on well enough for him to ask. "I never liked Clive."

"No? Does Elsa call you Harrigan?"

"She does, actually."

"Harrigan it is."

The questions continued and when they had all been answered to Nurse Emily's satisfaction, they moved onto blood. Harrigan put on his brave face when the needle went in and Nurse Emily proceeded to fill several colour-coded tubes.

"What did you do before you retired?" Making conversation was presumably another class that nurses took, alongside smiling.

"I was a detective. In Cambridge Police." He was more cautious of telling people that now than he had been when he lived in Cambridge, and particularly Nurse Emily, because... Well, the police had not exactly covered themselves in glory where race relations were concerned in recent years. Harrigan had always been proud of what he did and hated the idea of that pride being taken away. On the other hand he was an old, white, male, ex-policeman, which was perhaps the last thing a that young black woman wanted to be sitting opposite. On yet another hand, maybe he should let Nurse Emily make up her own mind rather than second-guessing what she might think of him based on the colour of her skin.

Once again, it was all a minefield to Harrigan.

"Interesting," murmured Emily, as she shook one of the tubes of his blood. She frowned, and Harrigan wondered what horrific thing she had spotted in the tube. "Cambridge? Were you there for that invisible man thing then?"

"Yes, I was in charge of that investigation."

"Really?"

The enthusiastic interest in Nurse Emily's voice raised the red flags and warning bells in Harrigan's head that should have gone off *before* he told her how heavily involved he had been.

"Err... Yes. Weird stuff."

"How did he do it all?"

Harrigan hemmed and hawed and waffled his way around an unsatisfying answer in which he used the word '*classified*' too many times and not very convincingly.

26

"Do you work here full-time?" he finished, moving the conversation away from stuff that he couldn't talk about or his girlfriend would have to kill him.

"No." Nurse Emily shook her head. "Most of the nurses here are volunteers, helping out in our spare time."

"I guess we all just want to help," said Harrigan.

Nurse Emily nodded, and Harrigan found himself looking at her properly for the first time and noticing how tired she looked. Careworn. Imagine being a nurse at a time like this and still feeling obligated to volunteer elsewhere – like you weren't doing enough already.

"You're all doing a really amazing job," said Harrigan. "I mean… I know that's not saying anything new but… you really are and we're all very grateful."

Nurse Emily ran a tired hand over her hair; straightened (though starting to bounce back) and tightly pulled into a pony tail.

"Thank you, Harrigan. It means a lot."

She really did look done in.

"You're all done for today. We'll get back to you and, all being well, we'll hopefully see you in a few days."

The tests came back positive or negative or whichever was the good one that allowed Harrigan to continue, and he returned a few days later so that Nurse Emily (they tried to make sure that you always saw the same face) could inject him with the trial drug. Harrigan went home feeling like a hero – like a caveman dragging a woolly mammoth behind him. A sensation that lasted until his weekly catch up with his sons.

"I just want to help," he tried to explain. "And look at it this way; I now get regular tests to check if I've got it."

"Fat lot of good that does," snorted Will. "You wouldn't need the tests if you just stayed indoors. I don't want to know *if* you've got it, I want to be sure you haven't." He sighed. "I'm sorry. I shouldn't go off at you. It's a pretty selfless thing you're doing."

It wasn't. He just hated feeling useless.

"We just want you to be safe," Will finished.

He felt safe. That was the problem. Everyone felt safe in

themselves, everyone was more worried about friends and family than themselves, and so everyone took risks and spread the damned virus themselves. It was the sort of thing that happened to other people. But, as the weeks passed, it became clearer and clearer that everyone was 'other people'. Slowly, those who, like Harrigan himself, had been initially dismissive, were won over by the science and by the dizzying death statistics, until the only hold-outs were die-hard conspiracy theorists and the terminally selfish.

The streets emptied even more, and the phrase '*spirit of the Blitz*' started getting dropped, because there is no event that the British public cannot somehow link to World War Two. It was not an inaccurate analogy; good Samaritans emerged as they always did in times of crisis. There were neighbourhood support groups, membership of volunteer organisations swelled and people started making their own masks and distributing them to those who couldn't afford them. Harrigan read about a tower block where some unseen do-gooder had started leaving anonymous care packages on people's doorsteps. People did what they could; a donation here, a few hours there. Some artist had built a statue to represent the spirit of London, which seemed idiotic to Harrigan but apparently it had brought people together. You did what you could with what you had.

That was the media-friendly face of the crisis, but, Harrigan considered, what everyone forgot about the Blitz was that criminals had taken advantage of it. Perhaps that was an old policeman's perspective but it was true, both then and now. Shops that stood silent and unprotected were easy prey for theft and looting, and no one asked where the contents of those anonymous care packages had come from. Frankly, Harrigan struggled to call the theft of toilet paper and hand sanitiser 'looting', but it never stopped there, because human nature said, '*If it's okay for me to take this, then I can take that as well*'. Then there were the big corporations, who remained operating out of public necessity and reaped huge financial benefits while insisting that their workers provide their own masks and gloves, because '*We're all in this together*'. That was a whole other type of crime.

But alongside the happy stories of human kindness, grey

areas of stolen bog roll and opportunists getting rich off a national disaster, there lurked the genuinely dark side that made Harrigan's blood boil.

"You would think," he roared down the phone to Don, "that at a time like this – when everyone is doing their best just to see another day – that people could be decent to each other! How do people like that look themselves in the face? What the hell has to happen to make a person like that? Can you be born a bastard or does shit have to happen to you?"

The empty streets were proving a hunting ground for some of society's most loathsome predators, and those who walked home alone at night had suddenly become much more vulnerable because there was no one else about. There had been some safety in numbers, but now the numbers were gone.

"And, you know, the only people going home at that time are key workers!" Harrigan ranted on furiously. "Care workers, medical staff, people working in supermarkets or some crappy menial job that we can't do without. They're all putting themselves at risk every damn day just by showing up and this is what they get?! What was this girl?" He grabbed the laptop on which he had read the news story. "See?! See?! She worked in an all-night pharmacy! Where is the justice in that?!"

The girl had been attacked on her way home. Precise details were not being made public, but she had not survived.

"What sort of scum does this?!"

"I don't know, Dad," Don had said, patiently. "But please tell me you're not going to start patrolling the streets with a baseball bat."

"Well somebody damn well should!"

It had been bad enough as a policeman, knowing that you couldn't save everybody. Now as a civilian he felt that he couldn't save anybody. London had been a nightmare for this sort of thing beforehand and it felt worse in Lockdown. The city was like a prison – one of those dodgy ones, run by the lowest bidder, where the inmates are in constant danger, and if you hear footsteps behind you then you don't look back, you just run.

Perhaps the country had always been like this and Lockdown just emphasised it, pushing people out to the extremes; the scum and the Samaritans.

Harrigan being Harrigan, and a career in the police being enough to imbue anyone with a healthy degree of cynicism, he wondered if the scum and the Samaritans were one and the same. Just because you handed out canned soup at the local foodbank didn't mean that you couldn't also prey on the vulnerable to whom you handed them. The world was never as black and white as it ought to be.

That was one thing he didn't miss about the police; too many decisions that left you choosing between fifty shades of grey.

It was three weeks after Harrigan had begun the drug trial. He had been back for twice weekly tests and check-ups since, and everything was fine; no ill-effects so far (although there was a fifty percent chance he was in the placebo group). Will had visited earlier that day to drop off the weekly shop, and had brought along John and May. The kids still struggled with the idea that they could not hug Grandad, but seeing them play together, answering their random questions and listening to their stream of consciousness accounts of what they had been doing made Harrigan's whole world brighter. Plus, he now had the ingredients to make chicken curry.

The rice was bubbling over as the phone rang and Harrigan juggled pots and pans while trying to answer.

"Harrigan."

"Hi." A small voice that was followed almost instantly by a big cough. Harrigan pulled away from the phone instinctively. Which was stupid, but if any cough could have infected a person through the airwaves then it was this one. "Is that Clive Harrigan?"

"Speaking," said Harrigan, coldly. Telemarketing fraud had increased during Lockdown, and Harrigan had lost count of the number of times he had been told that there was a problem with his computer.

"It's Emily Jennings. From the Trial Centre?"

"Yes, of course. Hi." Harrigan's heart jammed

30

uncomfortably into top gear. How bad were things that the Centre was calling him at this time of the evening? What had his bloodwork revealed? Would he even get to eat his last curry? "Is, is, is there a problem?"

"Well… Yes," said Nurse Emily. Then added. "Oh!" as she suddenly realised what Harrigan meant. "I mean no. Not with you. Sorry. I didn't think about how this would…" She broke off to cough some more.

"Are you alright?" Harrigan asked.

"Not great." Her voice sounded raw and weak. "I'll bounce back."

"You… errr…?" It was funny how the word had become taboo, like another 'C' word.

"Covid. Yeah," Emily confirmed. "Quarantining right now. Like I said, I'll bounce back."

She didn't sound too bouncy to Harrigan.

"Can I help?" He felt as if there had to be ninety or so people she could call before him, but if he could help then he would.

Emily laughed which turned into a coughing fit. "I'm sorted Covid-wise. One of my neighbours is shopping for me. All good. But… There's something else. Nothing to do with… you know. Something that happened before I got sick. I'd deal with it myself but I'm not breaking quarantine for anything – I *will not* be one of those people. I thought about calling the police but…" She sighed. "They wouldn't believe me. No one is going to believe me, they'll just think it's a fever dream. Covid brain. Even I'm starting to wonder, and *I know* it's real. It happened. It did."

She sounded as if she was trying to convince herself.

"I have to…" Emily paused. Coughed. Paused again. "I need you to hear me out. Don't tell me I'm nuts before I'm done."

"I wouldn't."

"Don't make any promises you can't keep, Harrigan," advised Emily. "Look, I…"

Another long pause, and her wheezing breathing made Harrigan wonder if she should even be talking.

"You never told me," she began to speak again, slow and

31

quiet. "You never told me how the invisible man did it."

"No," acknowledged Harrigan.

"I saw your face," Emily went on, the intensity in her tone mounting, straining her rasping voice still further. "The way you looked – there was stuff that didn't make the papers, right? Stuff you've never told anyone and if you did then they wouldn't believe you."

"Yes." He probably shouldn't have admitted that, but there was something going on here and he was going to be honest.

"Okay," she sounded relieved. "I'm going to tell you a story, and I think then you'll see why the only policeman I could turn to was one who believes in invisible men."

Chapter 4 – Emily Jennings

"So if you're a Taurus or a Leo then love is in your future. Or your past. Sometimes the two are the same. Now, if you're an Capricorn…"

As the bus reached her stop, Emily Jennings tugged out her earbuds and paused the video on her phone, cutting off Al the Astrologer mid-flow. She liked listening to Al on her way home, but the last leg of the journey was done on foot, and she preferred being able to hear. With a smiled '*thank you*' to the driver, she got off the bus, and walked down the road, between rows of darkened houses.

It was about five minutes later that she heard them; footsteps at her back.

Emily quickened her pace. It was late – or early, depending on your point of view. Either way it was dark, the streets were empty and quiet, and that quiet just magnified the sound of the footsteps.

The chances were in favour of them belonging to someone who, like Emily, had just finished a late shift and was on their way home. Or perhaps someone who had been unable to sleep and was taking advantage of the empty streets to go for a walk without having to worry about social distancing. It didn't have to be someone following her. The world was full of perfectly nice men who treated women respectfully.

Well… maybe not *full*.

Come to think of it, maybe they didn't even form a worldwide majority. But even if the balance was tilted in favour of men who could be jerks towards women, most of them kept that jerkish behaviour in their minds. Or at least on their tongues. They might say something unpleasant but would not actually act on it, and you could train yourself to let the words wash off. And Britain was, statistically, one of the better countries for this sort of thing, so that put the odds still more in Emily's favour. When you got right down to it (and it was not as if she had the statistics to hand), the chances of something bad happening to a woman walking home alone at night were probably about one in a million.

Which was very little comfort if you were the one. And still pretty horrifying when you considered how many million women were out there.

The footsteps seemed nearer now, and Emily was horribly aware of her heart beating somewhere towards the back of her throat. Her mouth was dry and she felt as if she couldn't breathe. She felt like a victim already, which was a bad mindset to get into.

The footsteps turned off somewhere behind her and Emily glanced back over her shoulder. The street was empty. She didn't even know if it had been a man or a woman.

Emily breathed again. Presumably there were people who walked the streets at night without being scared. She would have liked to try that. In fact, she had had cause to write down that wish recently, although in a fairly unusual context.

By the time Emily arrived at McDowall House, the tower block was attractively back-lit by the rising sun, burnishing the horizon. Emily couldn't help smiling. It was hardly the nicest place to live but at times like this you could only appreciate the old block. She was a city dweller by birth, and although that had been a more northerly city, she had taken to the capital like a pigeon to Trafalgar Square when she moved here, nearly ten years ago now, to study. London had a quiet beauty that most people missed while staring at their feet or grumbling about the transport, you had to look up to see it.

The lifts were working today and Emily went up to the 14th floor where she shared a flat with…

"Hi babe!" Jill greeted her, sprawled in her underwear on the sofa.

Emily forced a smile. "You're up early."

"Not gone to bed yet," Jill replied. "Only got in an hour ago."

Emily forced another shard of righteous anger to the back of her mind to go with all the others.

Jill – bone idle and apparently allergic to clothing – personified an attitude that some people (primarily in the sixteen to twenty five bracket, though Jill was twenty eight) had taken towards the pandemic; *I'm young, I'm fit, it won't hurt me, why should this interfere with my life?* Jill had not missed a single party since

34

Lockdown had come in, and seemed oblivious to Emily's barely stifled anger, as she recounted stories of fleeing through windows when the police arrived to break things up. Though Emily was only a year older than her flat-mate, Jill always made her feel like the uptight parent in an '80s teen comedy.

What made matters worse was that Emily was a nurse, working in a hospital, coming into daily contact with people who *definitely* had the virus, so Jill was potentially spreading what Emily brought back. She didn't like being made complicit.

"You had a good night?" Emily asked through gritted teeth.

"Just okay." Jill shook her head with a puzzled frown. "Not many people there."

"I wonder why," muttered Emily, darkly.

"You have a good night?"

The only thing that stopped Emily from gleefully strangling Jill (other than societal norms), was that Jill *genuinely* didn't get it. She genuinely didn't see that asking a nurse coming off a long shift, partway through a pandemic, if she had had 'a good night', was like asking someone vomiting off the side of a ship if they were enjoying the cruise.

"Not great," admitted Emily. There were precious few good nights. Or good days for that matter. Emily worried that her definition of 'good' had changed from not losing anyone to how few people they lost. London had been hit hard.

"I'm glad you're in." Jill sat up. "I wanted to tell you; I'm heading off for a bit."

"What?"

Jill shrugged. "London's a bit flat at the moment. Nobody's about, nobody wants to do anything. Some friends of mine have rented a place in the country and they've invited me down. So I'm going to ride out Lockdown with them. If that's okay with you."

It definitely wasn't okay with Emily. It was partying while the country burned and constituted the sort of unnecessary travel and social mixing that was one hundred percent illegal at the moment, not to mention vastly irresponsible. On the other hand, it got Jill out of the flat and out of Emily's high risk radius.

"Have a great time."

A week later, Emily woke in the silence of an empty flat, surrounded by an empty city, located in an empty country.

And yet, that emptiness was buffered by the population of McDowall House. The block was quieter than it once had been, but a community spirit remained, and if Mrs Ekman on the 7th floor couldn't asked her in for a cup of tea, then she still called hello from a safe distance and asked if Emily was eating properly. Eric Barry could no longer share the football scores with her, but he still told her what was wrong with the modern game, and Al the Astrologer (the only name by which Emily knew him) still gave her advice on when was a good time to date or a bad time to invest – neither of which she was doing much of, but it was nice to know.

McDowall House was owned and run by a corporation – a block of former council flats sold off to the highest bidder, who would probably, at some point, either tear it down and build something nicer or renovate the existing flats to attract a better (which was to say 'wealthier') class of resident. Either way, the current residents would be out. The corporation's public face was up and coming young developer, Paul Haworth, who visited the block from time to time, which was unusual for a monied corporate tycoon. Emily had spoken to him a few times and found him pleasant and approachable (which was even more unusual). She harboured the hope that he was too nice a man to just 'develop' the block with no concern for those who lived there. Who could say? Whatever its ultimate destiny, for now McDowall House was home to a wide cross-section of London's working class society, one of those places in which 'send them all home' Brexiteers rubbed shoulders (neither deliberately nor happily) with people fresh off the raft without a word of English. It was a melting pot, and like all melting pots it occasionally bubbled in worrying ways. But the residents were united in being from McDowall House, and that bond seemed to quiet things. That was true now more than ever. They were all separate, locked in their individual flats, forbidden to mix, and yet they were all in this together.

"Off to work?" asked Camilla, a working single mum two

36

doors down from Emily, looking out from her open doorway as Emily passed.

"Sort of. Volunteering," Emily replied with a smile.

"You never stop, do you?"

"Wouldn't know what to do with myself."

That was true, although Emily was starting to wonder if it might be nice to find out. Volunteering at the Vaccine Trial Centre had initially felt like a cheeky way out of Lockdown – she could go out while others could not. But it was still work, and the grind was starting to get her down. She had spent long minutes looking at herself in the mirror last night and was starting worry about the woman looking back. Emily had always been thin (She had never had a boyfriend whose mother had not attempted to feed her up), but she was now drifting into gaunt. Her eyes were shadowed, her cheeks seemed hollow, and the incised marks from the medical grade mask she wore at the hospital took longer to fade each time she wore it, her skin not springing back as it had used to.

She needed a break, but she wasn't the only one, and she'd only feel guilty about it.

"Emily!"

Camilla's daughter, Ursula (5 going on 6), charged past her mother in the direction of Emily, and had to be hauled back through the doorway by her hoodie. Ursula was an affectionate child who found it hard to adjust to not being able to hug people.

"Urs?" Camilla admonished.

"Sorry."

"Hi Ursula," Emily smiled.

"We've got flour!" the little girl enthused.

"You have? That's great."

Shops had suffered various shortages and the lack of flour had been a sore point with Ursula, because it meant that her Mummy was unable to make apple pie. Lockdown did not seem so bad to a five year old with access to apple pie.

"My Guardian Angel brought it," Ursula announced, proudly.

"Did he?" Emily did her best to sound impressed.

Ursula nodded in that way children have that makes it look as if their head is about to drop off. "He left it outside the door."

"Wow."

"Go play, Urs," her mother urged.

The child ran off and Emily gave Camilla a questioning look. "Guardian Angel? Or did Sainsburys come through with a slot?"

Camilla shrugged. "Well it wasn't bloody Sainsburys. Guardian Angel's as good an explanation as any. I've no idea who left it. (By the way, if you need flour, I now have white, brown, rye, self-raising – whatever you want, I've got it.) I heard a couple of people got toilet paper. Same deal. Just left on the doorstep."

"I wonder who's doing it." The gifts had been showing up here and there for days now.

Camilla shrugged. "If you hear anything – you know; around the block – let me know. I'd like to thank them. A little thing like that makes a world of difference to Urs. Do you know she asked the Golem for flour? Like she was writing a letter to Santa."

The Golem.

That was an odd one.

(The idea had first occurred to the artist, Henrik, during the London riots of 2011, and he had immediately recognised it as the perfect way to capture the shared frustrations of a disparate population, united in their sense that something was wrong. Unfortunately (for Henrik) the riots didn't last long enough for him to complete the project, and those tensions which had boiled over to create them were brought back to a light simmer once more. It was such a good idea that Henrik considered putting it out there anyway, commenting on events retrospectively. But he knew that it would never have the same impact that way. He decided instead to sit on it and wait for another suitable moment.

At times through the years, as protests swelled and waned, as movements came and went, and as the capital frequently threatened to erupt but remained forever rumbling like a volcano that couldn't make up its mind, his thoughts turned to *that* project. In his head it was The One, the work that would make his name, but he increasingly wondered if the opportunity to actually do it – that perfect moment – would ever arrive.

Then came 2020…

Along with the rest of the world, Henrik watched in slack-jawed disbelief as what many had dismissed as a bad dose of flu in a Chinese city they'd never heard of, became a global pandemic, driving the UK into Lockdown, something which had seemed science fiction a fortnight ago. Henrik was as shocked as anyone, but perhaps not as devastated as some. Looking out from his studio window at a caged populace, he knew the time had come; he would build the Golem.

Unlike the rioters, who had proved sadly lacking in staying power, the Corona virus seemed to be going nowhere fast. As Lockdown entered its second week, the consensus was that the end of the crisis was still weeks away, perhaps even months. For Henrik, it meant that he had time, but not a vast amount of it. Fortunately, the project – the Golem – had been on his mind for almost ten years. It loomed in his dreams and taunted him with its brilliance every time one of his concepts was described as '*poorly thought-out*', '*derivative*' or '*a waste of clay*'. He was more than ready to go.

The look of the thing was important, not just from an aesthetic standpoint but from a symbolic one. If the Golem was not for everyone then it was not for anyone; it had to represent The People, which wasn't easy in a city with as diverse a population as London. Henrik spent time creating a face that blended different racial characteristics into an harmonious whole, a face that could not be pinned down to a definite racial origin, but with which everyone could identify. In its costume too, he picked out delicate touches in the clay that tied it to this community or that (hints of a Bangladeshi fotua, Creole jewellery around its neck). All that said, he decided to retain the distinctive 'Egyptian' hair-do that was most associated with the Golem, because it looked right to him (although he suspected it was an invention of one film or another). Finally, as a nod to the modern world, he gave the Golem trainers, and, even though no one would ever see it, designed a bespoke tread for the soles inscribed with interlocking characters of the Hebrew alphabet, roughly spelling out '*left*' and '*right*'.

Interestingly, despite his focussed intent on inclusivity and making the Golem 'for everyone', it never even occurred to Henrik to make it female, or even androgynous. Because no one is perfect.

As he had with every other aspect of the Golem, Henrik had considered the question of cultural appropriation much over the years. Though clay people brought to life with magic were to be found in many cultures, the Golem was specifically Jewish, as was the method of giving it life via the written word (although Henrik would have to confess that his own vision was equally influenced by Terry Pratchett's *Feet of Clay*). Unavoidably, Henrik was literally appropriating a Jewish legend (and a religious one at that) for his own artistic purpose. On the other hand, his Golem would be as much for the Jewish community as it was for everyone else. There was a fine line between cultural appropriation and celebrating the diversity of London, and Henrik chose to believe that his project fell on the right side of that line. It was also true that, if you were going to appropriate elements of another culture to your own artistic and/or commercial ends, then, however wrong it might be, people were less likely to get angry if that culture was Semitic.

That sort of quiet discrimination was one reason that his Golem would be important; it would stand for the unspoken. All of them.

That was Henrik's next problem. He had always intended the Golem to represent London, and in a broader sense British society, but that scale made the idea impractical. He needed to reduce further, to base the Golem around a single community that would represent London, which would in turn represent Britain. But what discrete community was diverse enough to fulfil that brief?

It was late one night in 2015 when he started from his bed and snatched up the pen and paper that he always kept there in case of nocturnal inspiration. He scribbled down two words and then went to sleep, smiling happily. The words were '*tower block*'.

There were areas of London, which were still dominated by the tower block. They were an eyesore and people didn't really like them, yet could also be fiercely defensive of them. The tribal nature of humanity meant that people were very clear which block they were from and that became part of their identity. They housed hundreds of people of all backgrounds and cultures; those born here and those just arrived; all religions, races and creeds represented under one roof, and while they might not all know each other and had nothing else in common, they had that one roof. That was London.

But which block?

In an ideal world, Henrik would have gone out to study potential blocks to decide which was the best one around which to base his Golem. But the same circumstances that made now the perfect time for the Golem to appear also made this a world that was anything but 'ideal'. Much as he thought that the pursuit of Art should be considered 'essential travel', he had a hunch that the police would feel differently, and his research was therefore limited to online.

The enforced confinement of lockdown (something that particularly affected tower-dwellers) had led to an explosion of online creativity, and Henrik trawled through podcasts and YouTube videos made within the blocks, as people strove to stave off cabin fever any way they could. He did not know exactly what he was looking for, but assumed that he would know when he saw it.

"With Mars in the counter-clockwise aspect and Uranus in descension it's time to hunker down people, cos I'm seeing change on the horizon. Change is in the air."

Astrological symbolism played a role in more than one of the golem legends and Henrik was not one to ignore signs from fate, but it was Al the Astrologer's attitude that really drew the artist. He was relentlessly up-beat, even when delivering dire predictions about what 'change' might bring, seeming to embody the *'Keep Calm and Carry On'* spirit that Britons like to believe is a national trait.

"...and right here, right here in Lockdown London, I'm afraid we're looking at death, people. But that's the way of life. Death is just change and when I look at the arcs of the luminaries, I see us coming out the other side."

Al the Astrologer turned out to be a resident of McDowall House, a tower block in South-East London. Its inhabitants would soon play a pivotal role in the Golem Project.)

Three weeks ago, Emily, along with everyone else in McDowall House, had got a letter through her door from an artist who said that he was creating an artwork to unite spirits through the pandemic, and he needed people to contribute a slip of paper with a single declarative statement on it. He called them 'Truths'. It could be anything: something you wanted, something you cared about, something that mattered to you in these troubled times, a wish for the future, a plea for the present, a rant at the what made you mad, something you'd never told anyone or your personal soap box, *anything*, big or small.

Like a lot of art projects it had sounded a bit pointless to Emily, but it didn't seem to be pulling funding from healthcare so she decided to follow through, and actually spent a long time deciding what to write. In the end she went for something that was personal but also universal,

I'd like to be safe walking home at night.

It didn't seem a lot to ask and it didn't seem likely that an artist was going to fix the problem, but she actually felt better for writing it. Maybe it wasn't as dumb as it seemed; even if the only positive impact it could have was a mental one then that was still worth something.

After saying goodbye to Camilla, Emily carried on down through the block, taking the stairs. A few years ago when the lift was out she had been forced to walk the fourteen flights and she now did it regularly just to stay fit – she didn't have time to go running and was aware that, while she spent her days on her feet, she ate crap because it was quick, easy and cheap.

"Morning." She nodded a polite hello to the couple she often passed on the first floor, and felt the pang of guilt she always did that she had never learnt their names, which felt like something that she should have done. Emily was one of those people who spend their lives plagued by what they *should have done.*

The woman returned the nod with a shy smile, while her husband, who was taking out the rubbish, gave her a suspicious glower. They were, Emily believed, recent immigrants – Syrian perhaps, but she didn't even know that.

Leaving through the main doors and crossing the broken concrete of the plaza, Emily walked past the spot where the local council had re-erected the clay statue known as 'The Golem', after they had cleaned the graffiti off of it. It had first appeared directly outside the doors of McDowall House, but now stood some small distance away – still close but no longer an obstruction in case of fire alarm. There had been talk of a plinth, but the artist (who called himself Henrik, for reasons that were presumably artistic) insisted that it remain at ground level, on a par with the people it represented.

Because she saw it every day, Emily had quickly come to regard it as just another piece of the background landscape, and tended to walk straight past, but it was worth stopping now and then because there *was* something remarkable about it. For starters, it now had no graffiti on it. After that first time, when it had been removed for cleaning, there was an assumption that it would have to be cleaned again, perhaps regularly, but that hadn't happened. In a very brief time, the people of the block had adopted the McDowall Golem as their own, something to be treated with respect and protected. More than once, on her way to work, Emily had seen people from the block cleaning off graffiti, and that graffiti was certainly not the work of anyone from McDowall House – this was *their* Golem.

Its stern but not unfriendly features were unpainted, leaving it a uniform terracotta from head to foot. Its costume was decorated with various words and symbols which might have meant something or just be artistic embellishment. It stood in a neutral pose, very upright, arms down but held out from its sides, chest thrust forward, seeming almost to swell with what it contained. Baked within it were all the slips of paper – the 'Truths' – with the hopes, fears, dreams, pleas, rants, loves and hates of McDowall House.

The fact that it contained all this, combined with the way in which it had been adopted as an icon of the block, gave the Golem an almost religious significance, and so those slips of paper took on

43

the appearance of prayers, whether they said,

Tories out!

or,

We will survive.

Some were pleas for world peace, others just asked for toilet paper, a few pointed out what a waste of time this was, but, inevitably, the majority were about Covid:

Don't let CV come here.

I just want the pandemic to be over.

Keep us all safe from Corona Virus.

Protect me, my family, this block.

But Covid wasn't the only thing going on in the world; there was anguish and indignation from all sides of the political spectrum. Angry voices shouting at each other, buried within the clay. There was one hell of an argument going on behind the Golem's impassive features. The poor statue probably didn't know if it was coming or going.

Immigrants go home!

Smash the patriarchy!

Brexit now!

Lockdown is illegal!

Black lives matter!

People tended to assume a level of activism on Emily's part, partly because of her skin colour (which she mildly resented, as she did all assumptions made on that basis), and partly because of her father. Before moving north to marry Emily's mother, Abel Jennings had been a name in London's black community; he had marched to Portnall Road with the Mangrove demonstration in 1970 and to Hyde Park after the New Cross fire in '81. It was a formidable legacy, and Emily knew that her Dad was disappointed that she had not carried on that legacy (*'You've got to pick a side, Princess'*). But maybe inter-generational strife was a family trait.

Unusually, the majority of Emily's family (at least on her father's side) had been in Britain as long as anyone knew. They were presumably of African origin somewhere down the line, but how and when they had arrived no one had been able to find out (or perhaps had not looked, as it was unlikely to have been a voluntary arrival). Her Dad liked to tell the story of when The Windrush had arrived, bearing its influx of Caribbean immigrants; Emily's grandfather had been furiously opposed to *'All these foreigners coming over here'*. It had caused much friction between father and son. Her Dad saw himself as black first and British second, while her grandfather had been the reverse.

And Emily? She saw herself as Emily first. And she did feel guilty about that, as if she was letting everyone down by not being more... defined. Her grandfather (who had died when she was ten) had been proud to be British, her father was proud to be black, Emily was happy to be both but militant about neither, and preferred that her identity be linked to things she did rather than things she was.

What pride she had, therefore (and she was a fairly self-effacing person), Emily reserved for her role as a nurse in the NHS, the greatest health service in the world (and if you wanted to see Emily angry then just try denying it). It was all she had ever wanted to do, and even in such troubled times she did not regret it. She was eternally grateful to her Dad, and to the men and women like him who had given her generation the opportunities they took for granted, but that was *their* way of standing up to be counted, this was hers. It wasn't that she disagreed with what was being said at current rallies and protests, but Emily was not a natural shouter, and felt that quietly getting on with things that needed doing was an alternative form of protest. It was something on which she and her Dad would likely never agree, but she never the less carried his voice with her in her head (*'You have to stand up for what you believe in, Princess.'*). It was often a critical voice, but never a harsh one, and as she headed off for a half day of helping people through the vaccine trial process followed by a night shift in the busy Covid wards, caring for people, some of whom would never leave that building, she took comfort from the knowledge that *this* was what she believed in.

Which didn't stop the whole issue from being another of Emily's guilty '*should have done*'s, but it helped.

When had she last called home? There was something else to be guilty about.

The McDowall Golem watched her walk away. Its eyes were wide, the pupils scored into the clay, the irises gouged out, creating a shadow that gave the Golem a piercing stare.

Somehow, it did embody it all; the flour and the toilet paper, the hope and the hate. The Golem seemed a symbol for the whole seething, contradictory mass of it.

Things were slow at the Trial Centre that day, and one of the staff, knowing Emily's hectic schedule, covered for her while she slept an hour in the staff room under a pair of coats.

Unfortunately, though she felt as if she needed the sleep, a single hour of rest just left her feeling crappier than before as she headed off for her night shift at the hospital.

"Try to ration gloves today, we're getting low."

Here it was not slow. Here they prayed for things to just be fast. Fast would be a relief from furious.

"We have new Covid protocols, you need to learn these."

People were coming in faster than they were going out, the wards swelled and overflowed. Other patients were moved and more wards were made into Covid wards with hastily erected safety precautions.

"We're five people down. I'm ringing round for help but it's the same everywhere."

On her break, Emily huddled in a corner reading a much-thumbed copy of Terry Pratchett's *Guards, Guards!*. She had started re-reading all his books during Lockdown because they offered a fantasy world into which she could escape, and because they were one thing that could always make her smile.

"It's my husband – he's not breathing properly!"

And through it all there were the patients themselves. They all knew the score. They all knew the odds. They all knew that they might not see family again.

"How are you doing today?"

Some sat in silence, nothing to do but worry. Others liked to talk but lacked the breath to do so.

"The family needs an update. Whose turn is it?"

Once they reached a certain point they would not be able to do anything but lie there, unaware of their surroundings, a machine doing their breathing for them.

"He needs to go on a ventilator."

Everyone knew that once you hit that point, things were bad.

"Have we even got one free?"

When her shift ended, Emily went and sat quietly in the staff room for a while, breathing in and out. When things had first started to ratchet up, it was not uncommon to find people in tears at the end of a shift – Emily had been one of them more than once. That didn't happen so much anymore. Not because things had got better – in fact they had got worse – but because they had slowly become hardened to it. Maybe that was the worst of it.

Actually, no. That wasn't the worst of it. Not even close.

One of the good things about living in London was that you could not get stranded. No matter how late it was there was always a night bus to take you to at least within walking distance of where you were going.

"And if you want my opinion, friends, the stars are as good a guide to what happens next as the science. Better in many ways.

'*We're following the science,*' they say. I say; try following the stars."

Emily sat in a corner of the night bus, listening to Al the Astrologer, head against the window, slipping back and forth in the condensation. There was always at least one person not wearing a mask. They looked at Emily, seeing the uniform, daring her to say something. She never did. If you could look around and still think that it didn't apply to you, then nothing that Emily or anyone else could say would change your mind.

The nearest stop was still a twenty minute walk from McDowall House, which was why Emily had such strong feelings about walking home at night.

"Thanks." Emily nodded to the bus driver as she got off. There was another group doing a great job, and pretty thankless one at that. No one was clapping for bus drivers.

The streets were empty again as she walked for home, her feet feeling like lumps of lead.

The footsteps…

Why was it that the streets were always empty when she got off the damn bus and yet, minutes later, there was always someone behind her? They never seemed to mean her any harm, but at the end of a long night and a long day the last thing she needed was heart palpitations.

The footsteps kept coming, and Emily, as she usually did, sped up.

So did the footsteps.

They had not done that before.

Without meaning to, Emily went still faster, her heart racing. She did not want it to look as if she was running but her legs weren't listening to her.

The footsteps sped up again, keeping pace.

They were different tonight. They had purpose. And there was no ambiguity of gender; these were a *man's* footsteps, heavy and solid. Maybe it was a trick of the echo in amongst the houses but they sounded like cannon fire coming down, closing in, right on her heels.

Panicked and terrified, Emily turned off the main road. She didn't know where she was going but she was close enough to McDowall House now that she was sure all roads would lead there eventually. The footsteps would follow the main road of course, and then she would laugh about how foolish she had been.

But they didn't. They followed her. Not running, but fast, regular; long, determined strides pounding the pavement.

Emily broke into a run. She didn't have the strength for it but it was amazing the strength you could find when you had to. Normally she wouldn't have run, because it was probably just a passer-by and running made you look stupid, but stuff like that had now ceased to matter. She just wanted to get away, to not hear the footsteps, she just wanted…

I'd like to be safe walking home at night.

The words seemed to ring in her ear.

Still running, she took another random turn and choked out a half-cry half-sob as she came up against a chained gate, blocking her way.

The footsteps followed, coming to a sudden and complete stop behind her.

Emily spun around, her bag grasped like a weapon, ready to defend herself however she could.

The Golem stood before her.

Chapter 5 – The Guardian Angel

The Golem did not move. It was as if someone had crept up behind Emily and placed the statue there as a joke. Her breathing came in long, strained gasps as she stared into the unblinking ceramic eyes. Maybe it *was* a joke? Either that or she was losing her mind, because this could not be real. Maybe she was asleep on the bus and would wake up at the depot any moment – she had done that before.

She took a step to the side and was unable to suppress a squeak of hysterical terror as the Golem moved with her, going from immobile to moving to immobile again in a single fluid motion. Emily clamped a hand over her mouth, now just trying to stop herself from throwing up. It had been a long and emotional day, in a long and emotional week, part of a long and emotional month in the worst year that anyone could remember, and things showed no sign of getting any better. If she had started seeing things then she would not be the first. It didn't feel like a dream or a delusion, but if the delusional were able to identify their delusions then they wouldn't be deluded. Would they?

"Who's in there?" she hissed sharply. That was it. It was a costume. A mask. Some bastard thought this was funny. It was the sort of thing that people dreamed up to pass the time during Lockdown and never thought about how it might affect the victims of their dumb practical jokes. A film of it would probably show up on YouTube.

"Take the damn mask off. You fooled me, you frightened me. Well done. Hope that makes you feel like a big man. Now take it off!"

She needed it to be a joke. Because if it wasn't then it was in her head. There *was* no other option. She would admit no other option.

The Golem stood. When it was still, then it was *so* still that it gave the impression it could never have moved in the first place.

It was dark here, but the face did not look like a mask. It looked like the rough terracotta surface of the statue itself.

"Take it off." It was almost a whisper. A desperate plea.

The Golem did not move.

Gingerly, her hand shaking uncontrollably, Emily reached forward to touch the statue's cheek. It still did not move when she touched it and felt the cool surface of the fired clay. She pressed, but found no give in it. It did not feel like a mask. Hand still shaking, she rapped the cheek with a knuckle and heard the melodious '*dung*' of the terracotta.

It was real.

There was no way around it. This was not someone in a costume. It was not a dream or an hallucination (or if it was then she was too far gone to be helped). It was there in front of her, as solid and tangible as it was impossible.

She took a step forward and bit her lip almost to blood as the Golem stepped back.

She stepped back and the Golem stepped forward, keeping its position in relation to her.

Why in the hell was it doing this?

That was probably a lesser question compared to '*how* was it doing this?' or 'had she gone mad?', but it was odd behaviour. Then again, what was normal behaviour for a clay statue that had come to life?

"Why are you doing this to me?"

The Golem offered no answer.

To this point, Emily's eyes had been trained on the Golem's face, its impassive expression, that she had seen so many times, now oddly horrifying. But when she looked it up and down she spotted something else.

"You've been shopping."

She felt hysterical. It was such a stupid thing to say. But there, hanging from the Golem's hands, were a pair of shopping bags (re-useable, she noted, how environmentally sound of it).

"May I?"

The Golem made no move as Emily cautiously peeped inside one of the bags.

Flour.

"You're the Guardian Angel." Young Ursula had wanted

51

apple pie so much that she had asked the Golem for it.

We need flour. So my Mummy can make apple pie.

This was insane. But it triggered a new thought in Emily. She stepped forward again and the Golem stepped back. She took another few steps and it moved out of her way, allowing her to pass then falling in behind her like a presidential bodyguard. She came to a stop and the Golem did the same.

I'd like to be safe walking home at night.

Perhaps she should have said '*I'd like to not be scared*', but… Was she really considering this as a possibility? The Golem was following her because she had asked to be safe? Was that crazier than it bringing flour for the little girl two doors down?

In situations like this (not that there were many situations like this) then the most obvious answer was usually the right one. But the most obvious answer was that Emily had lost her mind, and she was not quite ready to accept that yet, despite some pretty compelling evidence. She was starting to think more clearly now, the panic fading.

"Okay. Thank you."

She started walking again and the Golem walked with her, its heavy feet pounding the rain-washed pavement, the steps metronomically exact. Emily did not look back at it, she just listened to the thudding of the footsteps, pounding above the thudding of her heart.

It did actually make her feel safer.

Back at the block, the Golem followed Emily through the doors, then walked briskly past her as if she no longer existed. It had done its job where she was concerned. Now their roles were reversed, Emily feeling compelled to follow the walking statue. It made a few stops, dropping off bags and boxes to those whose 'Truths' had been retail-based, like young Ollie Maxwell, whose slip of paper, written in a slow, round hand, had read;

I want to eat chocolate every day.

His parents might not let him, but they now had enough of the stuff for it to be feasible.

The flour went outside Camilla's door. Not all of it was the plain flour needed for apple pie, but Ursula had not specified so the Golem had picked up everything that qualified as flour, from self-raising to gluten-free.

Its errands complete, the Golem headed back the way it had come, hollow footsteps echoing up and down the stairwell. Emily trailed after it, exhausted but driven on by curiosity.

Out through the main doors the Golem stamped, across the poorly lit plaza. Here it came to another of those abrupt halts, going from fast motion (despite its bulk it could walk at quite a speed) to total stillness in the blink of an eye.

For a minute or so, Emily watched it. The sun was coming up, the sky creeping into bluey grey, smeared with dirty clouds that promised rain later.

The Golem did not move.

Emily stole up to the statue.

"Are you awake?" She gave it a little push then jumped back in case it moved.

But no reaction came.

"Hello?" She tapped it and waved a hand in front of its eyes.

Nothing. The Golem was done for the night.

So was Emily. As the adventure came to a close so the rush of adrenalin that had kept her going drained away and a tide of physical and mental exhaustion poured through her, leadening every limb. She needed sleep; it would all make sense after sleep. She couldn't imagine how, but... it had to.

The Golem towered over her. Its eyes crackled with green fire and when it opened its mouth a red light shone out. It reached down to her, picking her up and Emily suddenly realised that it was gigantic. Holding her in one hand, it climbed McDowall House, swatting

53

away bi-planes with the other. At the top, it beat its chest, opening its mouth to roar, though the only sound that came out was a ringing, that persisted even after its mouth closed...

Emily started awake, the doorbell breaking the bizarre dream. Her head felt as if it was full of cushions and her eyes refused to stay open. With a grunting groan like a stag in the mating season, she buried her head in the pillows, but the doorbell kept screaming.

She tried to focus on the clock by her bed. *Six?!* You had to be kidding! She had barely got an hour's sleep. What selfish, hell-spawned bastard was ringing her bell at six in the morning?

Not without an effort, Emily dragged her unwilling body out of bed, every inch of her begging to slink back under the covers, and tugged on a robe. A face mask hung on the door handle to remind her not to go out without it (Covid life hack #41), she put it on and opened the door.

"What?" Emily was the politest of people but everyone has their limit.

"Emily?" It was the wife from the probably Syrian family downstairs, and Emily was awake enough to feel guilty that she didn't know the woman's name.

"Yes?"

"You are a Nurse? Yes?"

Emily's mind was scrambled with exhaustion and the events of the night, to the extent that she was no longer sure those events had been real, but that was the sort of question that could wake you up. "Yes."

"My husband has a very bad cough." The woman had a strong accent but there was no mistaking the fear in her voice.

"He needs to stay in," Emily tried to speak kindly. "Isolate for ten days. You too. If he gets worse then call an ambulance."

"He says it is nothing. He wants to go to work."

Emily shook her head, though her brain stubbornly stayed where it was, rubbing on the inside of her skull. "No. He has to stay in."

"We cannot afford it." The woman sounded so plaintive.

"There's compensation available." She just wanted to go back to bed, not give a presentation on financial planning in the age Covid. "If he talks to his employer…"

"There will be forms." She said it quietly, but even Emily's sleep-deprived brain picked up on the dark tone in which the word *forms* was said. They didn't want to deal with anything 'Official', anything that might draw attention to them. Which probably meant that they were in the country illegally and were afraid of being sent back.

"Can you look at him?" the woman asked, desperately. "He might listen to you."

Emily rubbed a hand across her forehead, which seemed to throb with the confusion within. "Okay."

A few minutes later, Emily was downstairs, blinking back tiredness. After the wild fantasy of the night, this was a cold blast of reality. The husband came to the door, scowling irritably. He wore a bus driver's uniform – Emily hadn't known that. Bus drivers and transport staff were a high-risk group. She had seen a lot of them in the hospital and, statistically, they were more likely to catch the virus and to die from it. No wonder his wife was worried.

Keeping her distance, Emily went through the motions of a physical exam, peering into the man's open mouth from two metres away, asking him to take his temperature with a digital thermometer she had brought down from her flat. It was mostly for show – she knew the symptoms as well as everyone else did and already knew what she was going to tell the man.

"It could be Covid – Corona virus." People were still getting turned about by what the two terms meant. "You need to isolate."

The wife translated, but Emily had noticed that her husband had reacted dismissively as soon as Emily spoke. He understood English, perhaps could speak it too, but he chose not to.

"You say 'could'," the wife spoke back to Emily. "So it could not?"

"They're not uncommon symptoms, which is why everyone has to isolate as a matter of safety. The whole household."

Now it was the wife's turn to shake her head. "I have to go

shopping. I have to work. I clean."

It sometimes seemed as if London was cleaned exclusively by a quiet army of immigrant labour. How dirty would the city be if they all went home?

"I understand – someone can…" Emily sighed. "*I* can go shopping for you. But this is important. Most people get better quickly – do either of you have any other conditions? – No? In ten days…"

"We cannot lose ten days work."

"Then you have to see about sick pay. You won't lose out if…"

They were both shaking their heads, still scared of being discovered, of deportation.

"There is a test." The husband spoke, confirming Emily's suspicion.

"Yes," the wife nodded. "If we must miss work then we must be sure there is a reason."

Emily shook her head. "They're only testing people when they come into hospital."

There was talk of mass testing for everyone who had symptoms, or even those who didn't, but at the moment the capacity simply didn't exist. Even NHS staff were only tested on a semi-regular basis, and that depended on how many tests were available that week. There weren't enough tests, and every country in the world wanted them by the million right now.

"You work in a hospital." Again, the woman said it in that pleading tone that made Emily feel guilty before she even answered.

"It's not that simple."

It wasn't. But shouldn't it have been? Tests existed and here were two people who definitely needed them. Shouldn't that be the qualification? They stood outside the system so could not benefit from what compensation was available, and yet they both served that system as bus driver and cleaner. 'Key Workers' was one of a handful of phrases that had not existed two months ago and was now used every day.

From beyond the couple, from one of the rooms in their flat,

Emily heard a baby start to cry. It was as if someone had poked the child just to make Emily feel more guilty than she already did. Perhaps someone had. She hadn't known they had a child, she didn't know if they had more than one. You lived so close to your neighbours, saw them out and about, but you seldom knew much of what lay behind the closed door.

"If you don't go into work today, if you *stay here* and see no one, then I'll see what I can do."

The wife translated, even if it wasn't necessary, keeping up the pretence.

"You will get us a test?" her husband asked.

"I'll see what I can do." She was too tired to think about what she actually could do, too tired to be making decisions like this.

"Very well."

Head still whirling and utterly exhausted, Emily dragged herself back to her flat and to her bed. In the ordinary scheme of things, that conversation would have been enough to keep her awake, but she was simply too tired, and was asleep as soon as she dropped, full length onto the bed.

What the hell have I done?

Feeling better for a few more hours sleep, Emily got up at eleven and made coffee so strong it looked like tar, then added three sugars to make it drinkable.

What the hell had she done?

From a moral standpoint there were arguments to be made, but if you starting making them then pretty soon other arguments got in the way. The… (damn it! She still didn't know their names) …family deserved a test, but they were far from the only ones. The way things were, every test was needed. If she took one then it was depriving someone else, and who was she to say whose need was greater? That was why you left decisions like this to the people in charge, who had access to all the facts and figures. Plus, leaving it to them absolved you of blame.

She could not take a test from the hospital, not after all she had seen.

But the Trial Centre…

There were always surplus tests there, sitting on a shelf in case of emergency. They were *needed* – it wasn't like they were being wasted – but the need was not so urgent. They could be replaced before the need arose. She wouldn't be depriving anyone.

It was still theft, and that was something with which Emily remained uncomfortable. But wasn't theft occasionally justified? And if not in time of national crisis then when? '*There is a higher law,*' said her Dad's voice.

Unbidden, Emily's mind took her back to last night. Wherever the Golem had got those bags of flour, it certainly hadn't popped into Sainsburys with its Nectar card to buy them. It had stolen them. But hadn't the look on Ursula's face been worth that?

Emily threw together a meal that could have been breakfast or lunch (she just had generic 'meals' these days, her schedule too screwed up for anything else), ate quickly, then headed out. As she passed the Golem she took confidence from it, as if it was giving her enterprise a tacit thumbs up.

Of course, if everyone did stuff like this then that would be anarchy and…

Emily shook her head clear. She had made her decision and she didn't want to think about it. It might be wrong but she couldn't go back now and tell the family that she had changed her mind.

The Trial Centre was quiet when she arrived. No one questioned her being there when she wasn't rostered on, because volunteers came and went. It was actually very easy. She knew where the tests were kept, they weren't under lock and key, there weren't many people about and those there were knew her. She took a test (*one* – if the husband was ill the wife would have to isolate anyway), and left.

She did feel guilty. That was partly because she was Emily and guilt was her default state, and partly because she had something to feel guilty about. She had done something wrong and it might yet come back to bite her. Come to think of it, if she was found out and word got back to the hospital then…

Again she shook her head clear. Sometimes you had to

follow your conscience. It was unclear if this was one of those times, but it had better be.

When she started at the Trial Centre, Emily's plan had been to volunteer on those days when she was not working, but that had left her mentally and physically zombified, so she now tried to make sure that she had one complete day off each week, one day on which she was neither working nor volunteering and could just decompress.

But once she had taken care of the test (the result would be in tomorrow – one more thing for the husband to scowl about), her mind inevitably returned to the events of the night before. The shock of her early awakening, the subsequent decision and her low-key heist at the Trial Centre had left her with no brain space for anything else, even something as remarkable as last night's adventure. With all that other stuff taken care of (for now), she was again free to wonder if she was losing her mind.

Putting on her mask, she left the flat.

"Oh, hi Emily." Camilla's door was usually open, allowing Ursula the limited playground of the corridor, now that other areas were denied to her by Lockdown – a child's imagination could turn a stairwell into another world. Another Covid life hack.

"Hi," Emily returned. "Sorry to bother you, I was just wondering… Did you get another flour delivery last night?"

Camilla nodded. "I did. You don't want some, do you? I've got more than I can use."

"Not much of a baker."

"Well, if you change your mind. I don't suppose you found out who left it?"

Emily shook her head. "Sorry. How's Urs?"

"She's painting flowers on the walls of her bedroom," smiled Camilla. "Which is better than her bouncing off them."

"What do you do with a kid that age stuck inside all day?"

Camilla shrugged. "I make her apple pie."

Back in her own flat, Emily went and sat on the sofa. The flour had been delivered, so that part at least had not been in her head. And someone must have delivered it.

59

Was it possible that it had been Emily herself? She clearly had the capacity for theft. Had she unconsciously created this fantasy about the Golem to cushion her mind from her own actions?

If she had, then this was worse than she had feared.

There was only one thing to do. Much as Emily would have liked, and much as she really needed, a good night's sleep, she knew where she was going to be tonight.

Despite Lockdown, there were still people on the streets during the afternoon and early evening, although it was night and day compared to how busy they had been before. But as night fell, the streets emptied and London, a city that usually got about as much sleep as New York, became a ghost town.

Emily shivered, and wished that she hadn't thought the phrase 'ghost town'.

The Golem stood. That was all it did. Which was all you could really expect of a statue. Emily glanced at her watch, and considered that if she went home now she could still get a decent night's sleep.

But something kept her there.

Beforehand, she had decided that, if the Golem was going to move, then it was going to do so at some propitious moment; sunset or midnight. But it was in fact at eleven twenty seven – a time that seemed to have no significance at all – that the Golem came to life.

It did so on the instant. There was no gradual reawakening or stretching the stiffness from its pottery limbs; one instant it was a statue, the next a living thing, striding away down the street as if it had already been mid-stride.

For a moment, Emily remained frozen, until she had to remind herself to breathe, then she took off after it.

As it hit the high street, it became quickly apparent where the Golem was heading and Emily tried to get in front of it.

"No; there's no need. They're all set for flour. They don't need any more. You've done that one. They're grateful, but no more. You can cross it off your list."

But the Golem's list was baked into its body, part of its DNA

(DN-clay?). You could not cross something off of your soul. It kept walking.

"There are other people you could help," said Emily. She was not quite sure what she was doing now; saving an innocent bakery from yet another robbery or trying to help people whom the Golem had so far neglected. "People need…" What the hell did people need? "You'd be a great delivery person."

The stride did not slow. It had its orders.

"I know someone who lives not far from here who had to give up her cleaner when Lockdown came in. She's in her nineties and can't manage. I mean…" Emily paused. "We'd have to find a way to explain you (or keep her out while you're there) but we can get around that. That would be really helpful. And I bet you'd be a great cleaner." It certainly wouldn't leave the job half done.

But the Golem did not deviate from its course.

"Does it have to be stuff for the block?" asked Emily. "Is that all you can do? Cos there are people there who probably need a hand too. Maybe odd jobs. Picking up prescriptions. Collecting shopping rather than stealing it. You could do that. That would be really helpful to people."

If the Golem heard her then it gave no sign of it.

"In McDowall House." Emily tried treating the Golem like a computer; you had to find the correct command. "The people of McDowall House would be greatly helped by you picking up their shopping for them. Or doing odd jobs. Cleaning."

None of it had any affect. The Golem stomped on towards whatever bakery it was raiding tonight.

But it wasn't just about the block was it? That was part of it – it was the McDowall Golem – but everything she had seen it do so far had come from those slips of paper, the 'Truths'. She could reel off all the useful chores she wanted, but they had to relate back to what was inside it.

"You must have been asked for more than flour, chocolate and toilet paper."

She tried to remember what people had written. The trouble was that most of them had gone with big concepts that were very meaningful but not practical.

Antisemitism <u>is</u> racism!

Laudable, but what's a Golem to do?

Then there was all that stuff about Lockdown, Covid and the pandemic. The Golem wasn't really in a position to stop any of that.

Then again... maybe it was all a matter of how it was worded.

"Helping people through the pandemic – ending it, in fact," Emily tried to choose her words with care, "it's not just the big things, it's the little ones. Hand sanitiser kills Covid and... Whoa! That's not what I..."

Despite its size and the impressive momentum it could build up, the Golem could change direction on the head of a pin. The instant the words '*kills Covid*' were out of Emily's lips it veered off in a new direction. It was like watching an oil tanker execute a pirouette.

"Where are you going? What are you doing?"

The Golem kept walking. Perhaps Emily was imagining expressions onto its blank face but it seemed more determined now, as if it had been aware of its own shortcomings and was re-energised by the ability to fulfil more of its internal commands.

"Can we talk about this?" Emily suggested, jogging alongside to keep up. "I mean... Oh no..."

They were heading for a chemists.

"No... No. This isn't what I meant. I..."

The Golem did not even slow as it reached the metal shutter that covered the front of the shop, it ploughed through it, the metal buckling, the glass beyond shattering as the clay man just kept walking.

"Let's hope that takes out the security camera," muttered Emily. Although around here, most security cameras were fake. No one cared what happened to people in this area, even if you had video evidence.

On the bright side, this proved beyond doubt that it was not *her* committing the thefts and imagining the Golem, because she could not have done that. This was real. Very real.

From beyond the caved-in shop front, Emily could hear the Golem 'shopping', and her natural guilt level rose again. If she had known what it would do, then…

But there *was* a shortage of hand sanitiser. Certain bastards had bought it up and were now selling it at a jacked-up price, which people would pay because they were desperate. She hadn't wanted it to cause property damage – this was someone's livelihood – but… It might save lives.

It was never black and white. It would have been easier if someone could have laid out the pros and cons for her beforehand: how many lives were saved, what sort of insurance the chemist had, was the chemist a nice guy. That sort of information would have been helpful.

The Golem emerged carrying a bag. From the looks of it, the chemist had not had a great deal of hand sanitiser in stock. That would not stop the Golem, it was already on the move again.

This time, Emily did not follow.

By any measure, Emily could generate a healthy amount of guilt. She was good at beating herself up for pretty much everything. And yet, as she walked home, keen to grab what sleep she could, she did not feel as guilty as she would have expected. People were going to benefit from the Golem's crimes, this was stuff that was desperately needed by desperate people living through desperate times. Everyone was struggling, but for those towards the bottom of society's messy dog pile it was so much worse. If you had been living close to the edge beforehand then a compensation package, no matter how generous it might seem, was still a slap in the face. If you had three kids in a small flat, then, no matter how much you loved them, being told to stay indoors was a recipe for domestic strife. Everything was magnified, and anything that could alleviate that pressure, even a little, was worthwhile.

And yet, Emily knew that she would never have committed such crimes herself, and not just because she couldn't walk straight through a shop front. The Golem gave her distance. She might have put the idea in its head, or said the right words to make a connection to ideas that were already in there, but she hadn't told it to break in. It wasn't her fault. Once the Golem had made up its mind there was nothing that could stop it.

When she left for work the following day, Emily heard a buzz from behind the doors of McDowall House. The Guardian Angel had visited again. It almost did not matter what it brought, the fact that it existed and it had brought *something* gave people hope. Hope for the future, hope for humanity, hope that they had not been forgotten. And Emily smiled.

Over the next few days, through a series of casual enquiries, Emily tried to find out what people had written on those slips of paper that had gone into the Golem. It was a mixed bag; some were angry, some deeply personal, some seemed to be writing a shopping list. Some had taken it seriously, some had tried to be funny, some had just written;

Get a job.

But the majority, believing perhaps that they would be judged on what they wrote, went with Issues. So the Golem was stuffed with popular slogans, ideologies and bumper sticker wisdom.

Emily wrote down all she could find out, then puzzled over how these 'Truths' might be adapted. Left to its own devices, the Golem could not interpret, it could only take the words at face value (which actually made some of the more forthright statements quite worrying. '*Hang the bankers*' was probably not meant to be taken literally), but Emily could interpret for it.

Each night when it returned to life, she was there to meet it (though the time at which it did so seemed completely random, different every night). As it stomped along she jogged beside it, making a few leading comments about Covid and what people needed. Then she left it to go about its business, watching until its heavy silhouette was swallowed up into the night. If it chose to follow her suggestions then that was its own affair, all she had done was voice them.

Sometimes she would set her alarm so she could be there when the Golem returned, so she could see the fruits of its nightly labours. It did not follow all of her suggestions and she tried to determine what words had made the difference; why it had brought back disposable gloves but not surface cleanser.

Quickly she learned its limits. It was a slave to the words inside it, but if you could connect the big statements to something small and achievable in the real world, and if you could link it back to McDowall House, then you could almost program it. It would be too much to say that the Golem did her bidding, but she could push it in the right direction. With her guidance the Golem performed small acts of minor mercy.

"People with Covid have a cough, so cough sweets would help them."

"People with Covid often have a fever, so a thermometer would stop them from spreading it."

"General good health may make people less likely to contract the virus so fresh fruit could help them."

Sometimes the connections she made were too tenuous and the Golem simply ignored her, as if to say, '*You'll have to do better than that*'. It could only be led so far.

It was amazing to Emily how swiftly she accepted it as 'normal', stopped questioning her sanity and began to use it as a tool. Then again, there had been much in the last few months that had seemed unreal, like a dream or a horror movie, so why not this? The Golem gave her an opportunity to help people and she was not going to waste it just because it could not possibly exist. If she was going crazy then at least she was doing some good on her way there.

And so, hand sanitiser became common in McDowall House, along with other hygienic products like antiseptic wipes and bleach. Those staple foodstuffs that had been hard to come by as a consequence of panic-buying arrived, unasked for, on every doorstep. No one questioned it, because they all knew that it was not strictly legal, but they all appreciated it, and they all smiled more.

The fact that the Golem was *not* doing her bidding still worked in Emily's favour, giving her that precious distance. It made its own choices, she just suggested what sort of choices it might want to make. She was not profiting from it, so that stopped it from being a crime (by Emily's definition). And where it might have done unnecessary harm, then she could limit it – without her influence it would hit the same shops over and over and over, locked into a cycle of flour, toilet paper and chocolate for Ollie Maxwell. If it was going to rob people one way or the other, then wasn't it better that it stole the right things?

She still felt some guilt when she read angry articles online about the recent rise in looting or saw shop fronts boarded-up to cover a large Golem-shaped hole. But she balanced that against the quiet knowledge that her neighbours were safer, happier and healthier than they had been. The guilt she felt seemed fair recompense. She had made a deal with… not the Devil exactly, but with… chaos, perhaps. And while it was not a deal with which she was totally happy, it seemed a hell of a lot better than the alternative, since that alternative was to do nothing.

The doorbell rang and Emily turned down Capital Xtra, stopped dancing around her kitchen and pulled on a mask as she went to answer it.

"Oh. Hi Eric." Eric Barry (4th floor) was the football fan who frequently lectured her on why every England manager knew less than he did.

"Hi Emily. How's it going?"

"Okay. Did you need something?" In all the time she had lived here, Eric had never come to her door.

"Err… yeah. Feeling a bit… warm, you know?" He touched his forehead and lowered his voice. "I understand you can get hold of a test?"

Emily's stomach contracted and her skin went cold and clammy. The stolen test seemed a year ago now (it had come back negative) and she'd been happy to forget about it. "Who told you that?"

Eric shrugged, making his chins wobble. "You know this place; no secrets. You got a test for that immigrant family downstairs. Everyone knows."

Everyone…

"Right…" Now, Emily considered, would be an excellent time for the earth to open up and swallow her.

"So you can do the same for me, yeah." It wasn't a question.

"It's not that easy."

"Yeah, yeah, sure." Eric got out his wallet. "How 'not easy'? Fifty quid? Not exactly flush right now. Not working."

"It's not the money," Emily was suddenly very aware that every door on the landing had a peephole and she felt as if eyes were glued to every one. "I didn't do it for money."

"Oh right." Eric shrugged. "Well… bit peed off to pay for something that pair got for free but… not a lot of choice. I can stretch to a hundred."

"I can't." Emily's mouth felt dry. She wanted to slam the door and close the problem out.

"Can't?" Eric's tone was changing.

"I took a chance that one time but… Eric I could lose my job." Eric would understand that, he was a working man first and foremost, he took pride in it.

"You did it once. Twice is breaking point?"

"I shouldn't have done it once." Suddenly that seemed horribly true. "I was stupid. I got lucky. I can't… If I do it for you then sooner or later someone else…"

"I don't care about someone else. I'm here now."

He seemed closer to her now; threatening. Had he moved closer? He wasn't wearing a mask.

"I can't keep taking them from where they're needed. I'm sorry." She was firm, even if she didn't feel it.

"Sounds like it's not that you *can't*, more like you won't."

Emily tried to swallow but her mouth was too dry. "If that's the way you see it then, I guess; yeah. I am really sorry."

"Yeah. I bet." Eric turned as if to leave, but didn't actually go. "You'd do it for them but not for me, eh? Well colour me surprised." And from the way he stressed the word 'colour', Emily knew what was coming next. "You people always stick together."

67

And with that, he strode off.

Emily closed the door and put the latch across, as if that would help. Guilt and anger combined to make her feel sick to her stomach. She should have asked who '*you people*' were – her Dad would have, and it was a phrase she particularly hated. She'd been born in England and her ancestors were African; neither place particularly close to Syria. She should have pointed that out. But it wouldn't have helped. Eric was scared. He was in his late fifties and hardly a model of health, of course he wanted to know if he had the virus. That didn't excuse what he had said, but...

Emily wondered what words Eric had put in the Golem. Whatever they were, they were as much a part of it as all the others.

At least it was over.

But of course it wasn't. Eric had been right, word was around the block of what Emily had done to help that still nameless family on the first floor, and everyone with a cough or a fever, or any one of a dozen other symptoms, found their way to her door. Some begged, some cajoled, some shouted, swore and called her names, some offered money, some threatened to go to her boss. More than she would have expected – people she had known for years – brought race into it (which oughtn't to have been possible; what hell did that have to do with anything?!). She came to like those ones the most, because it was easy to reject them. Mothers terrified of infecting their children, sons and daughters living in multi-generational households scared of killing their parents; those were the worst.

Ellis, who'd lived in the area for sixty years and, according to block rumour, had never actually left London, pleaded on behalf of his niece, who was a teacher still working with the children of key workers. Maria had said it was all a Chinese plot last month, but this month had decided it was the government's way of 'thinning the herd', and that she was a target because she had been on a protest march last year (she'd quit partway through because it was boring). She called Emily a 'tool of the state', along with some other words as she got angrier and more emotional.

And Emily wanted to say to all of them; you don't know what I've done for you – all those gifts on your doorstep? I helped.

68

But that hadn't been her, that was the Golem.

The Golem…

As she looked out of her window one night, Emily seemed to see, reflected in the glass, the upraised hands of the residents of McDowall House, reaching out to her, begging for help. Pleading.

The Golem…

Things were changing quickly these days. Tests were not as hard to come by as they had been even a week ago. Would it be such a terrible crime?

Chapter 6 – It Hides

Unlike many of Its near and distant relations (those creatures of the night that were closest to It), It did not drain Its victims completely, though It always left them dead. To drain them would have been to leave a clue, and It lived in the shadows in every sense. Its existence was based on not being found, but also on no one knowing that it even existed.

It drew back from the throat of its latest victim, the slackness of death already distorting their features. Would he have died anyway? Perhaps. Perhaps not. That did not matter.

There was movement elsewhere in the house as It made Its way to the window, leaving the way It had come, crawling head first down the sheer wall of the house like a lizard, a bat or a cockroach, clawed fingers finding purchase with ease.

From the room behind It, It heard the shriek of the body being found. The screamer would now be hurrying for help, but too late. There were always screams. Sometimes they came long after It had left so It was not there to hear them, but the screams still happened. Always too late. The screams were not important, and yet they also defined It, in a way. If It had a name (though there was nothing It would call Itself for It had no clear sense of self) then that name was written in those screams. Its name was Terror.

Reaching the ground, It blended into the shadows of a tree in the garden. It wore clothes now, some instinct telling It that this was the best way to stay hidden – hidden in plain sight. They were dark and non-descript, and somehow made It seem less human rather than more because of the way It wore them.

It had come a long distance since It had risen, crossing borders – though such things meant nothing to It; there were only people, humans, prey. It spoke no languages and understood none either, so the changes in the jabberings of Its victims went unnoticed. It travelled without purpose, keeping moving because Its instincts, honed through millennia, told It to keep moving. Though It could not have put that drive into words, It understood that movement was the best way to avoid being caught. Stay in one place too long and, no matter how well It hid and how well Its victims blended in with all the others – so many others – people started to notice. Certain people.

Beyond the need to feed, there were few things of which It was actually 'aware', in any useful sense of the word, but one of them was that It had predators of Its own. There were people who knew, who saw, who tracked and hunted. That was why it was important to keep moving, to stay hidden.

But, as a predator Itself, It knew that prey can only stay safe and hidden for so long.

As It climbed the garden wall with scuttling ease and dropped into the alley behind the house, a sharp, blinding light cut through the darkness, finding Its face and making It hiss like a cornered animal.

"…!" It did not understand the words being shouted but It recognised the tone and instinctively knew that falling back into the shadows was not enough this time.

It fled.

Though It was built for stealth rather than speed, It could reach a swift pace when under attack and It moved like a whisper through the night, quick and silent, taking long, loping strides that made no sound on the ground beneath its feet.

Its pursuer was not so quiet. It could hear footfalls; heavy boots, running after It. The bright shaft of light waved this way and that as the hunter ran, always trying to keep the beam focussed on It, while It, in turn, undulated left and right to escape the scourge of the light, twisting sinuously like an eel, the light seeming to slip off Its body like oil on water.

The city through which the chase continued was an old one, riven with little back streets, nooks and crannies in which It could hide, but Its instinct was to go down. That was where It would be safest.

It dived through a narrow gap between two buildings, Its lean, slender body slipping between the walls, and It heard the pursuer spit out some expletive as she skidded to a halt, unable to follow. (She? Yes; she. It could smell her gender.)

The gap was so narrow that even the creature struggled to pry Itself free at the far end, Its long, bony fingers clawing their way out, tugging the rest of Its compressed body after, pulling Itself free. Once It was out, the gap looked far too slim to have every contained It, but the creature's body did not conform to regular physics, and It could fit through holes far smaller than appeared possible.

It hurried on, no longer hearing the footsteps but aware that Its hunter would not have given up and would be looking for another way around to cut It off. As It ran, Its wide eyes scanned the ground, searching, searching, searching, until It found what It was looking for. The drain cover came away easily in Its hands and It slithered Its body in, down through the hole to the sewer beneath. The open drain left an unavoidable clue to where It had gone, but that mattered less now that It was back in Its element. It felt safe down here.

In the dank of the sewer, It breathed in and relaxed a little. The infected were all on the streets above and in the houses that lined them, but the smell of that infection hung heavy in the thick, noisome atmosphere of the sewer. It was a comforting smell. This place felt like home. Perhaps it was from a place such as this that the creature had risen up, and to such a place that It would return when (if?) Its feeding season passed.

A loud clank of metal on stone rang through the sewer tunnel and It shrank back to the wall, baring its teeth. The hunter was persistent and knew what she was doing. Had she hunted Its kind before?

The strong beam of the torch cut through the blackness of the sewer and words echoed around It.

"....!" It did not know what they meant, but they said, '*I know you're here*' in any language.

In the dark of the sewer, perhaps It could have attacked and killed the hunter, but in situations like this, Its instinct was always to run and hide, that was how Its kind had stayed around so long. Besides, It did not like the smell of her. She was not food.

It ran. Even in the thick semi-liquid that gurgled along the sewer bed, It made little sound, Its limbs seeming to move through the dirty water as cleanly as a fish. But Its shadow in the bright torchlight gave it away. Damn the light. Damn the hunter. It could not hide from her as It could from others of her kind. It could not rely on the shadows to consume It, because she knew how to look. She saw It. More importantly, she knew that It was there to see.

Even so, down here It had the advantage. The hunter struggled in these surroundings while It was quite at home. It looked back, and for a moment caught sight of the hunter, silhouetted in the light from a shaft above, arms out to steady herself. She wore a long coat, and carried a light in one hand and a weapon in the other.

It ran on, then sprang from the water up to the ceiling, twisting in mid-air so It landed face to the bricks. In this position, It skittered along the roof of the tunnel like a bug, crawling faster than the hunter could run, putting distance between Itself and Its pursuer.

There.

There up ahead was an open pipe giving onto the stream beneath. It was not wide but it was wide enough. It scurried into the pipe, stretching out Its lean form to a still greater narrowness, squeezed in on every side.

It waited.

It heard the running feet pass.

It waited.

It heard the feet pass back again.

"…!"

It heard the frustrated voice.

The feet moved on.

It had survived.

It waited a long time before dropping back into the sewer, Its bones snapping back into place as It went. Though it was always night down here, It could sense the growing presence of daylight up above. Daylight was death. It would stay here for the night, silent and still amongst the shadows, unconcerned by the smell, the rats that ran over Its feet or the spiders scuttling across Its face.

Then would come the night. The chance to feed again.

But It also knew that it was time to move on. The hunter had gone, but had not given up. Time to find another city, another town, another country. Those concepts were alien to It, but It understood distance and It needed to put distance between Itself and the trailing hunter. It had crossed seas and oceans in Its time, lying in a ship's hold, emerging by night to feed, until the sailors began to talk of a curse aboard. It would do so again if necessary, and this had started to feel necessary. This hunter had come close, and the sewers could only afford It so much protection.

Besides, though the scent of infection here was rife, it also flowed. There was more; a richer hunting ground elsewhere, that It could sense even if It could not smell it yet. A slave to Its animal instincts, It always sought the greatest concentration of prey, even if It was already in an area where prey was abundant.

Come the night, time to move on.

Chapter 7 – Signed in Blood

"…if that's your sign then whoop-de-doo, because the late rising of Saturn is a clear indication of success in all your enterprises. But, be warned of a sharp reversal…"

Emily turned off Al the Astrologer and closed her laptop. She had wanted a distraction but Al just seemed to be talking directly to her.

She went back to pacing her room, frantic and nervous, bare feet slapping on the imitation wood floor, stopping every now and then to look out of the window, down onto the ill-lit plaza in front of McDowall House. Everyone called it 'the plaza' and by night it could almost live up to the name. By day it was a strip of dusty concrete, pitted and uneven, scattered with litter, the protruding foundations of a previous building that no one had known what to do with when McDowall House went up in the sixties. It had been forever in planning permission limbo, waiting to become a carpark, and with the block's future now in the hands of developers like Paul Howarth, it seemed likely to remain in that limbo until the block was torn down to make way for something more gentrified. Then the planning permission would come nice and quick. Money talked.

It was funny where your mind went when there was somewhere you very specifically did not want it to go.

Stepping away from the window, Emily paced some more, knotting her fingers together irritably, her heart loud in her ears, her thoughts racing. She tried putting on music (not too loud – it was late and she was a considerate neighbour). Then tried balancing a candle on one finger while tapping her feet back and forth in time to the music. She managed to dance her way around one complete lap of the room before the candle clattered to the floor, at which point she lost her temper, kicked it away, turned off the music and sat down, gasping for breath. Was she having a panic attack?

It had been so easy up to now, but, though she tried to tell herself otherwise, this one was different, and even distance from the event was not enough to separate her from it.

She still could not bring herself to take tests from the

hospital, even by proxy. That would have been a betrayal and an indefensible wrong – she knew how much the tests were needed there. The Trial Centre was easier to justify to herself but it was somewhere she worked, somewhere she would have to look people in the face the next day. Plus, she was not sure how many tests they even had. She wanted several, if only so she did not have to go through this again.

With the hospital and the Trial Centre ruled out that left the supply depot from which tests were sent out across the city. They would have enough tests, she would only be taking a *very* small proportion of the total and it could be re-stocked relatively quickly. When you looked at it like that then it was practically justifiable.

Her Dad would approve (*'Direct action, Princess, sometimes it's all that works.'*).

Getting the results would be difficult. She would have to space the tests out and slip them in on busy days when no one would notice one more or less. That shouldn't be hard; they were all busy days at the moment and, given the ever-increasing number of tests going through, there were always anomalies.

Emily looked out the window again and her heart sprang into her mouth as she saw movement below. But it was only someone taking a dog for a walk. Lockdown had changed people's habits and 3am dog-walkers were increasingly common.

She paced some more, her conscience tugging her this way and that. The bottom line was that there were people here who needed those tests and weren't getting them under the current system. What she was doing was what the government had *promised* would be happening next month anyway, so Emily was just getting ahead of the game. They might even thank her for it. Probably not, but maybe. The bottom line (she currently had several bottom lines) was that the rules did not make adequate provision for people on low income, people who could not get by on the proportion of their earnings that the government offered. For them, not going to work was a life or death decision, and didn't they deserve to have all the facts before making that decision?

It was all true of course, but there was another bottom line that she was trying hard not to think about. Every test was needed right now, and every one she took was one that someone else would not get. The people of McDowall House certainly needed them, but did they need them more than those who now would not get them? Who was Emily to make that decision? Come to think of it; how the hell had she ended up in a position where she was making it?

Maybe she had made a deal with the Devil.

But if she had, then the deal was done and the blood in which that pact had been signed was dry. This time she had not just suggested things to the Golem, she had given it carefully worded instructions, she had told it where to go, what it was looking for, how to avoid cameras and that it was on no account to damage the property within. It was done, it was happening. In fact, it was probably happening right now.

She went back to balancing the candle.

It was after an hour more of pacing and worrying herself into an ulcer that Emily recognised from her window the increasingly familiar striding gait of the Golem. From up here, and especially at night, it just looked like a man out for a brisk walk. Emily's heart went into her mouth; it was carrying a box.

Blood pounding in her ears, Emily ran out of the flat. As it was the dead of night and she was in a hurry she took the lift, but it had never seemed slower, creaking and groaning on its arrival, then continuing down with Emily aboard at a practically Victorian pace. The doors wheezed open on the ground floor and Emily shot out like a greased hare. Outside, the Golem was waiting for her, the box in its hands.

"You... You got them?"

The Golem made no response. No matter how much time she spent with it, Emily always found its stillness eerie.

She took the box from its unresisting hands and the Golem instantly turned away and walked back towards its spot.

Though it probably would have been prudent to wait until she was back in her flat, Emily could not help herself and tore open the box. A tremor passed through her as she saw the tests within. A tremor of... she hated to admit it, but it was excitement. Even pleasure. Being Emily, it was swiftly followed by guilt, both at what she had done and at the pleasure itself, but the sensation lingered, curled up in her stomach as she climbed the stairs back to her flat. She had done it.

Well… not her. She hadn't done anything (she was once again emphatic about that). But the Golem had done something more than the little chores and errands it had run so far. And if it could do this, then…What next? They had the opportunity to make a real difference to the lives of people in McDowall House.

Perhaps it was an ethical grey area, but why wasn't stuff like this happening already? It *should* have been happening. It wasn't her fault that the government was dragging its feet. She wasn't doing something wrong, she was *righting* a wrong. An unfamiliar sense of power flowed through Emily, waking up that ball of pleasure in her stomach and letting it stretch out like a contented cat.

Back in her flat, she collapsed on the sofa with the box of tests beside her. She wouldn't use them just yet; let some time elapse after the theft. But soon she would be able help her neighbours as never before. Emily smiled.

The smile was still there (albeit behind a mask) at work the following morning, even amongst the frantic day to day of the wards.

"You look cheery," remarked Saanvi, another nurse. "You get some last night?"

"Some what?" asked Emily, and then realised what she was being asked. "No. No. Just a good night."

"Not sure I believe you, but okay. Keep an eye on the guy in bed three. He's a policeman – came in last night with a broken leg and two broken arms."

Emily winced. "What happened to him?"

"Tried to stop a robbery at the NHS warehouse across the river. Can you believe that? Someone stealing from the NHS at a time like this. People are scum. He'll be fine, but just see that he's… Are you alright?"

Emily had stopped listening. The bottom had dropped out of

78

her world and her head was suddenly spinning as if it was disconnected from the rest of her. She'd never even considered the possibility that...

"Emily...?" Saanvi called after her as Emily ran out, rushing into the Ladies room to throw up.

That night, the Golem came to life as usual, and as usual, Emily was waiting for it.

"What the hell did you do?!" She ran at the Golem. But that was pointless, it was already moving, off on its next errand; whatever had floated to the top of its mind. Except that it didn't have a mind, it just had a task, and nothing got in the way of that.

"I told you not to hurt anyone!" Emily kept pace with the Golem, trying to face it down while it just kept walking. "I mean... I didn't say that specifically but it should go without saying! Isn't that in there somewhere? Didn't anyone think to write that down?"

But of course they hadn't, because it went without writing as much as it went without saying. And also because the artist had asked people for personal statements, not the Ten Commandments or Asimov's Laws of Robotics. It was an art project not a guide for living, and as the latter, the Golem's 'Truths' were left seriously wanting.

"You hurt someone. Don't you understand that's wrong?" Emily went on. "You can't do that. That's not what I told you to do!"

She didn't want it to hurt anyone else, but perhaps she also needed to attack the Golem because she did not want to believe that any part of the blame attached to her.

"Why did you attack him? Because he was in your way? Or just because he was a policeman?"

There had been a deal of animosity towards the police, and especially the Met, even before Lockdown, and their role in enforcing the Covid restrictions had not made them any more popular. It was not impossible that someone had put some anti-police statement into the Golem. More and more it seemed to Emily that, while the Golem could be given tasks (when properly worded),

79

it had no master but the 'Truths' inside it. So if it saw flour then it would go after flour, if it saw a policeman...

"No more. No more. You are not to attack any more policemen. Or anyone. It's bad for the block."

The Golem strode on, its impassive face giving no clue as to whether Emily's words had made any impression. She suspected not. There was no obvious way of adapting any of the messages inside it to say *'Don't hurt the police'* – particularly if one said, *'Screw all cops'*, or words to that effect. She knew from experience that just saying something was good for the block or bad for the block was not enough, it had to stem from the 'Truths'. She had tried pushing new ones in its ear but that didn't work either.

"I don't want you doing anything tonight. Take a night off. You deserve it. Stop!"

But the Golem did not have an off switch; this was what it did. This was *all* it did. Now it ploughed through the boarded-up front of a chemist's – one it had hit before. Emily started as an alarm went off. There hadn't been an alarm last time but that break-in had led to a change in security precautions. And an alarm could mean police.

"Get out of there! Now! Get out!"

She glanced up and down the street. The police were usually pretty slow around here and were stretched thin enough these days, but if one happened to be in the area… Was there anything she could do to stop the Golem?

It emerged now from the wrecked store front striding off, not back towards the block, but on towards its next target – it wasn't done yet. She had given it tools, given it a shopping list, given it the ability to better serve the words in its head and the block to which it felt a strange affinity. Suddenly, none of that seemed like a good thing any more.

"I'm telling you to stop. You will hurt the block if you go on like this. You don't like the police? They'll be coming to McDowall House if they find out that's where all the stolen stuff ends up. This isn't protecting anyone. Stop! Everything you're doing; stop!"

To her surprise, the Golem stopped.

"Okay. Now…"

The Golem reached up to grab a blue, diamond-shaped sign that was cable-tied to a lamppost, bearing the legend 'VOTE CONSERVATIVE'. It ripped the hardboard into shreds and dropped them to the pavement.

Emily paused. "Okay, that one I'll give you. But that's it for tonight."

But the Golem was already on the move again. Emily followed. She didn't want to, but she was responsible.

It was a thankfully short night. The Golem performed it usual robberies, taking what was needed, what was useful, what it had originally been asked for and those things Emily had interpreted for it.

They saw no one, and Emily was able to breathe a sigh of relief as they headed back towards the block. Perhaps it would not be so bad. It hadn't hurt anyone before last night. Maybe that was an anomaly, a one-off; unfortunate but never to be repeated. It was not as if she would be asking it to steal any more tests for her – she could not even bring herself to use the ones she had and was planning to return them anonymously first thing tomorrow. Perhaps it would be alright.

And if not, then what could she do? She couldn't follow it every night, and even if she could, there was nothing she could do to stop it if it tried to hurt someone else.

"I know you're probably not going to answer me, but is there anything I can do to make you take a night off?"

The Golem said nothing. Emily wiped a hand across her forehead. It was a cool night but she was sweating from the effort of keeping up with the creature. Or maybe it was guilt that was making her sweat.

They arrived back at McDowall House and Emily continued to trail after the Golem as it made its deliveries. She definitely couldn't do this every night; the events and activity of the past forty eight hours were now really starting to weigh in on her.

The last delivery was flour – for whatever reason, the Golem had decided that Camilla and Ursula needed more. As the bags cascaded to the floor in a cloud of white powder, a gasp came from the shadows at the end of the corridor, where a pair of bulbs had gone out six months ago and never been replaced.

"Are you my Guardian Angel?"

Ursula crept out of the shadows, wearing pyjamas and a dressing gown with a mermaid on it. There was a bright smile on her face as she gazed at the Golem with quiet wonder.

"I waited up for you – don't tell my Mummy. I brought you this." She held up a plate towards the Golem, a slice of apple pie on it. As she did so, she raised her other hand to her mouth, and coughed.

The Golem moved with sudden determination, striding towards the little girl with the unstoppable force of an avalanche. Emily saw its massive arm go back and heard her own shriek as if it came from someone else. She started forwards, diving past the hulking figure to shove Ursula back out of the way as the Golem's hand descended, clenched in a fist.

The fist stopped a half inch from Emily's cheek. In the frozen moment, Emily could hear nothing but the sound of her own breathing. She knew what those hands could do. She knew the strength in those massive arms. But its problem was not with her, it was with Ursula.

Emily's own words rang in her head; '*People with Covid have a cough, so cough sweets would help them*'. She had taught it that a cough meant Covid, and the 'Truths' inside it said that Covid was to be exterminated. The Golem's mind always took the most direct route, so even a casual comment could be fatal. She'd been a fool to think that she could control it.

"What's wrong with the Angel?" asked Ursula, a little surprised but otherwise untroubled.

Emily kept staring at the Golem. There was not a hint on its face of the violence it had been prepared to unleash against the child. There was nothing, and that blankness had never been so terrifying.

"She's from the block," Emily whispered. "She lives right there. You understand?"

The Golem straightened, its hand returning to its side. It did not hurt people from McDowall House; Ursula's 'Truth' was in its head.

It turned and marched away, and Emily heard its heavy, regular footfalls going down the stairs.

"Was that the Guardian Angel?" asked Ursula. How wonderful to be young enough that all this was like water off a duck's back. "He's not what I expected."

"No," acknowledged Emily. "But... he doesn't want people to know about him. Can you keep a secret?" She mimed a zip across her mouth.

Ursula nodded, excited that an adult had entrusted her with a secret. She mimed the zip.

"Good girl," said Emily. "You keep his secret, and I won't tell your Mummy that you sneaked out looking for angels."

Ursula flaunted a guilty smile, then looked down at the floor.

"I dropped his apple pie."

"I'll make sure he gets it."

Back in her flat, Emily collapsed onto her bed staring at the ceiling, fighting down the need to throw up, her mind filled only with the Golem's face. She recalled, vaguely, an old boyfriend who had been a film buff, telling her about an experiment done by some early filmmaker into the power of montage; of how putting images together changed their meaning. The filmmaker had shown an audience images of a blank-faced man alongside other images and the audience had interpreted the man's expression differently based on the images around it. The Golem's expression never changed, it had only the one, utterly impassive face. And yet, when it had taken a swing at Ursula, Emily could have sworn there was murderous intent in those ceramic eyes.

It would have done it, she was sure of that. It would have killed that little girl with the same unstoppable efficiency with which it did everything. It did not understand why that might have been wrong and it never would. Right and wrong were not in the Golem's vocabulary. Its head was full of absolutes; blacks and whites in a world of grey. And people who are certain never stop to justify their actions with 'right' or 'wrong' – there is only what *they* think.

83

She should have known better. It had been an old disagreement with her Dad; how quickly the good intentions of the individual vanished within the mob. And that was what the Golem was. When the will of the people is shorn of the intentions behind it, then what you are left with is the mob. In the hands of the mob, a slogan designed to make a point becomes a call to arms; an expression of dissent becomes justification for violence; a different point of view becomes Us and Them. She had known all that, but she had gone ahead and used it because it suited her to remain aloof from its actions.

It was too much to hope that it would not happen again. No matter how well-meaning the instruction, it had the potential to be terminally misinterpreted.

Emily stood back up, trying to ignore the dizzy rush that spun her head, and made for the door.

Back outside, she jogged over to where the Golem stood on its spot.

"I've come up with a way for you to protect the block from Covid."

The Golem looked at her. For the first time, Emily got the impression that it was thinking, analysing her words. It was only still for a second or two, then it stepped forward.

"Okay, we're not walking. It's too far. I'll get the car."

Though she didn't use it much, what with living in London, Emily did own a car. Her name was Gretchen (or so Emily had been told by the previous owner) and she was a third or fourth-hand Fiat Panda. Or, to put it another way, she was small and lacking in power, which was going to make this difficult.

The Golem regarded Gretchen, and again Emily found herself reading thoughts into its motionless features. Right now it seemed to be thinking, '*You've got to be kidding*'.

With the back seats down and the front jammed forward as far as they would go, Emily managed to manoeuvre the Golem in through the boot. Gretchen dipped considerably when the heavy bulk of solid clay got in, but she seemed to be holding up, even if she didn't like it much.

84

"We're not going far," Emily offered, not sure if she was talking to the Golem or the car.

Despite being curled into a very atypical position, the Golem had reverted to its motionless state. Even when it slid from one side to the other as they turned a corner, its weight threatening to roll the car, it made no move to stop itself, as if someone had crafted a second Golem, this one in repose, which Emily was delivering.

It was still night as they drove through East London, but the sky was starting to lighten. If dawn broke would the Golem still move? Or would she be stuck with an immobile ton of clay in the back of her car until night fell again?

Emily decided that she would rather not find out. Hopefully she could find somewhere suitable before morning because, from the sound of Gretchen's poor, straining engine, the car could not take much more of this.

"This should do."

They were still technically within the city limits (at least she thought they were – London's sprawl encompassed more than you imagined and it did not end so much as peter out), but the buildings were behind them and they were surrounded by the scrub of wasteland, sliced through by abandoned railway lines, now reclaimed by nature. The Golem stayed perfectly still as Emily pulled up, bringing Gretchen to a grateful stop.

"Here we are. Ready?"

She wasn't sure why she still talked to it, knowing that it would not and probably could not answer.

Emily got out of the car and closed the door. For a few moments she stood in the grey light, breathing in and out. The stress was getting to her, and she really wasn't sure what was going to happen now. Finally she went around to the boot and opened it.

"Out you get."

Every time the Golem was still she was surprised that it moved again. You never really thought about it, but living creatures were never still, not completely, there were always little micro-movements that you saw even if you didn't consciously notice them. The Golem was *still*. Wholly and completely. So utterly still that it seemed impossible it would ever move again.

Awkwardly, it managed to clamber out of the boot, Gretchen bouncing back up in relief, like a horse relieved of an overweight rider.

Keeping one eye on the ever-lightening sky, Emily walked into the wasteland, the Golem following. When she thought they had gone far enough, she led it down into one of the ditches, puddled with rancid water, that drew paths across the landscape – probably something to do with the old railway lines.

"Wait here and I will show you how you can *really* protect the block. Don't move."

The Golem stayed put as Emily scrabbled her way back up out of the ditch. She glanced back. The ditch was deep enough that the Golem could not see out. She began to walk faster, then broke into a run back to Gretchen, got into the car and started the engine.

Her mind was racing. This was the best way. Or at least the only way she could think of. She couldn't destroy the thing – who knew what it would do if she tried? She couldn't confine it; it was too strong. Out here there was no one it could hurt, and it was so far from McDowall House, the place that defined it, that perhaps it would just stop.

There was always the risk that it would find its way home like one of those stories you heard about cats, but she had to hope not.

She probably should have felt better. But, as sometimes happens when you have been worrying about something for a long time and are then suddenly relieved from that worry, Emily swiftly began to feel as if she had been hit by a bus. She had been through the stress and relief of the theft, then the horror of the aftermath; anxiety, more horror, fear, stress, tension and this final relief of taking her problems out into the wilderness and dumping them in a ditch, all alongside an almost terminal lack of sleep. It was natural that she feel a bit of mental whiplash.

But by the time she got back to her flat, Emily was beginning think that it might be more than that.

"Come on. Give me a break." Emily wasn't what you would

call a religious person, but occasionally asking God for stuff was a habit she had picked up from her Mum, and there was no harm in asking.

It was just past 6am when she fell into bed, and she slept for the next nine hours. She probably would have slept longer but was shaken awake by her own coughing. She had a fever too.

"Damn."

She located her jeans where she had left them the night before, lying on the floor beside the bed, clawed her phone out of the pocket and rang the hospital.

"I can't come in… Yeah… Cough and fever… Yeah. How many are you out today?... Shit. Sorry… I know, but, still; sorry… Yeah. Ten days."

Ten days quarantine. What did she do now?

After hanging up, Emily keeled over to lie on the bed again. It didn't *have* to be Covid. Given what she had been through she could have just overloaded her system, making her susceptible to flu. And yet, some part of her mind said; *Of course it's Covid, why wouldn't it be?*

She was young and in good health. She would be fine. But at the back of her mind lurked the knowledge with which all medical professionals are burdened; sometimes being young and in good health isn't enough.

Chapter 8 – It Travels

Though It had travelled before, and frequently, the means by which it did so seemed to change each time it re-emerged. It had little concept of time, particularly of how much passed while It slept.

It travelled in a direction dictated by instinct, by pursuit and, as always, by the scent of infection, though that scent seemed to be everywhere. But there was also a degree of chance involved. It followed Its nose to Its next victim and where they went, It went. If it found a pocket of potential victims then It might prey on them a while, though It had evolved to feed and move on for fear of drawing attention to Itself. But sometimes circumstances dictated Its behaviour and It was adaptable enough to roll with the changing situation.

Its options here were limited; a confined space, a small number of people and water all around, cutting It off. This was not a situation that It would have chosen. It had been moving fluidly between centres of habitation, picking off victims one by one, leaving no traces for the hunter to follow. That inexorable movement had led It to a camp of some sort, where It had moved with ease amongst people who were expected to die anyway and who few mourned when they did.

Suitable though this place was, it would be a mistake to remain and gorge Itself, for that would surely alert the hunter. So when the opportunity came to leave, It did so, following some of the camp's occupants onto what could, in the absence of a better word, be called a boat.

Here they huddled, and It huddled amongst them, unseen and unnoticed even in that proximity. Hopefully it would be a short crossing, and the next place at which they arrived would have wider possibilities; new cities for It to plunder, new victims for It to sniff out. Though the scent was weak yet, some inner sense told It that there were rich pickings up ahead, a land where infection hung heavy in the air.

It curled up beneath a pile of bags, insinuating Its body into the narrow gaps between them to sleep, eyes open and senses sharp, but essentially unconscious.

And then It dreamed…

It did not dream in the conventional, human sense, but Its mind wandered as It slept and so we might call that a dream – though any dream in a creature such as this might be more accurately termed a nightmare.

It dreamed of times past, of when It was last awake. That had been a rich time. In the wake of war, a deadlier enemy than guns and bombs stalked the streets, catching the world unawares and claiming lives in huge numbers. Amongst such death, no one noticed a few extra bodies, no one noticed that something else stalked the streets. They had been too caught up in their own problems to see It pass.

Before that there had been other opportunities, mostly small affairs but enough for It to feed. And then, further back still, the great event, the sort of thing It would have dreamed of, if It had the capacity to dream in such a fashion. In those times, when death was everywhere and people lived in constant fear, It had been dormant only fitfully, five years here, a decade there, because there was always some fresh outbreak to awaken It. It had never been awake for so long nor had such a glut of food to choose from.

Back then, It had been so prevalent that some had even begun to suspect Its presence, in their primitive way. 'King Death' they had called It, and had painted Its grinning image on walls, parchments and in religious texts. Or at least they painted what they imagined It might look like, for few had so much as caught a glimpse of It. Some of them weren't so very far out, though they got a lot of the details wrong and It would certainly never wear a crown or carry a scythe. Perhaps It saw some of those pictures in passing and stopped to look and wonder. But probably not.

King Death. The people whispered the name and imagined It a punishment sent by God, or perhaps by the Devil. Perhaps It had been. It did not know, nor would It have understood either concept. It had no purpose or mission, It had only the drive to feed and to survive, and, very occasionally, to procreate in the same manner as similar, related species, though not as often.

It lurked outside the churches where people prayed, night and day, for God's forgiveness. It lurked in their homes where they secretly cursed God for what He had done to them. It lurked on the streets where people preached repentance and flogged themselves in acts of over-enthusiastic and ultimately misguided contrition.

The people would have been disappointed to learn that It understood none of this.

Truthfully, 'King Death' as they called It, was not their main problem. Their main problem was the disease that ran riot through Europe and beyond. Their problem was the unsanitary conditions in which they lived and the vermin it attracted. If they had spent less time praying and more time cleaning then their problems might have at least been lessened. But though it was not their main problem, 'King Death' was there to take advantage of their situation, to feed on those unlucky enough to contract the disease, and turn a possible death sentence into a guaranteed one.

They had been good times. A human might have regretted such a bonanza coming to an end but It lacked the capacity for that. Animal-like, It enjoyed the good times while they lasted, feasted while It could, then retreated into dormancy to wait for the next feast.

Perhaps this was it.

It woke when they reached land, and followed the people, Its fellow travellers, into a sealed box. Its journey was not over yet.

Chapter 9 – Stake Out

Hidden around a brick wall, late at night, the cold spring drizzle dribbling down the back of his neck, his shoulders starting to ache and the feeling draining from his feet, Harrigan was increasingly aware that he was breaking Lockdown regulations and the only excuse he could give was not likely to get him a lot of sympathy.

"Bloody hell!" He started, jerking his head back awkwardly as a particularly large and icy drop of rain went down his spine.

He looked out around the corner again, squinting through the drizzle at the shadowy shape that stood, unmoving, thirty feet from his hiding place; the McDowall Golem.

How the hell had he ended up here?

"Wait," Harrigan interjected. "It came back?"

Nurse Emily's cough crackled again on the other end of the phone. "Sorry."

"It's okay. But... The Golem came back?"

"Two days later," Emily replied. Her voice had gotten weaker through the telling of her frankly unbelievable story, as if she was reliving it all. "Back on its spot like it'd never been gone. I guess it walked back, but... the council said it was off being cleaned. I mean... I don't know why they would say that! It's not true."

Not for the first time in her narrative, Nurse Emily sounded unsure of her own grip on reality.

"Maybe I shouldn't have just dumped it out there," she muttered. "Should have done something more permanent. Smashed it. But I was scared. I've seen what it can do. If I tried to harm it then... I don't know, I just... I don't know. It's all... I don't know."

Harrigan listened, not sure what to say. He understood why she hadn't gone to the police and why he had seemed like the best option, but...

He hadn't laughed at her – of course he hadn't – but he hadn't believed her either, and he was sure that she knew it. He felt bad about it and he *wanted* to believe her, but... A walking statue that ran errands for the residents of a tower block because the words

91

inside it told it to? He could be forgiven for thinking that those were the ravings of someone who was sick.

Very sick.

Maybe that was why he kept listening, and why he now said, "What do you need from me?"

Emily took a deep breath that bubbled unnaturally. "I need you to watch it. Just for one night, to see if it… To see what it does. I don't want it to hurt anyone else."

Since Lockdown, Nurse Emily had been Harrigan's only regular interaction with the outside world, and she had become almost an avatar of Britain's National Health Service to him, which had made him appreciate them even more than he already had. When he stood outside, once a week to 'clap for carers', he had a specific carer in mind and he knew how hard she was working. Nurse Emily always looked overworked, always tired and yet always smiling. That, to him, was the NHS.

He couldn't see her now, but he doubted that she was smiling.

"Emily, are you sure there's no one I can call? You sound awful."

"I'm okay. I've seen people way worse. I'm not complaining."

Of course she wasn't – she was the NHS.

"I know you don't believe me." Her voice was soft and low. "I get it. I wouldn't believe me either. If you had told me, when we first met, that the Invisible Man in Cambridge was real, and that he ran round the market singing kids' songs, then I wouldn't have believed you. But I believe it now, Harrigan – if you say it happened then I believe you." She paused. "You know… kind of. It's a lot to ask. Anyway, you don't have to believe me, but can you give me enough benefit of the doubt to do this one thing? I'd do it myself but… you know."

So he had said yes. Not because of the Invisible Man, although his own experiences had certainly stretched his mind open further, but because if ever a person deserved the benefit of the doubt then it was one who was working her arse off every day to help others, and whose reward had been to catch the bloody virus.

It wasn't that he regretted the decision, even as a drip of water located an opening at the front of his coat for a change, but he wasn't wild about it either. He did regret the rain. He was also starting to wonder if he had an obligation to report Nurse Emily to some relevant authority. He didn't want to (given what the NHS had been through this year it was amazing they weren't all seeing Golems tramping down the street, accompanied by pink elephants on parade), but the woman who was sticking needles into his and other people's arms on a daily basis was seeing things and that couldn't be good.

Then again, Emily had seemed almost ludicrously sincere. She was no fool, she was certain about what she had seen.

Harrigan looked out around the corner again. The statue was still there, as still as... well, a statue. Which was really all you could expect of it. He was almost willing it to move now (even if that would probably require a subsequent change of underwear). He didn't want Emily to be wrong. But of course she was; statues didn't move.

Harrigan wiped the rain from the face of his watch. It was past midnight now and the Golem had not so much as tottered. At what hour could he reasonably say that he had fulfilled his obligation, so that he could go home to dry off and warm up? If something bad was going to happen then surely it would have done so at midnight, as was traditional.

But he had promised Nurse Emily, and it wasn't really that big of an ask. Just one night.

He looked out once more. Nothing. Tugging out the pair of binoculars nestled under his coat, Harrigan took a closer look. The features of the Golem were striking but they were not moving. Rain ran down its arms to drip from its well-crafted fingers, forming a puddle about its incongruous trainers. It was a decent piece of work. Harrigan was firmly in the camp of '*I don't know much about art, but I know that I don't like art*', but even he was quietly impressed with the craftsmanship of the Golem. He would have been grudgingly willing to admit that there was something almost worthwhile about the concept behind it; all those statements crammed into it, giving the capital's unheard masses a voice. It was still a damn fool thing to do, but a damn fool with a good heart.

He lowered the binoculars and shivered, then checked his watch again. Half midnight. He had promised to watch through the night but that surely did not mean every second of the night. He could go for a coffee, couldn't he? As long as he came back afterwards. It was not as if the Golem was going anywhere (it really wasn't). And a coffee (maybe a snack of some sort) would get him through the next few hours. Harrigan had been on enough stake-outs to know that the early hours of the morning was when it really got difficult. He had also been on enough to know that smart people brought a thermos. But that was Hangdog Harrigan (as they had used to call him); always one step behind.

"Sod it," he muttered to himself. He took another look at the Golem. "Don't you dare go anywhere." Then he set off, trudging through the rain in the direction of an all-night takeaway coffee shop which he had spotted earlier.

As he went, he heard a door close and saw a brief flash of light from one of the boarded-up shops across the street. That was London; just because it was after midnight in the middle of a pandemic, didn't mean that people weren't working, the city stopped for nothing. Or possibly someone was squatting there. Either way, on a night like this; good luck to them.

Coffee 'shop' was a pretty big word for what had been reduced to a walk-through window sheltered by a striped awning (currently a dripping Niagara of rainwater), but as long as they had coffee Harrigan wasn't fussy.

"Black coffee, please. And one of those flapjacks." Two pound fifty for a flapjack? Why had he moved to the one city that was even more expensive than Cambridge?

The man behind the counter gave him a look. "Key worker?"

There were rules at the present. You weren't supposed to be out buying coffee without a good reason.

Harrigan pulled out his wallet and flashed his old warrant card. He probably should have given that back, but as far as he recalled no one had asked for it. He and his old boss had not been on the best of terms.

"Police." He had missed saying that.

The man at the counter nodded. Time was when being police might have got you a free cup of coffee, nowadays people were more likely to spit in it, although Harrigan did wonder if they had always spat in the coffee and were just more open about it now. He still preferred the old way; if you were going to drink spit one way or the other then he'd rather not know about it.

"Thanks." Harrigan paid and trudged back towards his corner, his shoes squelching as he went. He sipped at the coffee, finding it bitter and too hot to drink. He'd missed that too.

As he walked, he glanced at his watch again. He'd been gone about fifteen minutes. That wasn't so bad. It was not one hundred percent what Emily had had in mind but if he only missed fifteen minutes of a long night then that was pretty good going. Even if the Golem *had* walked off during his brief absence, the damn thing couldn't have got far; it didn't look light on its feet. Plus, it was a statue, and therefore didn't move.

Even so, Harrigan found himself unconsciously speeding up. A knot of anxiety had developed in his stomach, a sense that he had done something wrong and would have to pay for it. He was practically running by the time he got back to the corner and…

The Golem was still there.

Well of course it was. He breathed a sigh of relief and then felt like an idiot for doing so. Once again: statue. It wasn't going anywhere. Which doomed him to a very awkward conversation with Nurse Emily, who was probably already doubting her own sanity. Maybe his testimony could induce her to get the help she obviously needed. Although right now she had bigger worries. She really hadn't sounded good.

So far Harrigan had lost one friend and one acquaintance to the damned virus. That was a factor of his age; his social circle was not the *most* at risk but was at risk enough. Even though he barely knew Nurse Emily the fact of her youth would make it so much more tragic if…

Despite the rain and his certainty that this was a wasted errand, Harrigan resolved to do things right, and settled in for the night. At least he was out – there were plenty of people who'd have given a lot for that.

At about four in the morning, he decided that he had done his bit. The closest the Golem had come to moving was when an urban fox used its leg first as a back scratcher then as a lavatory. It would be hard to tell Nurse Emily that it was all in her head, but not totally unexpected.

Even so, he wanted to be able to tell her that he had left no stone unturned. Leaving his hiding place, Harrigan walked over to the Golem.

"Hello?" he suggested. "Anyone home?"

In close up it was even more impressive, and Harrigan looked it up and down, his gaze coming to rest on its deeply incised eyes.

"If you move now then I'm going to piss myself. That said, if you're ever going to move then now is the time."

The rain running down the Golem's terracotta cheeks looked almost like tears, but that was as near as it came to any sign of animation.

"If it helps I'm a friend of Emily's?" Harrigan tried. "Nice girl. You gave her a hand with some things. Remember? She dumped you in a ditch?"

At some point, you had to let go and admit that you were talking to a statue.

"Okay, it's gone four; I'm heading home. If Emily asks then maybe you could tell her I stuck it out till six." He wagged a finger in the Golem's face. "And if you move after I'm gone then I am not going to be happy."

In the shadow of the looming tower block, he gave the Golem a last once over, then walked away. At the corner he turned back, on the off-chance that the Golem had suddenly sprung to life and started tap-dancing to *Puttin' on the Ritz*. It hadn't. Out of loyalty to Nurse Emily, he gave it a long beat, a last chance to do something. But the Golem did not move. Maybe it didn't go out when it was raining.

Either way, Harrigan had had enough. His bed was calling, there was a mug of cocoa with his name on it, and he didn't think he could get any wetter if he tried.

Going by the main roads it was a longish walk to the nearest useful bus stop, so Harrigan struck out into the sides streets, pressing his limited London geography into service to find a shortcut. He tramped at a brisk pace, shoulders up, hands thrust into his pockets, body compressed in some small defence against the persistent rain which seemed to get heavier with every step. As he walked, he became aware that, despite the early hour, London was already awake and working. He could hear the regular, rhythmic thumping of some heavy machinery, growing louder as he grew increasingly doubtful of his shortcut.

"Bugger." He was lost, and the only safe thing to do was back-track to the main road and take the long way round.

"Bugger," he repeated, as he about-faced to tramp back the way he had come.

So far, Harrigan had only heard signs of activity, but as he turned he saw, up ahead of him, shrouded by night and rain, a figure walking in his direction. Whoever he was, he was a big chap, and Harrigan experienced a lightning flashback; a late night call-out to subdue a bouncer at a club in Cambridge city centre. The man had suffered a bad reaction to something he had taken and was feeling no pain, swinging wildly at police officers, passers-by and lamp posts without distinguishing between them. He'd been a beast of a man, it had taken five of them to get him to the ground and Harrigan had suffered a bloodied nose and bruised kidneys for his trouble. The man now approaching looked as if he could have picked up that bouncer and bounced him off the wall. Though Harrigan could see no more than a silhouette against a street light, he could make out the broad shoulders, barrel chest and thick arms. He seemed to be wearing some sort of hat, possibly with ear flaps.

With the convenient excuse of social distancing, Harrigan crossed the street, giving the giant a wide berth. He then felt a shiver of anxiety down his spine as the man crossed too, maintaining a collision course with Harrigan. His gait was heavy and lumbering, and his steps... His steps...

It was only when he looked at those steps that Harrigan realised that the man's feet were landing in perfect time with the thudding of what he had taken to be construction work. Those sounds were not some heavy machinery, they were the man's footfalls on the pavement. How much did he have to weigh? It was as if he was wearing lead boots.

Harrigan kept walking, ignoring the animal instinct, located at the back of his brain, that was urging flight. *It's just a big guy*, he told himself, *just a very big guy*. Too late, he realised that the silhouette should have been familiar; he'd been staring at it all night.

Passing into the light of a street lamp, the Golem's broad, hard features were illuminated and Harrigan found himself frozen to the spot in fear. It was the same immobile face he had said goodnight to mere minutes ago, but now that immobile expression seemed threatening, and it was looking right at him.

Harrigan staggered backwards, tripping over his own feet in haste and fear, tumbling to the wet pavement. The Golem saw him fall and sped up, its bulk bearing down on Harrigan. A massive arm shot out like a striking snake and Harrigan ducked just in time, so the solid fist slammed into the wall beside him, hard enough to break a clay knuckle on the brickwork.

Not wasting any time imagining what that fist might have done to his skull, Harrigan scrambled away on all fours, skidding in the wet as he tried to regain his feet. The Golem snatched at him, grabbing his coat with its left hand and taking a backhand swing with the right. Fortunately for Harrigan, the zip on his coat had bust a few months back and he had been too stubborn to buy a new one, insistent that the zip could be fixed when he had time. If he had been a more affluent man then his head would likely have been cracked like an egg by the Golem's swipe. As it was, he struggled out of the coat so the Golem caught him a only glancing blow on his left arm rather than a fatal one to his head.

Not that the 'glancing' blow wasn't enough to send Harrigan spinning back into a wall, hot pain shooting up and down his arm.

He cried out briefly before the wall knocked the wind out of him, then ran on, nursing his injured arm, as the Golem tossed away the coat and made for him once more. It must have weighed a ton but it moved with surprising speed, taking long, powerful strides while its footsteps echoed off the houses around them.

Harrigan rushed on ahead of it, his dead arm seeming to weigh him down. He now realised that he might also have twisted an ankle when he fell. That was the trouble with getting old; everything was reaching the end of its warranty period. But he ran on, terror blinding him to some of the pain he was in. The Golem strode after him, the intensity of its unchanging gaze locked on Harrigan.

What the hell did it want with him? This was not the creature that Emily had described. Then again, hadn't she wondered about its attitude towards policemen? But how could it know that Harrigan had been on the force?

They were good questions, but questions that could wait until Harrigan answered the far more pressing one; *How do I avoid getting beaten to a bloody pulp by a living statue?*

It was not a question he had expected to be asking himself tonight but you played the hand that life dealt you.

Taking a left between two buildings into an alleyway, Harrigan stumbled on, hoping the alley was too narrow for the Golem's hulking form.

No such luck. It had to turn sideways but it was not letting him get away, reaching for him with those long, tree trunk arms. If it got hold of him then one squeeze would crush flesh and bone into one sticky mass.

He really needed to stop thinking about these things.

The alley had at least slowed the monster down and given Harrigan the chance to put a bit of distance between him and it, though not enough to make much difference. He needed somewhere to hide but he did not know where he was or where he was going. And the latter of those was about to prove very important.

"Oh…"

In the Cambridge Police Force, his nickname had been 'Hangdog' Harrigan; always disappointed, always unlucky, always

99

able to snatch defeat from the jaws of victory. And he'd done it again. Only Hangdog Harrigan would have found the alley terminating in the river Thames. A flight of wet steps, made more slippery by green algae, led down to a broad mud flat bordering the river. Harrigan looked back, the Golem was approaching, its eyes still fixed on him.

Well, maybe it didn't like mud.

Harrigan hurried down the steps. Partway down, his foot slipped, shooting out from under him. His right thigh banged painfully against the corner of a step as he bounced off and fell to the blue-grey mud with a sucking splat. Was being swallowed by mud better or worse than being pounded to death by a Golem? Some people probably went their entire lives without having to ask that question.

Trying to ignore the screaming pain in his arm and leg, Harrigan began to drag himself across the mud flat. If he could get away from the wall and the steps then he would be safe; the Golem was far too heavy to walk across the mud. Just a few more feet and he would be alright. His groping hands found a length of rope, slippery with river ooze but knotted, which made it easy to pull, and – finally some good luck – the far end was attached to something solid. With a strain, and a suppressed scream as he tried to make his injured left arm do some work, he hauled himself a foot, then another and another. The Golem would not be able to reach him

Looking back, Harrigan saw the creature, standing on the wall, scanning the mud with its wide eyes. Again, it was probably all in his head but he thought he read frustration into its gaze. Despite the situation, he felt like singing.

"Try losing some weight!" he yelled back.

The Golem looked down in front of it, then stepped onto the top of the stairs.

"Go on, fall down," muttered Harrigan. It might shatter on the stone steps or land in the mud to wallow and struggle as it sank – either way was fine with him.

The Golem did not fall, it stepped forwards, not down the steps but off them to land in the mud with a splat, sending gobs of black goop spraying in every direction. As Harrigan had predicted, it instantly sank down to its waist.

Harrigan laughed. "Now what are you going to do?"

The Golem looked at him, and stepped forwards. It was not easy for the creature, the weight of the thick, glutinous mud through which it was pressing was incredible, but so too was the strength of the Golem.

Harrigan gaped. It wasn't possible. It couldn't be. More importantly it wasn't fair. He had won. He had got away. He had literally hauled himself to safety. But safety wasn't looking so very safe anymore.

Rolling back onto his belly, Harrigan resumed dragging himself across the flat in the direction of the river. The damn thing might be able to wade through mud, maybe it could even stroll along the bottom of the Thames, but it couldn't float! From behind him came the cloying, sucking sound of the mud clinging to the Golem as it drove itself onward like a bulldozer. He did not look back, he knew what he would see. It was like the end of *The Terminator* scored for mud rather than machines. It just kept coming.

The rope he had been using to drag himself along ran out, and Harrigan was forced to use his hands, burying his fingers in the stinking, oozing muck and kicking with his legs to haul himself on each precious inch. He was half-swimming across the flat, his face and underside smeared with the slime that formed the top coat of the mud, above the more viscous stuff beneath that threatened to take a hold of you and never let go (unless you were a damn Golem, of course!). His leg throbbed dully where he had caught it, while his arm screamed with savage pain each time he dragged himself on, but he kept going. And if he ever needed motivation, all he had to do was look behind. The Golem was gaining. Against all logic it was managing to build something like momentum as it ploughed through the mud, as unstoppable as a steamroller, its gaze forever fixed on Harrigan, its expression set. The lights from a passing boat, played briefly across its face, creating highlights and deep shadows that gave it the look of a demon raised from hell just to torture Harrigan.

"AHH!" Harrigan cried out in pain, exhaustion and a little

relief as the tidal wash of the Thames flowed over his outstretched fingers and receded again. He was almost there, but it was not just a case of reaching the water, he needed to get deep enough that the Golem would not be able to grab him from beneath.

He cried out again as he hauled himself on once more, the freezing water soaking his clothes but doing nothing to numb the fiery pain in his arm. He let the left hang limply at his side – he couldn't use it any more, the pain was so great that he was in danger of passing out. Fortunately, the water that now splashed him in the face, was making the mud less clinging, smoothing his passage and helping him along. Once more, Harrigan forced himself forward with his legs in a vaguely breast-stroke kick, inching on, further into the water, praying for the moment that it would take him. Although that was going to be a troubling moment too. Could he swim with one arm and, at best, one and a half legs, exhausted and with the weight of his clothes dragging him down? Less than eighteen months ago, Harrigan had almost drowned in the river Cam, just before Christmas. He hadn't been the surest of swimmers before and that had done nothing to bolster his confidence. The Thames was thicker, deeper and with more powerful currents than the Cam. If he sank here then there would be no saving him.

They were not comforting thoughts but they were excised from Harrigan's mind as he felt something brush against his foot. His head snapped back and panic surged through him, giving him new strength, as he saw the Golem at full stretch, reaching for him, its grasping hand clutching and the terracotta tip of its middle finger just brushing the sole of his right foot. Flopping like an elephant seal, Harrigan lurched forwards, landing with a splat and a faceful of water. Pain had slowed him, and he had not noticed how close the Golem had got. Nothing slowed it down.

And so, history's slowest, stickiest chase continued.

On his side, protecting his left arm (he was fairly sure now that something was broken), Harrigan undulated his awkward way forwards, like a sidewinder with sunburn. Each lolloping lunge took him into deeper water, and he was now swallowing more than was healthy (the Thames was only classified as water on the technicality that it was a river).

Behind him, the Golem struggled on. The water-logged mud through which it now pressed was harder going, and deeper too, reaching almost to the creature's chest, so each incoming wave washed over its helmet of hair. But it wasn't stopping; still coming, still reaching for Harrigan as if there was nothing else in the world.

"Blaech!"

As the water got deeper, Harrigan's low to the ground position got less and less tenable. He was struggling to keep his head above the surface but with only one arm it was hard to keep it any higher.

"Gah!"

You cannot know the symphony of sounds the human body will produce until you have tried to bellyflop your way across a mud flat at low tide pursued by an angry Golem.

Harrigan flung himself forward once more, this time hoping the water would bear him up. It did, though he could still touch the bottom with his hands and feet, and he used them to paddle his way on towards deeper water and safety.

Now he was putting real distance between himself and his pursuer. Harrigan looked back...

Nothing.

Not that he could see. The Golem would still be there, beneath the surface (he doubted that it needed to breathe), but surely it would have to give up at some point?

Unwilling to take chances, Harrigan effected a one-armed, uneven-legged doggie paddle – though not even the most unselfconscious of doggies would have swum like this in front of its peers. It was not the most efficient method of travel and so Harrigan was surprised when he looked back to see how far he had come. He was now unquestionably out of the Golem's reach, well above the bottom and a good twenty to twenty five feet from the shore.

And getting further.

With a cold shock, Harrigan realised that the admirable progress he had made was not down to a previously undiscovered swimming talent that would see him into the Olympic Doggie Style squad, but to the current that had grabbed him and was dragging him, not just into the middle of the river, but further downstream.

"Oh shit…" Harrigan bobbled as water flowed into his mouth.

He kicked hard to keep his head above the surface and his right leg complained bitterly. His right arm was having to work overtime to keep him afloat, but even trying to use the left brought stabbing pain so ferocious that he gave up.

Out of the frying pan and into the Thames. Bugger.

Unbidden memories of that night in Cambridge rose in his subconscious. There had been ice that night. He had crashed through it and been trapped beneath. He remembered the panic, the cold, the bursting of his lungs until he opened his mouth and water flowed in. He would have been dead if Elsa hadn't been there.

In the long run, it had been that near-death experience that had reunited him with Don and Will, so it had been all to the good. But did a man get that lucky twice?

Forced to give his aching right arm a break, Harrigan's head ducked beneath the surface and he got a mouthful of water before he kicked back up, spitting and struggling.

"Help!" He didn't have much energy with which to yell, and he wasn't sure if there was anyone to yell to, but, if nothing else, it was traditional.

Then, just before he sank again, he saw a shaft of light appear out of the night, illuminating a spot on the rippling surface. From beneath the water, he squinted and saw that same puddle of bright light – he had not imagined it. With the last of his strength, Harrigan kicked up again, trying to ignore the pain as he clawed his way back to the surface.

"There he is! That way."

The brilliant light landed on Harrigan, adding sudden blindness to the terror of drowning.

"Hold on!"

Thanks, that thought never occurred to me!

A life preserver landed in the water beside Harrigan and he made a desperate grab for it, missing and plunging below the surface again.

This time, he did not have the strength to swim back up, but a strong arm plunged down through the murky waters to grab him.

"I got you, I got you. Relax, buddy. You're okay."

Limp and barely able to breathe, let alone move, Harrigan allowed himself to be hauled onto the deck of a boat.

""You're a bit heavy, mate."

Witty ripostes failed Harrigan as he lay, choking up the Thames and willing the strength back into his body as his brain carried out a damage assessment.

He was vaguely aware of hands on him, checking him over, making sure he was breathing, and he issued a polite shriek as someone moved his arm to listen to his chest.

"Ooh... May have a problem with his arm," said one of his rescuers.

"You clumsy jackass," said another voice. "Would you try not to kill them after we've rescued them?"

"Well I didn't know."

"Leg... hurt... too..." Harrigan gasped. "Hospital... please..."

"It's our next stop," said the second voice. "Can you tell us your name?"

"Harrigan..."

"Okay, Harrigan, you relax there. You're safe now. You're going to be alright."

Safe. That was more by good fortune than anything else. Hangdog Harrigan had got lucky, and not for the first time where deep water was concerned. He was not destined to die by drowning. He closed his eyes.

"What do you reckon?" the second voice asked.

"He's definitely banged up. Hit and run maybe? That arm looks too much for a mugging. Either way, I don't reckon he jumped."

"Makes a nice change."

The pandemic, or more accurately the Lockdown, had led to a decrease in many other forms of death, notably car accident. But suicides were on the up. *Another grim reality of life in 2020,* thought Harrigan, and then passed out.

Chapter 10 – Harrigan Investigates

Though he was no longer as young as he had been, Harrigan had not yet reached the age at which trips to the hospital, or even the doctor, became a regular thing, so this was his first hospital visit since the pandemic had begun.

It was a grim sight, and one that the media struggled to convey. He had seen, on the News, glimpses of wards shrouded in protective plastic and medical staff rushed off their feet, close to tears, working shift after shift in a desperate attempt to get an uncontrollable situation under control. He had seen it and thought it looked bad, terrible in fact. But what he had seen was nothing. The version he had seen was edited for impact; the tragic highlights, flurried activity, then cut to heart-breaking close-up to bring it home. But condensing it softened it. The TV news could not convey the achingly slow passage of time, measured out in the beeps and whirrs of machines, it could not convey the atmosphere of frustration or the exhaustion on the faces. Above all, it could not capture the weight of despondency. You didn't need to focus in, you needed to step back and see the whole picture as it played out, moment by moment for the people trying to hold back the tide.

For Harrigan – for a lot of people – this would be over in a few weeks, and the fact that it had been 'over in a few weeks' for a few months now did not pour cold water on that optimism, because if it had been 'over in a few weeks' last month then it was *definitely* 'over in a few weeks' this month. That stood to reason. He listened to the News and watched the statistics (as Will had insisted) and saw that things were getting better. The people who were trained to read and interpret these numbers *said* that things were getting better, and Harrigan believed them.

But there was no sense of that here. Here you saw people worn down by the unendingness of it all, by the statistical reality of how many of their charges would die, crushed under constant demand, made worse by the blithe acceptance that they would always be there. '*Thank God for our NHS*,' public and politicians alike declared, '*They will cope*'. And they would. But too few people wondered what toll it might exact upon them. Certainly Harrigan hadn't until now. Even when he saw Nurse Emily, and recognised how tired she looked, he couldn't have guessed at this reality. He felt very guilty for having a broken arm.

"How did you do it?" asked the doctor.

"I fell down some steps by the river," said Harrigan – which he had.

The doctor nodded, sleepily. "You want to be more careful."

"I do."

"Your leg's not broken but it's a bad bruise. It's going to hurt for a while. Your arm is broken, and will be in the cast for six to eight weeks."

"Six weeks," nodded Harrigan.

"Six to eight," the doctor repeated patiently from behind his mask. "I wasn't giving you a choice. It'll take as long as it takes."

Harrigan nodded. "Thank you, doctor. For everything you and your colleagues are doing."

The doctor nodded, absently. Probably everyone said some variation on that, and Harrigan suspected that the doctors and nurses would all happily forego the thanks in return for everyone staying the hell indoors and following the rules.

Which Harrigan would have been happy to do, except that… Did investigating a Golem come under the heading of acceptable reasons to go out?

"We're going to keep you in for a day," the doctor said as he stood up from Harrigan's bed.

"Is that really necessary?"

The doctor looked down at Harrigan with a withering expression. "No. It's just that I find myself with nothing to do at present and we have so many free beds right now."

"Sorry," mumbled Harrigan.

"It's just a precaution."

And Harrigan could guess what it was a precaution against; when he'd been on the force they'd called it 'Suicide watch'. Too many people were going into the river right now, so they were taking twenty four hours to get an idea of his mental state. It wasn't enough, but it was all they could afford.

Once the doctor had gone, Harrigan turned awkwardly to the bedside cabinet with his belongings in it and fished out his mobile. It had survived the river (who knew how) and that left him with a decision to make; what the hell did he tell Nurse Emily? The truth was terrifying but a lie would make her think she was crazy. Neither seemed helpful, particularly with her health in so precarious a state, but he couldn't say nothing either.

He settled on a text, awkwardly typed one-handed. '*Have not forgotten what we talked about, but am in hospital. Nothing to worry about but please bear with me. Hope you are feeling better. Harrigan*'

All true, while thoroughly misleading. That was a line he seemed to be walking a lot of late. It was deferring the problem, but that would do until Emily was better. Or not.

He had hoped for a quick response but none came. Perhaps she had turned her phone off? Closing his eyes, Harrigan tried to sleep, repeatedly telling himself that everything was okay. But he was in the wrong place to believe that.

It was afternoon when Harrigan woke and he instantly checked his phone.

'*OK. Hope you are alright. E.*'

It wasn't much of a message, but it meant that Nurse Emily was… It meant that she had turned her phone back on.

There was a cold meal in front of Harrigan that looked to have been sitting there for an hour or so, but he was too hungry to be fussy. As he ate, he turned his attention to the TV mounted on the wall of the ward. The News was on and he watched, though there was nothing new in the News these days. There was only one story in 2020 and everything else connected back to it somehow. He almost fell out of bed when a familiar face came onto the screen, its terracotta glare apparently directed at him.

The subtitled reporter informed him that, '*The McDowall Golem is just one way the arts have been raising spirits during Lockdown.*'

109

"Not mine it bloody hasn't," muttered Harrigan.

The camera travelled down the statue, from its head to its trainers, and Harrigan frowned. Was this live? The caption said it was.

"Excuse me? Hello?" He spoke to the occupant of the next bed along, a grey-faced, man with hair that he must have been dyeing since the 80s. "Do you happen to know if this is live TV?"

The man nodded and said that, as far as he was aware, it was.

And it did seem to be; there was the time onscreen and there was the reporter standing beside the Golem. Except...

Harrigan sat back in his bed, his mind racing. There had been moments like this in some of his cases, when he knew that he had seen something important but wasn't sure what it meant. Nine times out of ten the connection eluded Hangdog Harrigan, but that tenth time was like drinking from the fountain of youth, you felt it tingle in your toes. Maybe it was the morphine talking, but Harrigan was starting to feel like his old self. He had purpose. He had a case.

Reaching for his phone again, he began his 'investigation', calling up images of the Golem. There was no shortage of those, people had been taking selfies alongside the statue since day one, and Harrigan pieced his way through them, looking for suitable pictures, squinting at his phone screen then checking the dates on which the images had been posted.

By the time dinner came around he was able to sit back and enjoy the tingling in his toes.

The following morning, Harrigan was released from hospital and took a taxi home, not wanting to bother his sons or deal with any of the questions they would have about what he was doing there. He spent the remainder of the day confirming his theory on a larger screen (one that required less squinting) and figuring out how to use the bathroom with one arm in plaster. By evening, his suspicions had grown to certainties, and he had a plan of action for tomorrow.

That night, he slept better than he had since the pandemic began. The sleep of a man who was feeling useful again. And of a man on prescription painkillers.

"Pluto in the 1st house can be a sign of new beginnings, new ventures, but beware of becoming obsessed with them…"

In the loneliness of Lockdown, it was nice to have another voice about the place and listening to Al the Astrologer as he made breakfast had become part of Harrigan's morning routine. It was Nurse Emily who had introduced him to the YouTuber, though Harrigan had initially demurred, saying he thought it was all so much crap. She had smiled and said, '*Yes. But it's surprising how, when you listen, you start to retrofit what he says to suit your own life.*'.

Harrigan finished his breakfast, turned off Al, and went to work.

It was not hard to track down the artist who called himself Henrik. The man had clearly modelled himself on Banksy, but while everyone wanted to know the identity of the Bristol artist, no one gave a toss who Henrik was, so he had been forced to be a lot less mysterious if he wanted to get any attention. And Henrik wanted attention.

Ideally Harrigan would have confronted the man in person but, after much backing and forthing on how important this was, he decided that he had pushed the Covid regulations far enough for one week. He *did* believe in them and felt strongly that people should follow them, it was just very inconvenient when *he* had to. Which was presumably how everyone felt, and if you didn't practice what you preached then, really, what use were you?

Posing as a reporter requesting an interview, Harrigan emailed Henrik's publicist (whom he strongly suspected was Henrik himself), then went to make a cup of coffee. The reply arrived before he had even had the chance to add sugar.

It took a little while, and two phone calls to Will, for him to figure out the minutiae of setting up a video call from his end, rather than being a passive video caller, but he managed it and sent the link through to Henrik, scheduling the interview for that afternoon. That gave him a few hours to get his thoughts in order and to scribble some notes on post-its that he stuck about the screen of his laptop.

Harrigan's heart was in his mouth as he began the call, although that was partly because he was nervous of the technology failing him. It had been a while since he had conducted any sort of 'interrogation', and this was a weird way to be doing it.

A face appeared on the screen. A man in his late thirties, with fashionable glasses and bleached hair.

"Mr Henrik?"

"Just Henrik, please."

Harrigan nodded and pretended to make a note. "Thanks for speaking to me, I'm sure you've been busy since the Golem."

Henrik's face broke into an involuntary smile. "It's been quite a ride, that's for sure. The way people have responded to it – not just in an aesthetic sense, but in terms of the concept behind it – has been really heartening. The public reaction has been exactly what I'd hoped; they've invested in the Golem, taken it as their representative and made it more than the sum of its clay. Right from the start I planned for the public to be integral – it's their words inside that make it what it is – but you can never predict how people will act, so it's been great."

Harrigan got the impression that Henrik had these responses ready to go. He'd done a few interviews recently and this was a man determined to seize his moment.

"Let me just make sure I'm getting my facts right; this wasn't a commission from the council or a private concern or anything like that, this was done off your own bat. That's right is it?"

"Absolutely," enthused Henrik. "It was all my idea, all my doing. Although I have to admit – another thing that's been really heartening – the response of local government has been great. You can never tell with public art; nine times out of ten, something that's erected without permission comes straight back down again. But all the council has done is clean it and move it. I guess the public response (which, like I said, has been so positive) will have guided them in that. I mean… maybe it's too much to say that there would have been *outcry* if it had been taken down, but people would have been angry."

"Sure," Harrigan nodded. "It obviously means something to

the local people but it must mean a lot to you too – how personal would you say it was?"

"Oh this comes right from my heart." Henrik was back on his internal script, words he had honed talking to himself in the mirror or in the shower. "It's my gift to the city – to the nation, really – but it remains a piece of myself. I mean, in these times you see everyone digging deep, doing what they can with what they've got and I wanted to be part of that. *This* is what I can do, *this* is what I've got. Obviously it's not as important as what doctors and nurses are doing but – I don't know – if it inspires people, uplifts them, gives them something to believe in then, maybe it *is* as important. More so even."

Harrigan bit back the response that had rushed to the tip of his tongue and, having put Henrik at ease, went for the jugular.

"So, given how much it means to you, how did you feel when it vanished?"

The question blindsided Henrik every bit as much as Harrigan had expected, he suddenly looked trapped by the sides of the screen. The old police instincts flickered within; you knew when you had a man on the ropes.

"You mean… You mean when they took it off for cleaning?" suggested Henrik.

"No." Harrigan shook his head. "I mean when it vanished and you made a replacement. Very quickly I have to say. What happened? Did the council get in touch?"

Henrik stared blankly, and Harrigan could see his hand hovering to cut them off.

"Mr Henrik, I know you don't want this made public – I imagine you signed something to promise you wouldn't reveal it – and I have some good news on that front; I'm not a reporter. The bad news is that if you hang up on me now, if you lie to me or hold anything back, then my next call will be to a *real* reporter, and we both know that I can prove this. You shouldn't have added the '2', Mr Henrik."

"Just Henrik," the artist muttered automatically. "You saw the '2'?"

"I was looking for it," admitted Harrigan. "You hid it well. I think you'd have to be looking for it to see it. But I was and I did, and my guess is that it's only a matter of time before other people notice. You should probably confess to the council and knock up another replacement before it's too late. And resist the urge to put '3' on it, eh?"

For a long beat, Henrik was silent. When he spoke, his voice was more subdued but there was hope in it. "You're not going to tell anyone?"

"You know my conditions." Harrigan had no reservations about playing hardball with an artist who had compared himself to NHS staff during a pandemic.

"I got the call the morning it vanished," Henrik murmured. "Early." He paused. "You're not recording this are you?"

"No."

"Thank you. Like you said; it was the council. They wanted to know if I'd removed the Golem." He smirked to himself. "If I remember rightly they wanted to know if it was *'part of the art'*." He shook his head. "Like they cared about Art. I told them no, and asked why and they said it was gone. No sign. They were going to look into it and get back to me. So I was… Well, if I'm honest, and as long as this isn't going out in print, I wasn't that bothered. Look at Banksy's stuff; up it goes and twenty four hours later someone's nicked the wall. That's the way it is with this sort of art – if it's not a vandal then it's a collector (fine line). It's finite, and that's okay. From my point of view (again; just between us) it was actually pretty good news. Everyone loved the Golem but the fuss was fading and this would have put it back in the spotlight. Might have got a few more commissions out of it." He looked dreamily off-camera. "Maybe an exhibition even. Anyway, I was getting ready for a call from *BBC Breakfast* or *Wake Up!* or whoever wanted me, figuring out what words I could say to express how heartbroken I was and watching a YouTube video about how to cry on cue, when the council called again."

"They wanted it back," said Harrigan.

Henrik nodded. "Do you know violent crime is down in that

area since the Golem arrived? I mean… not much, and there is also a national lockdown, and theft is actually up, but still. It's been good for the community. Or at least the council thought so."

Maybe it was, Harrigan thought, but it seemed just as likely that keeping the Golem there made the council popular in an area where they weren't. It was a cheaper way to buy public goodwill than fixing roads, increasing policing or making the blocks themselves less dangerously flammable.

"My first reaction was; no way," Henrik went on. "The Golem was a one-off. All those bits of paper inside it – hand-written – I couldn't replicate those and it wouldn't mean the same if people did it again *knowing* what they were for. It would look the same – I took moulds of the original – but it wouldn't *mean* anything."

Again, Harrigan thought the artist was wrong. Maybe the Golem without the words inside it meant nothing *artistically*, but it had come to mean something to the residents. To Henrik, the words of the people gave it meaning, but to Harrigan it was the people's reaction to it that made the Golem worth something. It was art that he could damn near get behind.

"I assume that the council suggested that maybe this time you might like to be paid?"

Henrik blushed, but sat up defensively at the same time. "Well what if they did? Where's the harm in that? I got paid nothing for something that brought people pleasure, that brought them together at a troubled time, that maybe even brought them some measure of peace. And what did I get out of it?"

"Publicity?" suggested Harrigan.

"Well… yes," admitted Henrik, slumping back again. "But I didn't know that going in. It could just as easily have got me nothing and I'd still be glad I did it. Let me tell you Mr Harrigan (believe me or not), I wouldn't have taken a penny for the first Golem. It meant too much. But the second," he shrugged, "that meant nothing. So if they wanted to pay a few thousand for a lump of fired clay, then let them."

It wasn't a totally unreasonable point.

"Is that why you put the '2' on it? Because I'm damn sure the

115

council didn't ask you to do that."

"I didn't want them to be identical," Henrik muttered irritably. "It was… You can say I sold out, and maybe I did, but I had enough integrity that I didn't want them identical. So if you looked, then you would know that one was art and the other was decoration. Or at least so I would know."

"So you're not going to tell the council?"

Henrik paused. "I suppose if they find out, they'll want their money back."

"I would think."

Henrik shrugged. "I'll make another one. Identical this time. The first one had the words inside it – if that isn't enough to make it different then what is?"

After Henrik had made Harrigan promise, once again, that he would not be telling the media or Twitter or making the truth public in any way, the interview came to a close. Harrigan hung up and smiled. His leg ached, his arm ached and he was still feeling a bit foggy, but he had done a nice little bit of police work there.

Of all things, it had been the Golem's hand that had done it. The memory of that hand, bunched into a fist, narrowly missing his head and slamming into the wall, was etched into Harrigan's mind, and if he closed his eyes he could still see the chunk of clay flying past his nose where the Golem had broken its own knuckle with the force of the blow. But the statue he had seen on the news had two pristine hands and the appropriate number of knuckles. That had been enough for him to take a closer look at the many pictures online and, peering closely, looking for any other differences, he had spotted the number '2', intertwined with the significant symbols and decorations on the Golem's front. By putting the pictures in chronological order, he then established that the number hadn't been there before the 10th of May, when Emily had taken the statue for a drive, but was in every subsequent picture.

It all led to one conclusion, which Henrik had now confirmed. The Golem he had spent more than half the night watching was nothing but a replica, and was never going to move no matter how long he stared at it. The one that had chased him however, Henrik's original; that was something else, and something that he was, at some point, going to have to deal with. The conversation with Henrik had also convinced Harrigan that the artist had no idea that his creation had come to life, and Harrigan saw no reason to share that information. Henrik would only take it as further evidence of his artistic genius.

Harrigan popped a painkiller and sat down to think.

The Invisible Man had been hard to believe in, but that had been 'science', which forgave an awful lot. If someone had sat down and explained to Harrigan how his phone worked then he would not have been able to understand it, and if they had said it was 'magic' then he couldn't have proved them wrong. When science reached a certain point then the division between it and magic became very thin indeed. Was an invisible man harder to believe than a device in your pocket that allowed you to talk to Australia? The only thing that made one more believable than the other was that everyone had a mobile phone and very few people were invisible. But if you went back two hundred years and asked a hundred people which sounded more likely, then the split would probably have been about fifty-fifty. Science did the impossible every day and then made it everyday. Right now the whole world was holding out for science to save them.

But the Golem wasn't science, it was... He didn't know what it was. Religion? Magic? Voodoo? Demonic possession? It was supernatural, and that meant bending the inflexible Harrigan mind in a whole new direction.

Perhaps the person he should have been talking to was his girlfriend.

Elsa occasionally let slip little nuggets about her job and, while they were vague, they all had that edge of the impossible. It was not all invisible men and mad science, she tackled stuff that was just 'other'. For all Harrigan knew, this one Golem was part of a global plague of them (like the globe didn't have plagues enough) and Elsa was off fighting them right now. The thought made him queasy – the Golem had come close to killing him, and the idea of Elsa up against one was troubling. Would anyone from her organisation tell him if something happened to her?

He shook his head, trying to dispel the idea. She would be fine. She was tough. She was always fine.

None of which helped him with the Golem.

Deal in facts. Henrik had got the call about the missing Golem the morning after Nurse Emily took it for a drive. That made sense.

So, at some point between then and three nights ago the Golem had made its way back to London (almost to its home), in time to menace Harrigan.

How didn't matter (presumably it had walked), what mattered was where it had ended up. Where was it, now that its spot was occupied by Golem #2?

How did you set about finding a Golem? The most reliable way was probably to wait for the inevitable carnage and work your way back. Even when it was doing good deeds, the Golem was as subtle as using a sledgehammer to perform heart surgery.

Harrigan's eyelids began to hang heavy as the painkillers started to kick in.

Even if he found the thing then what could he do? It didn't like him, and he'd been very lucky last time they met. He would not be so lucky again.

The room blurred and Harrigan blinked himself awake.

He would have to update Emily sometime. He couldn't tell her much that would ease her conscience, but nor could he leave her hanging forever.

But the room blurred again, and this time he did not fight it.

In his dream, Harrigan was with Elsa. They were both fighting against a Golem that seemed to get bigger each time he saw it.

"What do we do now?" Harrigan asked desperately.

And in answer, Elsa kissed him.

Harrigan started awake with a cry that turned into a scream as he jolted his broken arm.

"Well, that's not how it goes in the fairy tales," said Elsa, stepping back from him, hands on her hips. "Waking with a kiss always seems a pretty laid back affair."

"Wuh?" Confronted with his girlfriend, here in his home, Harrigan wasn't sure if he was awake or still dreaming.

Elsa looked him up and down, seeming to notice for the first time the cast on his arm. "Holy hell, Harrigan, what have you done to yourself?"

"You're back," breathed Harrigan.

"For now."

"For now?" That didn't sound so promising.

"I wanted to stop by, since I was in town," admitted Elsa. "But, truthfully, I'm here because this is where the trail led."

Chapter 11 – Eight Days Earlier

Maxie Feld was asleep in the flat which he, not quite legally, called home, on the sixteenth floor of McDowall House when the call came, jarring him awake.

He made a grab for his phone, knocking it across the floor in his haste, swearing repeatedly under his breath as he groped about for it in the dark, finally locating it and answering.

"Hello?" he croaked.

"Maxie?" The voice at the other end checked.

"Yes, it's Maxie. What the hell could you possibly… Do you know what time it is?" He had a look. "It's gone 2am. What could you possibly… Who is this?"

"It's Booth. I'm at the site. There's a problem."

Maxie rubbed his eyes. "I'll be right there."

It was a longish drive from McDowall House, and Maxie was completely (if unwillingly) awake by the time he strode into the abandoned railway tunnel, overgrown with vegetation, which rose like a Roman ruin from the wasteland that surrounded it on all sides.

"Alright, what's the problem?"

"It's stuck," explained Booth, simply.

Beyond Booth, who had come to meet him, Maxie could see the two small trucks, huddled in the anonymous shadows afforded by the tunnel. One was parked up, ready to go, but its headlights illuminated the rear wheels of the other, sunk deep into the wet mud; going nowhere.

"We thought we'd use the other to sort of – you know – nudge it free," Booth went on.

"What happened?"

"The second truck got stuck as well," replied Booth, briskly. "So we gunned the engine, it shot forward and gave the first one a bit more than a nudge, if you know what I mean."

Maxie could see exactly what he meant; the back doors of the stuck truck were badly buckled. Someone had used a bit of wood to jam them closed, but that was not a long-term solution.

"And it's still stuck," admitted Booth.

"Did you try towing it out with the other?"

Booth nodded. "Whole lot of skidding about, then the rope snapped."

Great. Just great. "How's the cargo?"

"Seems fine."

Maxie looked about, shifting to from foot to foot, somewhere between sleeplessly irritable and nervous. They were out in the middle of nowhere but you could never discount the possibility of late dog-walkers or early joggers (both occupations which Maxie mentally categorised as borderline psychotic). It would not do to be seen.

"It can't stay here."

"The cargo won't fit in the other truck."

"Make it fit." There was always room if you put your mind to it.

Booth sucked in air through his teeth. "You want to risk opening those doors?"

Maxie growled to himself. An hour ago he'd been in bed without a care in the world.

"Alright, everyone – and I mean *everyone* – get your arse behind the truck and push. And if I hear one comment about the mud then you can travel inside and see how you like that. And watch those doors! We lose *anything* and there'll be hell to pay"

As George took the wheel, the rest of them crowded around the back of the truck. *All five of us*, thought Maxie, *this is a waste of time.*

"On three! One... Two... Three!"

Mud spewed up as the tyres spun, digging deeper, leaving great treaded footprints in the muck. The five men pushed but they might as well have been trying to shift the Rock of Gibraltar.

"Sorry, Maxie." Booth spat mud, and wiped his eyes. "It's not going anywhere."

"Well it can't stay here." What was he supposed to do now? There were days when Maxie hated being the one in charge.

"Let's try again," he said, without much hope. "Can we find

something to put under the tyres? Get some grip?" He paused. "Can anyone else hear that?"

They all stopped to listen.

"George, cut the engine."

Now they could hear it clearly, coming from outside; a rhythmic thumping. For a beat, everyone was still, listening to the sound, then in the next instant they were all scurrying to turn off lights. It wasn't clear what the noise was but it had to be someone approaching. Possibly on a giant pogo stick...

Maxie loped through the shadows to the arch of the tunnel and peered out. It was still more night than morning, but a thin, grey mist was wafting across scrubland, gathering in the ditches and depressions and hanging above them like a lace curtain. He shivered in the cold, then drew breath as he spotted movement at the top of the slope. The fringes of mist seemed to part to admit a figure, barely visible in the darkness, given shape only by the outlining of mist. He strode down the incline with big thumping steps, proving himself the source of the mystery sound. What did he have in his boots? Maybe they were some kind of weighted fitness boots that athletes wore to train. Though the figure didn't look like a runner. Possibly a wrestler. Maxie had been a street fighter when he was a kid (everyone was where Maxie grew up), and a good one too, but if he'd come up against something like that then he'd have turned and run. The man was huge.

Reaching the bottom of the slope, the stranger paused and looked about him. Maxie ducked back. Had he been seen? The thumping started again, coming their way.

Maxie dashed back into the tunnel. "Right, it's some big bloke out for a walk. We're delivery drivers, our truck got stuck in the mud, we're trying to get it free. Keep the details light and keep that damn door closed!"

He ran over to join George, leaning against the second truck, a study in urban nonchalance and affected innocence.

"Lights on!" he hissed. "Don't make it look any more suspicious than it already does."

The lights of the trucks came on, partially illuminating the inside of the grimy tunnel and casting their light out beyond the arch to give the shifting mist a jaundiced pall. Now they got their first decent look at the stranger, still approaching, and Maxie felt his insides contract and the hairs on his arm rise up. It wasn't just a big man. It wasn't even a man. Now he could see it, he knew that face, that form. He walked past it every day, and always experienced a short but noticeable stab of guilt, that he probably deserved, when he thought of the words he'd written that lay within its clay body:

I hope my parents never find out what I became.

It was the McDowall Golem, thumping towards them, and just looking at it, he knew – they all knew – that this was not a man in a suit or someone wearing a mask.

Sometimes when you watched a horror film you wondered; how would I react? What would I do? Would I be a believer or a sceptic? You might dismiss films in which characters too quickly jumped to the supernatural conclusion. But right now, as the figure strode out of the murk of night into the yellow beams of the headlights, its footfalls echoing about the tunnel, there was no room for any other conclusion. It *was* the Golem.

And it was coming right for Maxie.

With a cry of terror, George, who had been standing beside him, took off, the rest of the gang following. Booth was the last, torn between fear and the embarrassment of looking as if he was afraid. The former won out and he scurried away, almost tripping over his own feet as he went.

Maxie stayed. He didn't know if he was too afraid to move or just… not afraid. Or at least, not afraid in the same way.

Ethnically speaking, Maxie's ancestry gave him roughly equal shares across the Moslem/Jewish divide. Philosophically speaking he belonged to neither side and had no time for religion of any variety. His closest tie to his heritage was his Grandfather; barnstormingly Jewish and a great teller of stories '*from the old country*'. Maxie had never bothered to learn what old country that might be (as a boy he had misheard it as '*odd country*' and got a smack about the head for being disrespectful), but he adored listening to the stories, which were dark and depressing but fascinated him. Golem stories had been a particular favourite, his Grandfather intoning them with the gravitas of a true believer combined with the panache of a natural performer.

Maxie knew about Golems; he knew the legends and the rules, and he was willing to believe.

The Golem stopped in front of Maxie, its eyes fixed on him. It was the same stare he saw every day and yet it was very different when it was so obviously *on* him. What did it want? It had been heading for him before the others had fled. Why him? Did it recognise him as being in charge?

Or was it because he lived in the block?

The golems in his Grandfather's stories had come from the ghettos of eastern Europe and they embodied those places. They were servants of the chosen people. This latter day example had a mixed heritage (Maxie could identify), but it had the same drives, didn't it? And its chosen people were the residents of McDowall House, who had all given a little bit of themselves to make it real.

"Our truck is stuck." He couldn't quite believe he was speaking to it. "Can you help?"

The Golem kept looking at him.

Of course it wasn't enough to serve a single resident; it was supposed to serve the community.

"There's supplies inside for McDowall House," said Maxie. "Stuff to help them through Covid."

It wasn't a one hundred percent lie, and even if it had been the Golem did not ask for proof. Before Maxie had finished speaking it was striding towards the truck.

"George, get in that cab!" yelled Maxie. "Gun it."

George looked nervous but did as he was told.

The engine started just as the Golem bent down to lay hands on the back of the truck.

For once in his life, Maxie was lost for swear words. As the engine roared and the wheels churned once more, the Golem straightened up, bringing the rear end of the truck with it, the wheels spinning in the air, flinging off mud. The truck was four-wheel drive and as George started to creep it forward, the Golem went with it, carrying the back of the vehicle like a huge wheelbarrow.

Maxie could only watch. He wished his Grandfather could have seen this.

Once they were out of the mud, Maxie called for George to cut the engine, leaving the Golem still standing there, apparently untroubled by the weight resting in its huge clay hands. Maxie hurried over.

"That'll do. That's great, thanks. You can put it down now."

The Golem did as it was told, and then was motionless.

Maxie was still staring at it as Booth crept cautiously up.

"What is it? I mean… What *is* it?"

"It's a Golem," replied Maxie, simply.

Booth frowned. "Like in *Lord of the Rings*?"

"No, that's Gollum."

Booth blinked a few times, reflecting that none of this answered his question. "It picked up the truck."

"They're very strong."

Booth nodded, his Adam's apple bobbing nervously. "So… it's like a robot?"

"Kind of." A robot from a time when no one knew what robots were.

Booth nodded again. He felt more comfortable with a familiar word like 'robot'. "Is it on our side?"

That was a question Maxie wasn't sure how to answer, and Booth had another one.

"What do we do with it?"

For starters they got it to step back from the truck so Bill could open the doors and check inside.

"I'll have to tell the Boss about it," judged Maxie. It was all a bit *Little Caesar* referring to him as 'the Boss' (you needed a fedora and a tommy gun to talk like that), but only Maxie knew his name, and at least this way there were no confusing aliases to deal with.

Booth shook his head. "He'll never believe it. I'm standing right here and I don't believe it."

"Maxie!" Bill called from the back of the truck.

"What?"

"You'd best get over here. There's a problem with the cargo."

Chapter 12 – Jakeem

For the first few days of her infection, Emily did not even check in online; she barely had the strength to leave her bed.

The Corona virus, officially identified as Covid 19, could have very different effects on different people, ranging from no symptoms at all to death. The reasons for this were not yet fully understood, but there did seem to be a racial component. Statistically, black people got hit harder, and although biology didn't discriminate, Emily still found herself thinking, '*Typical*'. Her Dad insisted that it was social factors that made them more susceptible, and he might well be right.

Emily found herself somewhere in the middle of the Covid spectrum. The virus metaphorically whacked her over the head, stole her lunch money and left her curled up in bed too sick to even re-read a Terry Pratchett book – and when a person is too sick for Terry Pratchett then they are *sick*.

But in the midst of fever, breathlessness and brooding on how bad she knew this *could* get, the spectre of the Golem still lurked at the back of her mind. At her worst, the fever convinced her that the whole thing had been a dream. When she was lucid enough to know that it had been real, she took comfort from the fact that she had dealt with it, but still worried about what might have happened next.

Then she went online.

There was not a word about the Golem's disappearance. What there was, was an article about it being back in its usual spot after being removed for cleaning.

Emily read it three times, finishing the last with a scream of frustration before collapsing back onto her bed, her mind a fever-boiled stew of worry and self-doubt.

It had been real. It *had*!

She needed to go out there and prove it to herself, but that was out of the question for another week yet. If the Golem remained at large then she ought to call the police; the thing was dangerous. But they would never believe her.

That was when she thought of Clive Harrigan.

It was difficult to form personal connections with all the people she saw via the vaccine trial, but she did try, and Harrigan was one with whom she had genuinely got on. He seemed a nice man, and as an ex-policeman he presumably carried some authority – people were more likely to listen to him. More importantly, she had seen his face when he talked about the Invisible Man. At the time, Emily had been stunned that Cambridge Police employed someone who believed in invisible people, and wondered if that that had hastened his departure from the Force. Now she had encountered something equally inexplicable, and a man open-minded enough to believe in invisible men might also be open-minded enough to admit the existence of a golem.

She made the call, had the conversation, and while he clearly hadn't believed her, she was sure that he would do as he had promised and spend a night watching the Golem.

Telling someone else had an unexpected side-effect. The morning after talking to Harrigan, Emily found herself reaching for the dog-eared copy of *Eric* on her bedside table (not Pratchett's best but she hadn't read it for a while). She was still sick as a dog but a weight had been lifted from her shoulders that had clearly been making her worse. Pretty soon she was starting to feel guilty for making such a fuss, and when Emily started feeling guilty then it was a fair bet that she was on the mend.

She could not completely absolve herself of responsibility, nor would she have wanted to; the Golem was *her* problem. But a problem shared was a problem that did not consume her every waking moment. By calling Harrigan, she had taken appropriate action, and she now worried more about not hearing back from him than about the creature itself. What was taking so long? Each time her phone made a sound her heart jumped up a gear.

In fact, it only took Harrigan three days to get back to her, though it seemed far longer to the isolated Emily (time did funny things in Lockdown), but when the message came it was not the one she had been hoping for.

'*Have not forgotten what we talked about, but am in hospital.*

128

Nothing to worry about but please bear with me. Hope you are feeling better. Harrigan.'

Actually, she was not sure what message she had been hoping for; one way she was crazy, the other there was a potentially violent living statue on the loose. But something *definitive* would have been better than more waiting.

Would Harrigan even go through with it? Or was he making excuses to cover the fact that he thought she was nuts?

She texted back a terse *'OK'*, then regretted it and hastily added *'Hope you are alright. E.'*, because if he genuinely was in hospital then she was being a bitch.

It was a few days later, as Emily's quarantine was about to end (by which time she was starting to quite enjoy the break – more guilt), when she received another text, which managed to be, in turn, comforting, cryptic and unnerving.

'Have reported Golem to the appropriate authorities. The one outside M. House is not the same one you saw. Nothing to worry about. Best, Harrigan.'

That suggested that he too had seen the Golem come to life – so she wasn't crazy – but the rest of it was perplexing. Particularly one phrase.

Emily texted back *'There are appropriate authorities?'* Who the hell took care of golems?

And Harrigan had replied, *'Apparently so.'*

Emily recognised when she was being shut down – he didn't want to talk any more. Which just raised further questions of the pressing variety. Maybe he *hadn't* seen it move, maybe he was humouring her and the *'appropriate authorities'* would be arriving on her doorstep in white coats, bearing a straitjacket and a large butterfly net. Or maybe the existence of golems was all top secret, hush-hush, and it was the Men in Black who would be showing up, with that flashy thing to blank her memory. What she wouldn't have given for that flashy thing.

Emily made herself a cup of herbal tea (her Mum's secret recipe), sat on her sofa and read the messages through a few more times.

He'd said '*Nothing to worry about*' twice. That actually made her worry more.

She felt let down. Part of her reason for involving Harrigan had been to pass the responsibility onto someone in a more official position. It seemed to have worked, but almost too well. There were so many questions still unanswered. If this wasn't '*the same one*', then what was it and where had it come from? What guarantee did she get that there was '*Nothing to worry about*'?

She couldn't let it go.

In twelve hours her quarantine period would be up. Tomorrow night, *she* would watch the Golem, and make her own decision about it. And before that she was going to buy a large hammer. One way or another, this ended tomorrow night.

"You're out?" Robert smiled as Emily passed him on the stairs the following afternoon, doing the awkward social distance dance that was becoming increasingly familiar to those living in cramped spaces. Robert lived on fifth; a quiet man in his late thirties, hair starting to thin and always seeming slightly scared of the world. He was one those who was actually quite well-suited to Lockdown. "Do I need to keep my distance? More than usual, I mean."

"No." Emily returned his smile. "I am virus-free and feeling good." A few years ago he had shyly asked her on a date, and she had invented a fictitious boyfriend to let him down gently. She wished she hadn't, because then she either had to maintain the fiction or risk being asked again.

"That's a relief," nodded Robert. "Maybe it'd be better if people just went out and caught it. Get it over with."

It was horrifying to Emily how many people – well-meaning and intelligent people – thought that. One look inside a Covid ward would change their minds.

"No." She shook her head. "Trust me on this."

Robert nodded again. "I'm sure you're right."

But he wasn't sure. Emily could hear it in his voice. Even Robert, who had not exactly been a social butterfly before Lockdown, was starting to feel the confinement. That was a bad sign.

"Guess what I got last night." Robert beamed. "Bleach."

"Okay." Emily nodded politely. Robert sometimes struggled with everyday interactions, but even for him this seemed an unpromising conversation starter.

"From the Guardian Angel," Robert quickly added. "I wasn't just bragging on buying bleach, it was the – you know? I mean he's probably not an actual angel but – you know what I'm talking about, yeah?"

"Yeah." Emily nodded again. She knew. So the Golem outside was '*not the same one*', huh? Harrigan had clearly been humouring her. Her resolve to go buy that hammer doubled.

"Nice to have him back," Robert went on. "Sooner would have been better. I ran out of bleach days ago."

It was a quirk of human nature that when something like the Angel happened, everyone was grateful for about five minutes and then assumed it to be their right, so when the free gifts on their doorstep stopped, they felt as if they had been robbed of something.

Continuing down, Emily heard voices from the first floor landing and recognised one of them as belonging to the wife of the Syrian family whose name remained an enigma. She had not spoken to them recently and it would be good to check in. Though her days of Golem-assisted theft were over, she still wanted to contribute to the block if she could. Her steps slowed as she approached, hoping to catch a name.

Reaching the landing she saw the wife standing in the doorway, talking with a tall, dark-haired man in an immaculate powder blue shirt and infeasibly shiny shoes. The mask he wore meant that Emily took a moment to recognise him, but it also helped with that identification because it bore his own corporate logo.

It would be too much to say that Paul Haworth owned McDowall House, but he was the smiling figurehead of the corporation that did. Far from most faceless developers, who prefer not to look people in the eye before bulldozing their home, Haworth visited, met with residents and was on first name terms with several, which gave Emily hope that the block might continue to stand. It was not the greatest place to live, and she certainly did not plan to be there forever, but it was an affordable home for people who needed one, and that was increasingly rare in London.

"Hi." Emily raised a hand like a schoolgirl needing to be excused. "Am I interrupting?"

She was specifically talking to the wife, but Haworth answered, used to being the most important individual in any room he entered. "Not at all – Emily, isn't it? Yes? Hard to tell behind the mask. Nice mask by the way. Lydia and I were just chatting."

Lydia! Thank God for Paul Haworth and his assumption that everyone must be talking to him.

"Thanks," nodded Emily. "I like your mask too."

Haworth waved this off. "It was in my pocket (don't you find you have masks everywhere now?), I wear it when I'm at the office – you know; tow the company line. If I'd seen what it was then I'd have worn another one. It's just embarrassing. I might as well be wearing a T-Shirt that says *'How Great Am I?'*."

"Well it's your colour." Emily turned to *Lydia*. "I just wanted to check in and see how you guys were doing? I've been out of it recently." No need to go into details.

Lydia nodded, and seemed to be smiling behind her own mask (a scarf tied about the bottom of her face) though with some anxiety. "Everything is fine. Thank you for asking. We are fine. But I am concerned about my brother-in-law. He was supposed to be arriving. We believe he left the camp in France where he was living, but he has not arrived here yet."

She seemed quite comfortable talking about this subject in front of Haworth, who now chipped in.

"I'd offered him a room here and a job but, like Lydia says, no sign."

"I wondered," Lydia's voice was low, "if there was anything Mr Haworth could do to help find what might have happened to him. He was kind enough to…" she shot a look at Haworth, who nodded as if to say *'I have no secrets from Emily'*. "He helped Masud and I when we first arrived."

Lydia and Masud. Emily wondered if she ought to write that

down now before she forgot.

Haworth made a helpless gesture with his hands. "You know I would if I could, Lydia, but I wouldn't even know where to start. It was just good luck I came across you guys. And it's 'Paul' please, Mr Haworth is my… well, actually I didn't know my father but that's another story."

"Do you have any idea where he would have come into the country?" asked Emily. She seemed to be bouncing from one illegal activity to another, but this one seemed pretty well-justified.

"I know where the men who brought us here, took us," said Lydia. Her concern was evident, even behind the mask. "They were not good men. I worry about what they may have done with Jakeem."

"Now, they didn't bring him here just for their health," Haworth interposed.

"But they have already been paid," pointed out Lydia.

Haworth rallied well. "Yes, but – not wanting to make it sound like Jakeem is just cargo, but he's worth more to them alive. It's not a pretty trade and these bastards want stamping out. Although then of course it's even harder for refugees to get here, so… Oh, the whole system is just bordering on the inhuman but we're not going to fix it in this corridor – the point is; these traffickers? It's not in their interests to harm Jakeem. It may not be easy to find him but he'll be out there somewhere."

Lydia looked comforted.

"Look, tell me where you and Masud were dropped off and I'll go and have a poke around, see if I can find anything." He looked at Emily. "Maybe Emily can come to? Just in case."

Because she was a nurse. For all his affected optimism in front of Lydia, Haworth was far from confident of Jakeem's safety.

"I'd be happy to." The damn Golem could wait, this was important.

"Paul, please," Paul corrected Emily, as they left the block, walking a carefully maintained two metres apart. "How do you want to do this?"

"Separate cars," said Emily, firmly. "The rules are there for a reason. I just had Covid and I don't want it again."

Paul frowned. "You can get it twice?"

"Yes."

"Are you sure?"

"Pretty sure."

Paul rubbed a hand through his dark hair. "I feel like they ought to make that clearer to people."

Emily thought it had been made abundantly clear, but the facts had little chance against the tremendous weight of '*everyone knows*'. Everyone knew that you could only catch it once and were then immune, so no amount of telling them that this was *not* the case did any good. Stuff said by a doctor or a scientist carried little traction when placed against something you heard from the friend of a friend down the pub ('*And he works at Superdrug, so he'd know*').

"We'll meet there then," said Paul. "I don't know if we'll find anything but it's got to be worth a look."

Emily nodded. "You were giving him a job?"

Paul shrugged. "Just handy man or something. Same thing I did for Lydia; she works as a cleaner in the block and I give her and Masud a break on rent. Everyone wins."

"It's a pretty decent thing to do," Emily judged.

Paul demurred. "She's a good cleaner. She works hard. And, let's be honest, it's a sticking plaster for my conscience. I could afford to do more, but I don't." He shook his head. "She told me about Masud's brother when he was still in one of the refugee camps near Calais. I said I'd give him a job if he made it across. Maybe if I hadn't said that…"

"You can't blame yourself."

"I blame the bastards who are taking advantage of desperate people and selling them into virtual (or actual) slavery," snapped Paul. "I blame a government willing to turn a blind eye to people in need if it wins them a few extra votes with the Britain First mob. And yes, I blame myself and people like me for picking up cheap labour when we know damn well where it comes from. You get a choice; employ them and give them a reason to keep coming across, or don't and watch them starve on the streets." He gave a rueful smile. "Option three would be to actually do something useful, but that's too much like hard work for people like me. Come on. I'll meet you there."

Emily had always marked Paul Haworth out as being different from other corporate executives, but she wouldn't have put any of those words into his mouth. That said, he had a way of talking quickly and saying all the right things in a bright, busy tone, that made you almost miss the fact that he was openly admitting to using a broken system to his own advantage. He didn't make excuses for himself, but did that self-awareness make him better or worse? Emily wasn't sure, partly because her Dad would have been ('*You can't trust rich people, Princess*'), and partly because Paul was likeable and seemed genuine in his desire to help, even if it was only a little. Sooner or later the other shoe was sure to drop, presumably in the form of an eviction notice on her doormat.

But there were other things on her mind right now.

When Lydia had given her the directions, Emily had become nervous. The area she had described was safely out of the way, a place where illegal activities could go uninterrupted. The same reason that Emily had dumped the Golem there eleven days ago. It was not the same spot, but it was that same area. It was a big area but... The fear of finding a boatload of refugees beaten to a pulp by heavy, clay hands tortured her during the drive.

She parked Gretchen close to where Lydia's directions led and looked about her. No sign of Paul yet, but it had probably taken a little while for him to walk to his car – if you left an expensive car in that area then the least you could expect was a penis drawn on the bonnet, and Paul surely had an expensive car. BMW probably.

The sensible thing to do was to wait until Paul arrived; who knew what they were walking into and there was safety in numbers. On the other hand if there were people who needed help then every second might be precious, and they would need a nurse more than a property developer.

Emily left the road, skidding down the rough verge scattered with loose stones and thick with weeds. There had been rain recently

135

and there was no drainage, so the ground remained soggy, squelching beneath her trainers as she walked. Here and there, lengths of plastic pipe lay abandoned, choked by bindweed and bramble. A scatter of litter had spread evenly over time; crisp packets, Coke cans, deteriorating plastic bags, brittle and flaking. A shopping trolley lay, belly up with its wheels in the air, providing a perch for a wren that seemed untroubled by how its home had been treated. Though the wild was reclaiming the area, Emily could see where heavy vehicles had passed recently, tyres ploughing muddy furrows now filled with dirty water, rimed with a film of rainbow scum.

The path of the tyres followed a broad ditch that had once been a railway line. It was hard to tell if the line had slowly decayed after going out of use, or if it had been begun and never finished. It led towards the dark mouth of a tunnel, no more than twenty feet long, where the line burrowed through a mound.

Parked inside was a truck.

Emily held back a moment, looking around and listening. There was bird song, the buzz of a thousand insects and, in the distance, the constant background hum of the city; the trains, cars and people blended into one atonal noise. There was no suggestion of anyone else being around. Which didn't mean no one was there.

This was such a bad idea.

As she got closer, Emily noticed that the back doors of the truck were buckled, as if it had been in a minor accident. At the bottom, a piece of wood had been thrust across as a makeshift bolt to keep them closed, but at the top the twisted metal pulled away from the truck roof, making a gap about eight inches wide. A slight downward slope had channelled the rain into the tunnel, turning the ground into a quagmire, and around the back of the truck was a riot of squelched footprints. In amongst the prints were the marks of tyre treads, sunk into the mud. It looked as if the truck had been stuck and it had been all hands on deck to push it clear. The vehicle must have skidded from side to side because those deeply impressed tread marks were all over the place, two particularly prominent ones directly behind the truck's buckled door.

136

But it *did* seem to be clear of the mud. So why abandon it? Maybe the engine was dead too.

There was a smell on the air that Emily didn't like, and a stillness that was making her edgy. Sometimes on a late shift you got this sort of feeling, when it had been quiet for a few hours and you had the sense of something about to happen, the moment before the shit hit the fan.

Emily reached for the door.

Chapter 13 – It Waits

This had not gone as It would have hoped. It would be too much to say that the creature was disappointed or concerned – those were human traits – but It did not know where to go or what to do next. Its instincts did battle with Its situation and with Its increasing hunger. It had come here with plenty of potential victims, but they now lay about the floor of the conveyance in which It had arrived, all dead, some by Its hand, others not.

It remained. The box was a suitable lair – a little warm in the day but good enough. The rotting corpses gave it a smell the creature appreciated and the darkness suited It.

The problem lay outside. Outside the box It now called home was nothing. There were no people about, no dwellings to investigate, just acres of scrubland on every side. No one to feed on, no clue as to where Its next meal might come from.

Every night It crawled out through a narrow gap where the metal of the box had been warped somehow and went on the hunt. It had fallen back on Its oldest instincts – those inherited from distant ancestors who had lived in a very different and less densely populated world than this one. Starting from the box, It prowled the surrounding countryside, moving in ever widening circles, searching with Its eyes, sniffing the air for someone nearby who could be called 'prey'.

Invariably It found no one, and as the end of the night drew near, It climbed to a high point and stared at the horizon, hissing in furious indecision. There, out in front of It, growing clearer against the hazy sky, was the outline of a city. Even at this remove It could taste the infection on the air, and with it the thin, yellow tang of fear. There was food there, It knew it. Not so very far away there was a feast just waiting for It, and the knowledge and the smell drew It with tangible force. But then there was the distance, and the chance of being caught in the open come the morning. Its every instinct told It to stay close to home, not to risk the journey; something would turn up. The internal conflict made it twist and twitch.

It needed to feed. Food was there. But not *right* there. And the gulf that lay between It and food was a broad and an unknown one. Could It make that journey in one night? It would be a one-way journey, there was no coming back. If It was caught in the sun with nowhere to hide then It was dead. But if It went much longer without feeding then It would starve to death. It needed the crush of people, the press of humanity – that was where It thrived. Out here It was dying by degrees.

And yet It still could not quite force Itself to take the risk, Its common sense unable to override Its most basic instincts. As dawn worried at the night sky, It slunk back into the box to sleep another day as best It could in hunger.

But before the next night fell It was woken by noises. Someone was outside the box.

The creature tensed Its lean body in the darkness, and waited.

Chapter 14 – The Truck

Emily's hands were trembling as she slid free the piece of wood that had been used to hold the door closed. The metal door of the truck swung back on its hinges, scraping as it went with a noise like fingernails down a blackboard.

"Oahh…" Emily recoiled. The smell within was so much stronger than it was outside.

People assumed that doctors and nurses got used to the scent of death, but that scent was very different in a hospital setting to what you got when the deceased was left out in the wilds for a few days. The smell of the hospital morgue was chemical, antiseptic, like bleached sadness. You could still catch the odour of death behind it but that odour had been scrubbed down and wrapped up. It was nothing like the smell that now hit her from the thick, oily warmth of the truck's interior. This was death as nature intended; the smell of slow rot, choking and cloying, reaching down your throat, urging you to vomit. It was raw and eye-wateringly sharp, yet also smothering, enveloping Emily like a noxious cloud and advertising what lay within.

When the smell hit her, Emily had turned away, but now, taking control of her lurching stomach, she turned back to look. That was lesson one of being a Nurse; you had to look. The rest of world seemed suddenly quieter as Emily stood in the cool shadow of the tunnel, listening to the flies within, their buzzing gaining a tinny echo in that hollow interior. She was grateful that the dark hid some of the horrors from her; if it had been lighter she knew that she would have seen the bodies moving with maggots.

Bodies. Plural. It was dark but she was quite sure of that, the shadowy outlines within leaving no room for doubt. Maybe ten people? Maybe more? Was Jakeem among them? Would anyone even be able to tell now?

It didn't take a detective to work out what had happened here; they were refugees or illegal immigrants, maybe a mixture of both, who had made it here courtesy of people traffickers, who had then… What? Locked them in here to die? Why? It didn't matter really. Perhaps the police had been closing in, perhaps they had been unable to pay what had been agreed. Whatever the reason, the result was the same. It was not the first time that something like this had happened to those optimistically seeking a new life in a safer country, and it wouldn't be the last.

The outlines were too vague for Emily to see if there were children amongst their number. She hoped not, but it wouldn't be a surprise. The people who did this had no souls.

The only thing she could make out clearly was the corner of a woollen blanket, near enough to the door that it caught what little light there was. It was bright and colourful with a vivid pattern; a small, sad detail of a life lost.

Emily started. That had been a noise, coming from within the truck.

There had been various noises since she her arrival, because the decomposition of the human body is neither a silent process nor a still one. But this had been different, it had not sounded like the wet, sibilant, and occasionally flatulent sounds that characterised body rot. It had sounded like movement. *Deliberate* movement.

It wasn't possible. Was it?

"Hello?"

If there was someone alive in there then what would their mental state be?

"Anyone?"

There was no answer, but again she heard movement; slow but certain.

"You don't have to be scared. I'm not the police, or any authority. I'm not one of the people who locked you in here. I'm… Well I'm not anybody really. I'm a nurse. I can help you."

There was a good chance that whoever was in there did not speak English and had no idea what Emily was or was not, but was hiding because, after what they had been through, it seemed like the best thing to do.

"Damn it," Emily muttered to herself in resignation. She had to go in. She could not stay out here if there was someone in there who needed help.

"I'm coming in," she said, loudly and clearly. "Don't panic. I'm here to help."

Fat lot of good any of that did if they couldn't understand English. Emily had a sudden flashback to her Grandfather, ranting about how '...*most of them can't even speak English!*'. But he would have been as horrified by this as she was. Life would easier if everyone who disagreed with you was a terrible person and *vice versa*, but that wasn't how it worked.

Emily took the mask from her pocket and put it on – it wouldn't be much protection against the smell but anything was better than nothing. She grabbed the swinging door in one hand, gave it a tug to make sure it was stable, then used it to haul herself up, managing to get a foot onto the floor of the truck's interior. She almost fell back out again as her foot skidded in… in whatever it was that was making the floor slippery, and Emily tried hard not to think about what that might be. She rather liked these trainers but they were going straight in the bin when she got home.

"Hello?" She kept talking in a friendly tone of voice. Though that was probably exactly the tone of voice that the traffickers had used.

In here, the darkness was darker and the atmosphere was claustrophobically oppressive, closing in on her, heavy with the scent of rotting flesh. The flies buzzed around her, loud as helicopters, and if she listened she could hear the movement of their larvae at floor level.

"If there's anyone there, please say something." She trod extremely carefully, aware that there were trip hazards everywhere, and that most of them had been people a short while ago.

There was that noise again! Where was it coming from? In the closeness of the truck's interior it seemed to be all around her.

"Anyone?"

She knew what she had to do, but really didn't want to do it.

"I… I'm putting on a torch. Don't be scared."

The phone shook in her hands as she took it from her pocket. Horrifying though all this was in the dark, she had a hunch that adding light was only going to make things worse. The idea of

142

seeing all these poor individuals clearly... But she had to look.

The noise again! It was closer this time, but it sounded... It sounded like the skittering of insects over a metallic surface, but louder. Was it coming from above her? With trembling fingers she turned on the torch on her phone.

As she did so, she heard the noise again, this time to her side, and she whipped the torch around...

...and almost swallowed her tongue in fright. There, for an instant, she could have sworn she saw a face, pale and cadaverous, its skin as lifeless as that of the corpses on the floor, eyes wide and staring, hands raised, fingers spread in defence against the sudden light, hissing mouth wide to reveal sharp, rat-like teeth.

"Emily?"

Emily leapt out of her skin and spun around to see Paul standing just outside the truck.

"What in the name of God have you found?"

He meant the truck with its cargo of bodies, but Emily turned her torch back to the wall where she had seen (or thought she had seen) the apparition. There was no sign of it. She scoured the interior of the truck, ignoring the horrors of the dead for now, searching the floor, the walls, the corners, the ceiling. But there was no sign of it.

"I... I don't know..." She stuttered a belated reply to Paul's question. "I don't know."

Though it went against the grain for Emily, they did mislead the police on one point.

"Just out for a walk," Paul lied with the fluid ease of a career businessman.

The officer shot a suspicious look at Emily. "The two of you live together?"

"No, but we've been seeing each other for a bit and..."

"You shouldn't be mixing with people from other households."

It sounded like a police state: going out walking with someone you didn't live with was a crime. And yet it *was* all for the best. Emily had seen what came out the other side when people were

143

irresponsible and didn't stick to the rules. Perhaps she should never have agreed to this errand.

"We both live alone," Paul answered smoothly. "We're bubbled together."

Bubbling. A relatively recent addition to the rules that allowed people living alone to have some company – the longer this went on, the more the mental toll of isolation was being recognised.

The officer nodded. "So, out for a walk, you see an abandoned truck. What made you look inside?"

Emily was grateful that Paul had gone first. She tried hard to listen to his lies so she could copy them, but she was struggling to focus. Right now the whole world seemed to be just fuzz and noise. They might not even bother talking to her; it was not as if they were suspected of anything.

It was a shame they had to lie at all but Lydia and Masud trusted them. They could not tell the police that they had come here following up on information from a pair of illegal immigrants in the hope of finding a third.

Jakeem...

There was no way of knowing if he had been one of those bodies but... there they were, exactly where Lydia had said they might find Masud's brother. That wasn't a coincidence. What the hell was Emily going to tell them?

"Officer, it's getting late, I've told you all I know about these poor people."

The officer nodded and raised a hand. "Alright. Thank you, Mr Haworth. We've got contact details for yourself and Miss Jennings. We'll be in touch if we need anything more."

The police moved on. When they had first arrived, one had asked to search Emily's bag, and, though he had neither reason nor legal right to do so, Emily had let him, partly because she was in shock, but mainly because it felt wrong to complain about anything while standing so close to that truck.

The inside of her car felt close and strangely silent to Emily as she sat there a few minutes later, breathing steadily in and out. It was evening now, the night closing in. Time to get going, but she

144

needed a moment.

This year had been a horror movie. Nothing about the pandemic had been believable until they were in the thick of it, at which point it had become horribly real. Then there was the Golem; just as impossible to believe and it too had ended badly – if it had even ended. Now this.

This was different. The pandemic was almost too big to take in, the Golem too fantastical. This... There was something very immediate and personal about this. She had seen more than her share of death this year and spoken to more than her share of grieving families, giving the pandemic a personal face. But this... It was so unnecessary. And such a dreadful way to die. It was horrific in the truest sense of that word.

And it had happened not so far from where she had dumped the Golem.

That thought had come back to her again and again, but at least it was one fear she could lay to rest. They hadn't been pounded to death or trampled, they had been left, locked up in there to die. People had done this. If you could call them people.

She started up Gretchen. She and Paul would travel back as they had arrived, each in their separate cars. So the rules insisted. They had exchanged a few words before parting but Emily now found that she couldn't recall any of it; fuzz and noise. She barely knew the man and yet now wished that he was here with her. She didn't want to be alone. Welcome to a pandemic; get used to being on your own.

She stirred uncomfortably in her seat as she drove away. There was a prickling sensation on the back of her neck and she wondered if a spider or fly or some other small insect had got in with her. She brushed at her neck and the sensation seemed to pass.

But there was still something wrong. Which was normal after what she had seen today but...

Emily started around to look at the back seat – something had moved in the mirror!

The seat was empty. Of course it was. She turned her attention back to the road and twitched her head, rubbing it against the headrest – there was that prickly sensation again, almost as if someone was blowing lightly at her neck, making the small hairs stand up on end. She squirmed in her seat. That was the problem with nature; it was all very pretty but there was always some tiny thing with too many legs crawling on you to ruin it.

The smell from the inside of the truck was still in her nostrils but that was probably her. She needed a shower, and then a bonfire of her clothes – even if they were salvageable she would never wear them again.

She would not be going out again tonight. The Golem could wait.

She snatched another glance at the back seat – the roads were quiet anyway. For a moment she thought that she had heard something, perhaps a breath being drawn, slow and low and directly behind her. But there was nothing there, even when she craned her head awkwardly to check the footwell.

She was imagining it.

But it was not just the sounds, the movement in the mirror or the tickling at the back of her neck. It was… it was nothing she could put her finger on, just the overwhelming sensation of not being alone. Sometimes the human body had a sixth sense about these things, telling you when to be on your guard. Other times it was just screwing with you.

Without her wanting it to, her mind took her back to the interior of the truck just before Paul arrived. There had been nothing there (she had searched *really* thoroughly), but at the time it had been so real. If 'real' was the right word for what she had seen. That face had been straight out of a nightmare.

But there again, that had been 2020 all over; the world had become a nightmare. And if that nightmare was starting to make her see things then she would not be the first. It was kept quiet, but many nurses and doctors were suffering from mental health problems brought on by overwork, stress and the constant tragedy that had become their everyday. Because no one makes a worse patient than a doctor or a nurse they all tried to push through it, telling themselves that it wasn't a *real* problem, not when you stacked it up against

146

wards full of the dying. But mental problems were as real as physical ones.

Was that what it had been? Something in her head? What else could it be?

She remembered reading of a syndrome, recognised during the Spanish Flu pandemic that had followed the First World War; people imagined that they had seen Death.

As a Terry Pratchett reader, Emily had a very clear image of Death, and even anticipated his personality. But what she had seen in the truck had not looked as if it might make the occasional dry quip, eat curry or ride a horse called Binky.

There in the mirror!

Emily tugged violently at the wheel to pull the car over and slammed on the brakes. She leapt out and opened the back door.

There was *nothing* there.

By the side of the road, Emily leant against Gretchen, eyes closed, head in her hands, waiting to get her breath back, waiting until she felt more or less safe to drive again. What were the symptoms of Long Covid? Did you get hallucinations?

The back seat remained quiet as Emily drove the rest of the way home, resisting the urge to floor it. But the sensation of someone else in there with her remained. When she parked and walked across the plaza to McDowall House, she found herself checking behind, feeling as if she was being followed. So many times on her walk home she had heard footsteps at her back and imagined who they might be. This time there were no footsteps, but the sensation was no less unnerving.

On her way, Emily passed the Golem. Despite what Harrigan claimed, it *looked* the same as ever. If she was being followed, would it help? Would that be better or worse? Better the Devil you know?

The sensation stayed with her as she went through the doors of McDowall House, but by the time she reached the base of the stairs (she was too frightened to even contemplate the narrow confines of the lift) it had gone. The difference was extraordinary. She felt as if a weight had been lifted, the whole atmosphere about her changed.

She jogged up the stairs and, by the time she reached her door, was happy to dismiss the whole thing as her imagination.

Chapter 15 – It Follows

The door to the metal box opened and It watched a female peer inside, covering her nose against the smell, which It would have called homely (had It spoken). It moved to get a closer look at her and the female seemed to hear It. She spoke some meaningless syllables, peering into the gloom, looking straight at It but seeing nothing, because they never did.

It breathed in her scent, tasting the faint hint of an old infection. A week ago It would have attacked her instantly, but now she was of no interest as food, unless It was really desperate.

But she might still be of use to It, as a means of escape. Might she have transport to the city? The sun was still up – how long might she stay?

She was not leaving yet, and was, in fact, now climbing into the metal box. It could taste her fear on the air, and for a moment wondered about consuming her regardless. It was so hungry now, and her fear was almost as delicious as infection.

It turned to the wall and began to climb, Its long claws easily finding purchase on the box's smooth interior. At the top of the wall It started across the roof, hanging like a giant bat, its head twisted so It could keep Its wide eyes on the female at all times. She was still speaking, looking around her.

Continuing across the roof, It crawled down the wall on the other side of the female, descending head-first as easily as It had ascended, still watching her sheep-like movements, scenting the ever-increasing levels of her fear that hung in the air about her like an aura.

She was doing something now and It watched in a detached way. It took little interest in Its prey, but by watching It could sometimes learn to hunt them better. It observed that she had now taken something out of her pocket, something that glowed dimly in her hand, and It automatically backed away from the light.

But as It moved, that dim light was suddenly transformed into an intense, hideous glare, turned directly on It. Raising Its hands against the searing light, It hissed and darted back, the cool shadows a relief to Its eyes.

It could hear another voice; male this time, talking to the female. It ignored them for the moment, huddled up, nursing Its eyes, head buried in Its thin arms.

The male joined the female in the box, and now a pair of light beams cut into the darkness where It had made Its home. It skittered up the wall, out of their way, alert to wherever the light beams pointed, keeping ahead of them, hanging to the shadows until they felt that they had swept every corner and left the box. It waited a moment, then followed, still on the roof, hanging by the door, watching to see if they were staying or going.

There was still daylight outside, beyond the arch, but the male and the female did not seem to be leaving yet. If only they stayed until after dark.

Not long after, more people arrived with ugly lights on their vehicles, and It realised that Its brief home in the metal box was no longer a safe one.

As the new people entered the box – all wearing similar clothing – so It left, unnoticed even as It passed amongst them. It clung to the shadows by the wall, but the light outside was starting to fade. Soon It would be able to pass beyond the arch, and surely *one* of these people would provide transport to the city.

From where It hid, It could see the male and female talking to one of the uniformed people – another male – and It kept Its eyes on them.

When the sun finally vanished below the horizon, It slunk out, darting sinuously from cover to cover, crawling beneath their vehicles and hiding behind shrubs.

The female was on the move. It watched her. She was heading for a vehicle.

The decision did not take long to make – anywhere was better than here, and It could always fall back on the female as a food of last resort.

As she opened her car door, It slipped in before she could seat herself, insinuating Its way through the gap and making Itself comfortable on the seat behind her.

She was unusually perceptive, for on more than one occasion during the following journey she seemed to sense Its presence. Sometimes people were born that way, but it was also true that tired people, at the sharp end of their own narrow control, could have such perception, though they invariably wrote it off as a symptom of exhaustion.

When the car stopped, It followed her out and was delighted to recognise that It was in the city. The gamble had paid off and the smell of infection was heavy on the air. There were trails going this way and that, criss-crossing, cross-contaminating, leading every which way. It was spoilt for choice and so It stuck with the tactic that had worked for It thus far; It followed the female. She was presumably on her way to some centre of habitation, and there It was sure to find food.

As It had hoped, the female led the way into a mass hive of people, and Its nostrils twitched with the scent of fresh meat and recent infections within. One particular smell beckoned to It, a smell that It recognised.

Abandoning the female, It passed through a door and went down a dark flight of stairs. The room below was disappointingly empty; the people who had been here, whose smell had drawn It, had not stopped long. But though the room contained nothing for It to eat, it would make a suitable lair, a place to sleep through the day and digest the food It would track by night.

It made Itself comfortable. Soon the lights would be turned off and the sharp sounds of activity would be blunted to murmurs. The people would sleep. Then It would steal out of Its hiding place and find Its first meal in this new home. Tonight, It would feed.

Chapter 16 – The Schreck

"A Schreck?" Harrigan frowned as he dumped more chips onto his girlfriend's plate.

It was the night of Elsa's sudden return (two days before Emily's discovery of the truck) and Harrigan was learning that her week had been as eventful as his own.

"Schreck means 'terror' in German," Elsa explained. "That's where it was first discovered. Or at least where it was officially described. Eighteen thirty eight if my memory holds."

"Yes, but… what is a Schreck?"

Elsa used a mouthful of chips as an excuse not to answer the question while she thought.

"Okay," she said, after finally swallowing, "I need to tell you some things and I need you to be cool about them. You probably won't believe them, but… well it would be useful if you did."

Harrigan snorted. "We met chasing an invisible man and a few nights ago I was almost killed by a living statue (which, by the way, you have shown oddly little surprise about), I think I can deal with whatever you throw at me."

Elsa shrugged. "I know you think that, but…" Again she paused to think before going on. "There's supposed to be a limited amount I can tell you. In reality, we bend and stretch that rule a lot, because not telling people what's trying to kill them has worse results than telling them. Because you're my 'boyfriend'…"

"Do you have to use the air quotes?"

"You don't like the word any more than I do. Because you are my *'partner'* (another one I don't like), I have been extra careful about not sharing stuff. But since you have, through no fault of mine, come into contact with a golem, I think I have licence to fill you in. This is my job, Harrigan. I work for an organisation called Universal and… Invisible Men, Golems, Schrecks, things that go bump in the night – that's what we do. We protect people from the stuff that shouldn't really exist, and we try to do it without anyone finding out that it does. All the stuff out of folklore (well… not all, but much) it's real. That's what I'm talking about."

Harrigan considered this. "I can handle that."

"You only think you can."

"You have a very low opinion of me."

"If that was true then I wouldn't be telling you any of this."

"I've never heard of a Schreck," said Harrigan. "You said 'all the stuff out of folklore' – I've never heard of that."

Elsa nodded, grimly. "They are thankfully not common. They're what you might call 'situational' monsters. They only turn up at certain times."

"What times?"

"They're a type of vampire," Elsa went on. "And I'm just going to breeze past the fact that vampires exist because you're cool with all this. But Schrecks have a more specialised diet, or at least a different way of feeding. They still drink blood, although they seldom drain their victims as the more common vampires do…"

"'The more common vampires'?"

"This'll go quicker if you don't interrupt. This specialised feeding pattern makes it much harder to find a Schreck. As does the fact that they only emerge at times when death is excessively common."

A light bulb went on above Harrigan's head. "Pandemics."

Elsa finished eating and pushed her plate away. "Epidemics will do, if they happen to be in the vicinity. Schrecks can sleep for decades – centuries even – completely dormant, not needing to eat. They wake at times like this and they feed, every night if they can, fuelling their next period of dormancy. The one I've been tracking has probably slept since the Spanish flu. Now it's awake and it's managed to elude me, and several other Universal agents, all across Europe." She clenched her teeth irritably. "Thought I had it in France but the damn thing gave me the slip in the Paris sewers. Who knows how many people it's killed since then."

Harrigan knew better than to tell her it wasn't her fault and that she had done all she could. Such excuses cut no ice with Elsa.

"And now it's here?"

"I think so." Elsa pulled a face. "Damn things are hard to track and harder to spot."

"They blend in?" Popular culture suggested that vampires look just like us.

"Yes. But perhaps not in the way you mean," said Elsa. "They don't look like humans. At all." She paused, her green eyes suddenly distant. "I got a look at it in France. Only briefly but... I've seen a few monsters, but this thing gave me chills. That's why they're called Schrecks. They *are* terror. Nightmares come to life. You can't look at one without it haunting you." She shook her head. "So yeah; they don't blend in like your common or garden vamp, you just can't see them."

Harrigan puffed out his cheeks. "Another invisible killer."

"Yes and no. Mostly no. They're visible. You just can't see them. Unless you look."

Harrigan frowned. "They hide well?"

"Again; yes. But that's not it." Elsa seemed frustrated by her own inability to explain. "It's almost as if the human brain rebels against seeing something like that, something that *can't* exist."

"I'm almost certain that's not how sight works."

"You've never seen an optical illusion?" retorted Elsa. "Besides, this would be the problem with the supernatural; it does not conform to the rules. Try to explain it in everyday terms and you come a cropper. Our vision seems to slide off the Schreck like water off a duck's back. You have to concentrate to see it. Which means you have to know it's there in advance to know to concentrate."

"How did you get to see it?"

Elsa smiled. "Got lucky. I'd tracked it there so I was already looking, then I heard a noise and caught it in my torch beam. They don't like light. If you can catch them off-guard in the light then you get a glimpse." She swallowed. "Which I wouldn't recommend."

"What does it look like?" Harrigan had to ask.

"Like Edvard Munch had a bad LSD trip."

"And that's what you've been off doing? Chasing monsters?" Harrigan had always had only the vaguest idea of what his girlfriend did for a living, but he had known that it was important and dangerous and... weird. He wouldn't have guessed this, but, just to look at her, he knew it was true. "You're pretty incredible."

154

How many men could say that their girlfriend hunted vampires?

"Incredible would have been catching it." Elsa got up from the table and flopped down on the sofa. "Now it's here. And London is as good a hunting ground as it will find in Europe. The virus is everywhere, people are everywhere and I don't know where to start." She rubbed her eyes. "It will find a lair – somewhere to spend the days. Somewhere dank, filthy and horrible."

Harrigan shook his head. "You just described London."

"Yes." Elsa started to unlace her boots. "So all I can do is wait for the dead. Except there are already so many. Unless you know what you're looking for, victims of the Schreck just look like they died of the virus. That's why they've evolved to feed on infected people; so no one notices. These creatures gorged themselves through the bubonic plague and no one noticed them because their victims were just piled up alongside the rest of the dead." She lay back on the sofa, putting her feet up and closing her eyes. "So many dead."

Harrigan got the impression that there was more going on here than a viral vampire. "Elsa?"

Elsa didn't open her eyes. "It's bad out there, Harrigan. Covid. I was in Spain and… I guess it's bad all over but still; you can't imagine." She looked at him. "I've spent my adult life with Universal, chasing the worst things you can imagine, and then something like this comes along and… you start to wonder what's the point? Saving… What? One, two, three lives, in amongst all this?"

"Who was it said that thing about lighting a candle rather than cursing the dark?"

It wasn't the best delivered proverb, but it made Elsa smile. "You always know the right thing to say."

"I really don't."

"That's true, you don't. But on this occasion you nailed it." She sat up again. "Tell me more about your thing. The Golem."

Harrigan roughed out events, telling her about Nurse Emily and his nocturnal stake-out (lightly embellishing his own heroics on the mud flats) and his video call with Henrik.

"That's incredible."

"I know, I was there."

"Not the Golem," dismissed Elsa. "You made a video call without Will?"

"Next time you can cook your own chips."

Elsa laughed.

"Is there some reason these things are happening at the same time?" asked Harrigan. "The Golem and the Schreck."

Elsa moved her head back and forth. "Probably yes, but not directly linked."

"You're not big on straight answers tonight."

"The supernatural is not big on straight answers full stop," Elsa acknowledged. "You have to get used to grey areas. You're accustomed to a world governed by science, by rules. I live in a world where that doesn't apply. Universal studies these creatures and the one thing we know for sure is that we know nothing. Some werewolves retain full memory of being the wolf, others don't. Some vampires can't pass running water, others can. There are few hard and fast rules and that inconsistency takes some getting used to."

"Werewolves?"

"Roll with the punches, Harrigan. It's not a coincidence that these things are happening at the same time when that time is a pandemic," Elsa returned to the subject of the Schreck and the Golem. "Ninety nine times out of a hundred if you build a clay man stuffed with the *cri de coeur* of hundreds of angry and distressed people, then nothing will happen, but it's that hundredth time that people will tend to remember. You could recreate the circumstances exactly and it wouldn't happen, but this time it did. The pandemic is probably part of that. Emotions are high and people poured those emotions onto those little slips of paper. That's not *why* it happened (I can't really tell you *why* it happened), but it's why it worked. Understand?"

"No," admitted Harrigan.

"Good. Now you just have to work on accepting that. Point is; they've both turned up now because of the pandemic. That they

156

both ended up *here*, I suspect, is a coincidence."

Harrigan considered this. "That doesn't seem fair."

"These things never do."

"So…" Harrigan tried to get his head as far around this as his mind could stretch. "The words in its head – all the things people wrote – it's trying to live up to those?"

"Simpler than that," replied Elsa. "Those words are what it is. They're *all* it is. It's just clay and paper. The words give it life. They define it. Now, normally a Golem is brought to life with one word, or a handful, which keeps things simple (although, if you bring your Golem to life with the word 'Truth' then you might want to be sure that the two of you agree on what truth is). This one has a whole damn chorus inside it. Because 'Art'. What that does, I don't know, but I very much doubt that everyone said the same thing. It must disagree with itself from time to time."

"Seemed pretty single-minded when I met it," said Harrigan, darkly.

"Based on what you and Nurse Emily have seen," ventured Elsa, "I'd say that it's responding to the notes one at a time. Not in order. And I don't mean like; it's done that one so it won't come back to it. It doesn't have a 'To Do' list. But nor does it feel the need to do everything at once. If it was trying to act on all of them, all the time, then it wouldn't know if it was helping little old ladies cross the street or patrolling the beaches for foreigners. So it might start with the most achievable."

"Flour."

"Exactly. Then, if it happens to see something pertaining to another of its instructions, it will act on that."

"Like tearing down a 'Vote Tory' sign."

Elsa nodded. "Or attacking a policeman."

"I still don't understand how it knew I was a policeman."

"That is odd," Elsa mused. "Especially as you're not. The Golem is nothing if not literal – ex-policeman wouldn't cut it. Maybe it had another reason." She ran a frustrated hand back and forth through the tangled mane of her red hair. "It's hard to know what's going on in its head. Which is odd because, in a very real

157

sense, we know *exactly* what is going on in its head. The trouble is, your nurse friend, though very well-meaning (if somewhat criminal), has made the Golem potentially much more dangerous."

"She has?"

"She's given it the tools to think outside the box. It's still very limited in what it will do, but she has expanded its repertoire by connecting events to consequences."

"So if one of the notes says '*Stop Covid*'," Harrigan slowly reasoned, "there's nothing it can do; it can't pummel a virus. But then along comes Emily saying, 'Here's how you stop it'."

"And suddenly no chemist's window is safe," nodded Elsa. "The question is; can it only make those extrapolations when a third party points them out, or has Nurse Emily given it the mental tools to make those jumps itself?"

"You mean," Harrigan was not liking the way this conversation was heading, "if there's a shortage of hospital beds for Covid patients then it might start hurling other sick people out?"

"That's one example," replied Elsa. "There are others. Lots of others. And it doesn't just apply to Covid. There are probably statements in there that are harmless in isolation but which become terrifying if you take the literal route. The Golem thinks in straight lines and it doesn't get nuance or metaphor. If someone wrote '*Kill all Tory bastards*' then members of the government born outside of wedlock should watch their backs."

Harrigan sat back in his chair and shook his head. "Damn thing's a maniac."

Elsa smiled. "It's the voice of the people."

"Hardly."

"Oh but it is." She leaned forward. "People as individuals are generally intelligent and considered – maybe they have views you don't agree with, but they'll talk and listen and you can part amicably without coming to blows. But put them in a group – 'people' *en masse* – and the smartest can become idiots. The mob. Ever wonder why, no matter how well-intentioned the protest, it always seems to end in looting and violence? People in a group do things they would never do alone. Being around other likeminded persons seems to justify your actions; he's doing this so I can too; our cause is just so the rules don't apply. Someone said that the IQ of the mob is the IQ of its dumbest member divided by the number of people. *That's* the Golem. It doesn't have access to the thoughts behind those statements inside it; just the headlines, the soundbites, the things you write on a placard or scream into Twitter. That's what its mind is composed of. It's capable of extraordinary good but also horrendous bad, both with the same intensity. And it can't tell the difference. There's no knowing what it might do next."

Chapter 17- What It Did Next

Help the homeless.

Ernest Salmonova had been homeless since his arrival in Britain, and sometimes asked himself if coming here had been the right thing to do. It wasn't as if he had been one of those fleeing a war-torn nation, there had just been nothing there for him but bad memories.

Things would turn around. One of these days.

Take today for example; today he had found an unopened can of food. The label had sloughed off in the damp so it remained simply 'food', but it still promised a meal of a sort that he did not usually get. If he could get it open.

Thoughtful people often brought him scarves or blankets, bottled water or fruit, and he was grateful for it, but no one ever thought about a can-opener.

"Open, you bastard." He had learnt English in school and had always been good at it. He had thought that would put him in a strong position when he arrived in this country.

Positioning a plastic bag on the ground at the base of the stone step on which he was sitting, Ernest proceeded to whack the can against the corner of the step, hoping the bag would stop anything going to waste once the can split, which it *surely* would eventually.

The sound of the metal can against the stone step rang in Ernest's ears, so it was a few seconds before he realised that the sound continued after he had stopped and the echoes had died away. Now he listened, he realised that it was a different sound, but with the same regular beat.

The alley in which he sat was lit like a 1940s horror film (one of Val Lewton's RKO classics), the street lights illuminating one end brightly enough to make the shadows deeper and darker within. Into that blaze of light, a massive silhouette now stepped, walking heavily but briskly, feet slamming into the ground as if they stamped every step in lead divers' boots.

English words failed Ernest as the figure came closer,

looming over him, and he muttered a handful of swearwords in his mother tongue.

The figure reached down to pluck the can from Ernest's unresisting grasp, then, with surprising delicacy given the size of its thick fingers, it pinched the lip of the can and peeled back the top as easily as if it was opening a yoghurt, the metal tearing like foil in its grip.

The figure handed the open can back to Ernest.

"Thank you." Ernest smiled. The man was gigantic and no looker, but you met all sorts down here and it did not do to judge people on first impressions. Frankly he seemed like a pretty useful friend to have.

"Did you want some?" Ernest had been brought up to share.

The figure said nothing, its attention seemingly taken by something on the ground. Possibly Ernest's foot.

Ernest tried not to flinch as the big man reached down and tied Ernest's shoelaces, which were forever coming undone.

"Thank you again."

The figure straightened and strode off past Ernest, walking at the same hard pace.

A man with a place to be, thought Ernest. He looked at the can in front of him. It contained peach slices in syrup. They were delicious.

Reopen the schools! The teachers are just lazy.

Hanna Holt was one of those for whom the pandemic had meant the end of various sporting opportunities, or at least their deferment. She had always taken adversity in her stride and had, in the past, treated disappointments and injuries as challenges to overcome, but the cancellation of races and championships was a bitter blow.

Not to be cheated by the virus, she had kept up her training as best she could, and had altered her whole sleep schedule so she could run at night when the streets were empty.

Tonight she was taking her usual run, accompanied by the music of her i-phone. By sticking to the same playlist she could time how well she was doing, knowing what song to expect when she hit certain landmarks, trying to reach home before Europe's *The Final Countdown* played. This also meant that the scene onto which she stumbled outside the Duvivier Preparatory School was scored by The White Stripes' *Seven Nation Army*.

Though she had self-confidence by the bucketload, Hanna was not immune to that fear of a woman alone at night encountering a man coming the other way. The man in question was on the far side of the road, still some distance away, and, to Hanna, seemed to be walking in time to the insistent drum beat pummelled out by Meg White.

Reaching the school gates – a row of iron bars topped with arrow spikes – the man stopped, while Jack White began to sing in Hanna's ears. He looked at the gate a few moments, then took hold of the chain that fastened them and pulled.

Hanna almost tripped over her own carefully paced steps as she saw the chain snap like wet spaghetti in the man's grip.

The man paused a beat, as the song went into the second verse, then threw the gates wide open and strode through.

Now was probably the time to run faster, but instead, Hanna found herself slowing, almost stopping to see what happened next.

As the song entered its raw, chaotic instrumental, the man yanked open the school's main doors, splintered wood flying about him as the lock burst. On to the next set of doors, which he opened with a single shove and an echoing 'crack!', as the handles were driven into the plaster of the walls within. The third door put up even less resistance, its hinges giving way, leaving the man staring at it, as it hung from his hand. He looked almost apologetic.

By the time Jack White was '*Goin' to Wichita*' in the final verse, all the doors into the building were open and/or removed.

But the man didn't go in.

Hanna had jogged on a bit now but was still casting backward glances, wondering if she should have called the police earlier (it was too late now). But the man didn't go in. He wasn't robbing the place, and if it was vandalism then it seemed odd to leave the windows and everything else intact.

At the gate, a sign had been posted announcing that the school was closed to due to government restrictions. On his way out, the man removed the sign, and then strode off, his steps still matching the beat as the song ended.

Clap for carers.

There were bigger things to worry about, but Ellen Pimm did find herself wondering why, the older she got, the less able she was to sleep at night *and* the less able to stop herself from sleeping during the day. It seemed unfair, and it was roundabout this time, in the early hours of the morning, that that unfairness always struck her.

It could be worse. It could always be worse and she was reminded of that every day.

Ellen's room in the nursing home placed her between two women suffering from dementia. One believed that she was twelve years old, the other was so far gone that it was hard to say if she believed anything anymore. Though she felt bad for even thinking it, Ellen privately considered that it would have been better for everyone if one of them had succumbed to the virus, rather than Aubrey Clark, who had been frail but mentally like a rock.

It had taken him in mere days.

The staff had done everything they could, as they always did, and Ellen thought that it was perhaps hardest on them. Aubrey had not been the first and he would not be the last, and they had to deal with each, struggling to bear up in the face of grieving relatives and the callous disregard of those in power.

With difficulty, Ellen got out of bed and made it to the chair by the window, where she spent many nights. She slept better seated upright, but doing so felt like surrender.

It was as she settled into the chair that she became aware of a noise from outside. It sounded like someone hitting two bricks together, over and over.

Locating her glasses and twitching back the curtain, Ellen peered out into the night. Standing outside the gates of the nursing home was a large man clapping his hands. The applause came at such a regular rate that you could have played piano to it.

The man continued for fifteen minutes, uninterrupted, the rhythm never changing, before he went away.

We don't need 'art'! All we need to make this country great again is for all the immigrants to go back where they came from.

Though he was still working from home, navigating the minefield of online teaching, Lakshay Mehta felt that if he didn't help out in some other way, then he was a worthless person. A well-educated man with an English wife, Lakshay had had little difficulty relocating to England and, while he had inevitably come up against some of the more engrained prejudices that an Indian teacher working in a British school will face, he knew that he was one of the lucky ones and was aware that his experience was not necessarily the norm. He didn't feel guilty about how easy he had it, but he did try to give back.

Right now, he was on his way to the local homeless shelter, where he had volunteered (somewhat erratically if he was honest) for the last five years.

He had left his house and made it almost to the end of the street when someone grabbed his collar from behind. Lakshay cried out and struggled but that made no difference to the unseen attacker, who now proceeded to drag him back the way he had come. The man's grip was like iron and, though Lakshay was carrying a few extra Lockdown pounds, he dragged the teacher with ease.

Before he knew what was happening, Lakshay found himself back at his front door where he was unceremoniously dumped. He had assumed that this would be when his attacker forced him to open the door, prior to ransacking his home, but instead, the man simply walked away, leaving Lakshay shaken but unharmed.

Later, over a soothing cup of tea, Lakshay wondered what the hell the point had been in dragging him back to where he had just come from.

Let's all give doctors a hand, they're killing themselves.

At the end of his shift, junior doctor Adi Paz felt as if someone had slipped weights into the soles of his shoes. Possibly into his eyelids as well. It was just so damn hard to keep moving. He'd spent the day on his feet and the only rest he seemed to get was when he sat down to deliver bad news, which was more exhausting than any of the physical stuff. He just wanted to get home, have something to eat, and fall into bed. Maybe just fall into bed. He really hoped he wouldn't fall asleep on the bus. He had done that twice in the last week, and there was nothing more disheartening when you were dead tired than the knowledge that you would now have to get off and wait for another bus when you could have been in your bed half an hour ago.

He also hoped that he would not have to wait too long. There was always another bus – that was a great thing about living in London – but how long you had to wait varied a great deal.

"No, no, no, no, no!"

There was the bus, at the stop, people getting on, and he was still thirty feet away.

Adi started to run. Or at least, he thought he that he had started to run, that was definitely the message that his brain had sent to his legs, but the message that his legs had sent back was not one that could be repeated in polite company.

The last people got on and the doors closed.

"HEY!" Adi waved wildly. There was no way the driver could miss him, but London bus drivers are trained to be brutal about this sort of thing or the buses start backing up and the whole system breaks down.

Adi felt his heart sinking as the bus pulled away from the kerb.

"HEY!" he tried again, but without much optimism.

How long would he have to wait now?

As the bus left, up ahead of it, Adi saw a man walking in his direction. He wouldn't have been noteworthy were it not for his size, reminding Adi of the wrestlers he had used to watch with his Gran on a Sunday afternoon, back when the main requirement was to be shaped liked a barrel with a head and legs. The man seemed to notice Adi waving and his gaze switched from the doctor to the bus.

"NO!" Adi screamed as the man stepped out into the road in front of the oncoming vehicle. He heard the shriek of brakes as the driver tried to force the bus into the impossible. He heard the thump of the collision. Though it did not sound quite as he would have expected.

Adi had looked away when the man stepped out, but he now looked up again and stared. The bus had stopped, but the man was still standing there, apparently unharmed. He looked at Adi as if to say, '*Come on if you're coming*'.

Hurrying, as much as he was able, Adi caught up to the bus. The doors were open and he got on, nodding a '*thank you*' to the driver, whose white-faced gaze was fixed out in front. Adi followed that gaze to where the wrestler stood, as solid and immoveable as the Statue of Liberty. His left hand was straight out in front of him, touching the front of the bus, and where it touched, Adi could see an impressed dent in the metal.

The bus driver looked at Adi, wide-eyed. "Do you think he's getting on?"

But the man was already on the move again, striding down the street.

"I guess not," said Adi.

The driver nodded. He was not altogether sorry about that.

No means no, and men who don't get that need it beaten into them.

The date had gone even better than Rebecca had expected. They probably shouldn't have gone out, but there was only so much online chatting you could stand when you both liked each other and when a burgeoning relationship had reached that point of wanting more. Covid could do many things but when it took away a girl's love-life then that was a step too far. Besides, Antonne had said it was cool and that they were both young and healthy so it wouldn't matter, and Rebecca was currently in a place where everything Antonne said was right because he said it. That said, Rebecca didn't feel comfortable going to the house of a man she had never even met in person, and still less comfortable having him come to hers, so she used the restrictions as a way to avoid that and keep things moving slowly.

It had been great. They'd had coffee together, seated by the river. They'd chatted in person as easily as they had online (Antonne was even better looking in the flesh than he was onscreen). They'd gone for a walk as evening threatened and were now heading home as night fell.

There was then some tension, as Antonne wanted the evening to continue at her place or his and she was adamant not. He at first seemed irritated by this, as if she had misled him (which she did not think she had and did not think it actually mattered whether she had or not). It seemed to resolve and they walked partway home together.

Rebecca had given some thought to the goodnight kiss and had decided definitely not, then definitely maybe, then, what the hell, he wasn't getting anything else and a kiss was the least she could do. So as they reached the point of parting company she was happy to make the first move and kiss him, and he kissed her back and it was a rather lovely moment.

If only it had stopped there.

"No…"

At first Rebecca said it in a playful way as Antonne's hands got carried away.

"No."

Then more firmly, because this was fast getting out of hand.

"I said, no!"

She felt trapped and under attack, and then realised that she felt that way because she was both those things.

"No. Antonne, stop… No!"

Eyes tightly shut, Rebecca did not see what happened next. One moment she was pinned to the wall struggling, the next there was a yelp and Antonne was gone.

She opened her eyes in time to see a huge figure standing over Antonne, who looked dazed and possibly hurt. The figure raised a massive arm, hand balled into a fist ready to strike.

"NO!" Rebecca screamed.

And the figure stopped on her command.

Rebecca ran. She later learned through friends that Antonne had been taken to hospital with a broken collar bone, and Rebecca wondered why the strange figure had stopped there.

My cat has gone missing and I miss him and his name is Toothless.

Sarah was up early that morning (she'd been waking earlier and earlier as financial worries played around her head), and was in the kitchen obsessively re-washing last night's washing-up, cursing herself for doing so but unable to stop.

"...in the 7th house, meaning a new relationship (could be professional, could be hey-hey, here we go!). But if you're on the cusp, then that same mysterious stranger could be something else entirely."

Listening to Al the Astrologer sometimes helped her break the obsessive behaviours that seemed to have been magnified by Lockdown, but he was now interrupted by the doorbell.

"Benjamin! Will you see who that is please!"

Benjamin too had been waking early since Lockdown started, but that was general *joie de vivre* at not having to go to school.

"Mum!" Perhaps it was Sarah's imagination but Benjamin seemed to have used this time to perfect his petulant whine.

""I said go."

Sarah heard the sound of reluctant feet going to the door. She heard the door open.

"Mum!" This time her son's voice was thrilled and excited. "Come here."

Sarah sighed, and went to the front door.

Seated on the doormat was a black and white cat that looked up at Sarah expectantly.

It was not Toothless, the cat that had gone missing a month ago, and nor were the other six cats that wandered about the corridor of McDowall House.

"Can we keep them?" asked Benjamin.

168

Chapter 18 – An Island of Normality

The first thing Emily did when she got in after finding the truck and… its contents, was to put the shower on. It always took a while for the water to heat so she left it running while she vigorously stripped, grabbed a black rubbish bag from a drawer in the kitchen and shoved her clothes into it. She twisted the top and tied it off. A moment's consideration and she pulled out another bag, put the first one inside it, twisted and tied once more then dumped the bag by the door to take down to the bins later. She still felt as if she could smell the thick, putrid atmosphere of the truck's interior, but that might just be her.

She took a long shower, the water as hot as she could bear it, soaping every part of her body obsessively, wringing the stink from her hair. On an impulse she switched the water to cold, gasping with the sudden shock that made her body cringe inwards. For as long as she could stand it she stood under the frigid stream, head bowed, palms flat against the wall. There was something cleansing about cold water – maybe this would do the trick.

For a moment she was overcome with the desperate urge to call home. But that never seemed to go well. She wouldn't have known what to say anyway.

She was making dinner later, her still wet hair up in a towel, when the doorbell went. Feeling the twinges of anxiety return, Emily cinched her bathrobe tighter about her waist, slipped on her mask and went to answer it.

"Paul?"

"Hi." Paul too had changed and, by the look of him, showered, though he was one of those people who always looked freshly laundered. "I just thought I'd drop by and see how you were doing. We didn't have chance to talk after the police and… Hell, I don't know what to say about today."

"No," agreed Emily. Pausing to think before adding, "Me neither."

"I also wanted you to know that I've spoken to Lydia and Masud," said Paul.

Though she knew she shouldn't, Emily felt a rush of relief. "Oh. That must have been awful."

"Yeah," said Paul. "I think Lydia's clinging to whatever hope there is in the fact that they couldn't actually identify Jakeem."

"And Masud?" It had been his brother after all.

"He didn't say anything."

Owing to his mask, much of Paul's face was hidden from Emily, but there was trauma written in his eyes.

He looked up again, forcing a smile that made his mask crease. "But you're okay?"

"I… I had a bit of a moment on the drive back." Why was she telling him this? "I think it all just caught up with me. But I'm feeling better now. Just cooking dinner."

"Oh. Sorry." Paul held up his hands. "Didn't mean to disturb you…"

"You weren't, I was…"

"I just…

"I was glad to see you."

They paused, rather than continuing to talk over each other.

"Look," Paul tugged absently at the elastic of his mask where it seemed to rub awkwardly behind his ear, "this is clearly the most inappropriate thing I've ever done and God knows it probably ought to wait, but I'm not a man who waits. Business credo, you know? You take the opportunities when they come cos they might not be there tomorrow. Not sure it's best to apply that outside of work, but that's who I am – love me or leave me. Anyway, when I started this speech (which seems like a very long time ago) I was going to ask if you would like to, sometime, have dinner or coffee or a drink or whatever passes for a date in this socially distant new normal in which we find ourselves?"

"Oh," said Emily.

Dating had not been a major priority of her life before the pandemic and had become a complete non-issue since. It wasn't that she hadn't thought about men; when her flat-mate Jill had been in residence Emily had been regularly reminded of what she was missing (usually via a rhythmic thumping late at night and again in the morning). She knew that some of her colleagues used their breaks to get a quick hit of intimacy in the backseat of a parked car – taking what chances they had in these difficult times. But that wasn't really Emily's style.

"Can I think about it?"

"Sure. I'd actually prefer that to a knee-jerk response," nodded Paul. "I like to think I'm at least worth considering."

"Definitely worth considering," Emily confirmed. He was. He was a nice man who said the right things and seemed to share many of her values, albeit coming at them from a very different angle. He was also wealthy and privileged and maybe anybody could be nice when they had so little to worry about. Then again, he made her smile, which cancelled out a lot of negatives.

Her Dad would hate him.

"I feel I should point out," Paul went on, "especially with the mask, that (I know you're probably already aware of it, but I'd regret it if I didn't remind you) I am *very* handsome."

Emily couldn't help laughing.

"Good," nodded Paul. "You recognised it as a joke. But, like all the best jokes, it's funny because it's true."

"Yes it is," admitted Emily.

"Rich too," added Paul with a rueful shake of his head. "Not everyone sees that as a positive. Still; there it is. No point in pretending otherwise."

"I will definitely think on it," said Emily.

"Good. I'll let you get back to dinner. And remember," he pointed to his masked face. "Handsome."

Emily closed the door and was pleased to find that she was smiling. A genuine smile went a long way these days; you had treasure them.

If nothing else it was nice to be asked.

The rich business man whose shoes probably cost more than her entire wardrobe was not her usual type but… At the very least it would be nice to get to know him well enough to know what *type* he really was; the person behind the wallet. If you judged people for their wealth then you were as bad as those who judged people for their poverty. And if a man could make you end a day like today with a smile, then that wasn't nothing.

Emily woke with the sound of the ambulances, which was just as well because she had slept through all her alarms (she increasingly used multiple alarms). Fortunately, the sirens had roused her only ten minutes late so she had little time to make up. But her fortune was someone else's tragedy.

Looking out the window as she made coffee, Emily saw the stretcher leave. The person on it had their face covered. That was never a good sign.

She showered again (the smell seemed to be inside her head and she wished she could scrub out her own skull), wolfed down coffee and a breakfast bar, then pulled on her uniform. It had been two weeks since she had worn it and she felt like a soldier back from leave, returning to the trenches; not happy to be going back but also guilty at having been away. A little part of her thought; *maybe things have gotten better*, and the rest of her laughed.

Camilla's door was open as she passed.

"Did you see?"

Emily nodded. "Do you know who it was?"

"Mrs McCulloch. Fourth floor. I spoke to her only last week (did a bit of shopping for her and we chatted on the doorstep). She was so proud of the fact she'd dodged it."

"It was definitely Covid?" Emily held back from asking if the old woman had been killed by powerful hands.

"That's the word," nodded Camilla. "I guess she was old."

That was something you heard a lot. The majority of Covid deaths were amongst the elderly, and if you were a parent like Camilla then the increasing evidence that children were not so badly affected was a relief. But people lived long lives these days. And they filled those lives with things; they played with grandchildren, they contributed, volunteered here and there, took up hobbies, did the things they had always intended to do once their time was finally their own. They *lived*. They had earned that time and it wasn't fair to cut it short. It would be very wrong to start accepting those deaths as a best case scenario.

On her way across the plaza, Emily looked towards the Golem. Had the Guardian Angel been out last night? She hadn't heard of any unexpected gifts, but the talk around the block was all of Mrs McCulloch. She would have to ask around. Then, tonight, she would watch it, as she had planned to last night. And, if necessary, she would take more final action than dumping it in a ditch.

The hospital was as she had left it; busy and chaotic, desperate and sad, and even more shorthanded now than it had been two weeks ago – the inevitable result of working alongside such a contagious virus on a daily basis. The tiredness hung in the air as before and the despondency alongside it, even as people found ways to combat it as best they could. Saanvi had taken to reading out letters from the public and posting them in the break room, just to remind them that they *were* appreciated, even if they did not always feel it. Pictures of rainbows, pictures of nurses, '*thank you for helping my Gran/Uncle/Mother*', boxes of biscuits and chocolates. All heartfelt, all helpful in their way, something to keep in mind when you were staring a dying person in the face, holding their hand because none of their relatives were allowed to be there. Then you might take five minutes out to cry before doing it all over again.

And yet, Emily was glad to be back. It was horrible, but it was necessary, and she would rather be part of the fight than sitting at home wishing it was all over. What was it someone had said about lighting a candle rather than swearing in the dark? Something like that. Besides, it would all be over by summer. That was what they were saying on TV and on the streets. Emily didn't know anyone in the profession who thought that was going to happen.

It was good to start back with a day shift, something to ease her back in, and it was nice to walk home in the light; no ominous footsteps, no Golems. On the bus home, an old man wearing a homemade mask in a bright tartan, came up to her.

"I just wanted to say thank you for all you people are doing. Nurses," he added, just in case she got the wrong idea from '*you people*'.

Emily could have burst into tears. She never used to be this weepy.

As she arrived back at McDowall House, Emily saw a familiar figure, leaning against the wall, and could not help smiling.

"Hi Paul." Of course he was here. Paul Haworth might try to keep business tactics out of his personal life, but that proactivity was just a part of who he was.

"I bought you a tea," said Paul, as he strung his mask on. He placed the takeaway cup on the ground and backed up. "It is, at best, lukewarm."

Emily felt the sides of the cup. It was stone cold. "Okay. I'm not going to drink this, but thank you for the thought."

"How was your day?"

Emily sighed. She didn't really want to answer that question. It was harder to put the days out of your mind if you had to talk about them. "It was a day. I didn't love it, but I'm glad to be back."

Paul nodded. "I imagine it didn't afford you much time for deep consideration of important, maybe even life-changing, questions asked to you in the last twenty four hours."

"Not really," lied Emily. He'd actually been on her mind a bit.

"Perfectly understandable," said Paul. "In business, as you can well imagine, I don't take no for an answer, but in my personal life, if you were to give the answer 'no' (for whatever reason – I can't think of one right this minute), I would simply nod with sad resignation, give a half-smile and say, 'I hope we can be friends because I genuinely enjoy your company'. I do this because I respect you and, I must confess, because I got it badly wrong when I was younger – there was this time when I was a student in Prague…" he waved his hands. "Story for another day. And do you know who I blame?"

"Yourself?" Emily suggested.

Paul frowned. "You clearly don't know me at all. No, I blame Richard Curtis."

"Richard Curtis?"

"Writer, sometime director. *Four Weddings*, *Notting Hill*, *Love Actually*, latterly the excellent *Yesterday* directed by Danny

174

Boyle (there's versatility for you; *Trainspotting* and that). He's not solely to blame, but the genre of romantic comedy in which Richard Curtis made his name has lied to successive generations of men to make them believe that persistence gets results *and* is what women look for in a man, resulting in behaviour which in real life will, quite rightly, get you nothing but a restraining order (no, I have not had one taken out against me). It's an attitude that has no place in the modern romantical dating sphere and I try my best to steer clear of it."

"And yet here we are," commented Emily.

"Just bringing you tea," replied Paul, defensively. "Let's bear in mind that I could just as easily have bought you a car. But that would have been presumptuous. Third date stuff. If I'd done nothing then it might have seemed like I wasn't invested in the answer to my question – an impression I definitely did not want to give. This seemed like a happy medium; just a cup of tea. Low pressure, but a quiet reminder that I am eager to know where you stand because I rather like you."

There was a character named Moist Von Lipwig, who had appeared relatively late in Terry Pratchett's Discworld novels, and although the books centred around him were perfectly enjoyable, Emily had always struggled to warm to the character himself. And not just because his name was Moist. He was a rogue, a chancer, a rich kid off the rails who always fell on his feet no matter what, and trusted that his immense charm and personal magnetism would see him through. That sort of attitude sat poorly with Emily and she wondered what his girlfriend, Adora Bell Dearheart (who seemed a sensible and level-headed woman) saw in a man like Moist. She understood it a bit more now.

Generally, Emily ended up with men more in the vein of Captain Carrot Ironfoundersson (sticking with her Discworld system for classifying men), men who were honest and sweet, easily embarrassed and boring in a very well-meaning fashion. A Moist type might be a good change of pace, though she still hoped that her rough around the edges Sam Vimes was out there somewhere.

"What would a date even look like right now?" she chanced.

Paul's eyes lit up. "It would be well-considered, quite safe and abiding with all current guidelines. I am #TeamFollowTheRules all the way. No matter how much I might want to hold your hand or kiss you goodnight, you'll be getting none of that from me."

Emily snapped her fingers theatrically. "Damn."

"But I think," Paul went on, ignoring her, "that a man of my resources and imagination can come up with a date that is socially distant yet intimate, rule-abiding yet world-rocking. If you were to give me a few hours to make some calls and... You're shaking your head."

Emily poured the cold tea down a convenient drain and tossed the cup into a recycling bin. "I'm calling bullshit on that."

"You don't think I can do it?"

"I don't think you have to," Emily corrected. "Right now, I'd bet you another cup of tea that you've already got the date planned out, set up and ready to go."

Paul's expression was hard to read from behind the mask. "What makes you think that?"

Emily shrugged. "I don't think you leave anything to chance. *And* I don't think the possibility of me saying 'no', ever even entered your head."

"Now that's not true." Paul held up a finger. "The possibility *did* enter my head, but I naturally dismissed it as madness. Other than that... seems like you *do* know me. Should I make a call to cancel it?"

"Yes," said Emily, allowing Paul's face to fall before adding. "I'll organise it."

Paul grinned. "You had me there for a minute."

"And I enjoyed it."

"You really won't let me organise? It would be incredible."

"It will be. Be at mine at eight thirty."

"I'll see you then. Dress? Smart casual?"

"Whatever you feel comfortable in."

It was the wrong time to be starting a relationship, or even just dating, but you needed these islands of normality just to stay sane. It was good to have something to look forward to, and Emily

176

allowed herself the luxury of optimism. Why shouldn't it go well? Why shouldn't she have fun? Why shouldn't she enjoy the present and dare to consider a future? 2020 couldn't last forever.

It was only after she had returned to her flat and begun preparations that Emily remembered she had planned to watch the Golem that night. For a moment she considered calling Paul and bumping the date back, but that would have looked as if she needed more time to prepare, and after getting him to cancel his plans... She didn't want to be any more on the back foot with Paul than she already felt. The Golem watch could be deferred one more night.

The doorbell went at exactly eight thirty and Emily found Paul waiting – smart but casual as promised, right down to his mask, which looked to have been tailored.

"I got you those."

There were flowers on the doorstep while Paul remained two metres away.

"Thank you. I'll put them in hand sanitiser."

Paul laughed and Emily put the flowers to one side.

"So where are we going? I am agog."

"Follow me," smiled Emily.

"With pleasure."

Emily led the way up the stairs – the lift being too small for two people in the age of Covid.

"Do you always commence your dates with cardio?" asked Paul as they climbed higher.

"I like to make sure a man is up to the task," teased Emily.

Paul shook his head. "After this I won't be up to anything. Thank God for social distancing."

At the top of the stairs, Emily pushed open the emergency exit, ignoring the 'This door is alarmed' sign, which had been irrelevant for years, and led Paul out onto the roof.

"Wow," breathed Paul.

The view was spectacular. It was hard to call this part of London beautiful, and yet, with the sun starting to set across it and the monolithic tower blocks in silhouette like a brutalist Stonehenge, there was an almost gothic splendour to it that was not apparent from the ground.

"Do you know I've never been up here."

"Well it's usually occupied," said Emily. "Speaking of which; Al?"

"Good evening!" Al the Astrologer announced himself with a flourish, leaping out from behind his telescope as Emily had one hundred percent not asked him to. "I understand some love birds are looking for a personal reading. Let me get your star charts."

"Is he staying for dinner?" whispered Paul, as Al the Astrologer fetched out some papers.

"I don't think so, but it's a little hard to tell," admitted Emily.

"Ah yes, ah yes, ah yes. Here we are, here we are." Al laid out the hand-drawn star charts with lines linking the constellations. "This is you and this is you. And what we do first is we look at them individually; ladies first, of course. What do we see in the stars for Emily? I see... change. Yes, change. I see big decisions to be made. Life and death? Could be, could be. You live an interesting life. And you sir, what do I see? I see... change. Definitely change, change is in the air. Might be a work change, might be a life change, maybe a bit of both. And... death. I see death. Doesn't *have* to be yours though, and we're all seeing death at the moment."

Emily kept a rictus smile and wished that she had nixed this idea when Al suggested it. It had seemed cute at the time, but Al said what he saw no matter how repeatedly it was proved to be so much nonsense.

"But now," Al the Astrologer waggled his fingers as he approached his big finale, "what we do now is we take yours, and we overlay it on yours and – this would be easier if I had something more see-through, but tracing paper more or less does the job – you see the lines and the intersections where your lives meet and... Oh, ho, ho, these are some intersecting lives. You two are tangled together. Look at that, you're intersecting all over the place. Like rabbits it is. You know what I see here?"

"Change?" guessed Paul.

"I see change," Al the Astrologer continued, unabashed.

"His, hers, both of yours? Who can say? But it brings you together, all mixed up in each other's lives. Will it last? I can't tell, but it's there and you know it'll happen because Al the Astrologer says so."

That seemed to be the end of the show and Emily and Paul applauded politely.

"Thanks Al," said Emily, trying to herd the man in the general direction of the stairs while maintaining a two metre distance.

"Any time, any time," Al enthused. "Al the Astrologer is always there for couples in love. It's in the stars, my friends. And if it's in the stars then Al the Astrologer can read it."

He always spoke, Emily noted, as if he was addressing his audience. She couldn't help but like him; a genuine English Eccentric.

"Are there many like him in the block?" wondered Paul, as Emily returned with Al safely gone from the roof.

"I don't think there are many like Al, full stop," replied Emily. "But there are some characters. You should get to know them."

"Maybe I will, if I'm around more. Sorry. Am I going too fast?"

Yes, probably, Emily's cautious mind responded. But she shook her head. "Like you said; you have to take the chances when they come. Tomorrow's not a promise."

Paul puffed out his cheeks. "Tell me about it. There's death in my stars!"

Emily tried not to laugh. "I hope he didn't freak you out. He's very seldom right. In fact, by the law of averages he ought to be right way more often than he is."

"Well that's a relief."

There was a moment's awkwardness as the conversational possibilities of Al the Astrologer dried up and they stood face to face looking at each other. Emily felt as if she was just now realising where she was and what she was doing. It had all happened so fast that she hadn't really had a chance to stop and think. It was nice. It was… normal.

"I was promised food," Paul broke the silence. "Maybe drink. I did – I hope you don't mind – slip a bottle of wine into my pocket. I know nothing about wine but it's expensive so it must be good – I am assured that's how it works."

It was funny how he could be amusing and charming at the same time as conspicuously flaunting his wealth. That was a tightrope.

"I made a picnic." It suddenly felt like a tremendously childish thing to have done. Why had she not just let him organise this? It would have been as spectacular as advertised rather than silly and small.

But, as he took off his mask, Paul's smile could have lit up the night. "That's a brilliant idea. Picnic on the roof under the stars. What could be better?"

One thing that could have been better was that Emily could have had time to go shopping before deciding on the picnic. The contents of the basket (originally a chocolate gift basket sent by her Mum at the start of Lockdown) were overwhelmingly '*what happened to be in the fridge*', and it was more like a ploughman's lunch than a romantic dinner. There was bread and cheese, some ham, fruit and salad, and two bags of crisps mixed up in a bowl. For dessert there was butterscotch Angel Delight (something else her Mum had sent, because it fitted comfortably in an envelope).

And they talked. Seated on the edge of the roof, London sprawled before them, glowing with its myriad pinpoint lights, they talked.

"It's like an island," said Emily, looking out across the city.

"The block?"

"Yeah." But there was more. "Tonight. It's like an island in all the insanity. I don't know when I last paused to enjoy a meal without thinking about... everything. I don't know when I last sat down without feeling guilty for it, because there's always more."

Paul smiled softly. "You can't take it all on you. It's not your job to fix the world."

Yeah, her Dad definitely wouldn't like him.

"Thank you. For this."

"You organised it."

"Whatever we'd done," said Emily, earnestly, "I think it would have felt like this. Like an island of peace in the middle of 2020."

Paul considered this, for once not taking the compliment and blowing it up even further.

"If I can be that to you," he said, finally, "if I can be the place where you can take a breath, then that would make me very happy."

Emily thought that it would make her happy too.

They drank more of Paul's wine (which paired surprisingly well with butterscotch) and Emily put on music from her phone.

"You know what?" Paul seemed suddenly struck.

"What?"

"We should be dancing."

"We can't…"

"Sure we can."

Paul stood up and, keeping a two metre distance, held out his hand to Emily. "Would you?"

Maintaining the distance, Emily held out her hand and stood, facing Paul.

"Shall I lead?"

"If you like."

At first they were a little clumsy. Emily felt that if she got out of synch with Paul then it would break the spell, so she focussed on his feet and on following his movements as they sashayed in stumble-footed tandem across the rooftop. But looking into Paul's eyes she found the awkwardness slough away and they both began to move with more freedom. Somehow they read each other's minds, somehow they moved as one while always apart, somehow Emily felt Paul's hands on her though he never touched her, felt his breath on her cheek and the thump of his heart against her chest. Somehow it was the most intimate dance she had ever had with a man.

"One more? Or call it a night?" asked Paul, as the song faded.

"Let's stop before we blow it."

They cleared up the picnic things in silence and headed for

181

the stairs, still distant, but moving as one.

Chapter 19 – The Hunters (Part 1)

Wednesday (The day before Emily found the truck)
"…and where do we find Pluto? I know it's not considered a planet any more but that doesn't make it any less significant in astrological terms."

"What are you listening to?" yawned Elsa as she entered the kitchen.

It was the morning after Elsa's dramatic reappearance, and it was testament to how hard she must have been pushing herself lately that Harrigan was up and about before her. They had stayed up late into the night, talking about the Golem and the Schreck and what they might do about either, before Harrigan had noticed his girlfriend's drooping eyelids and nodding head, and suggested they go to bed. Naturally, Elsa's response had been '*Well, if you're tired*' and Harrigan was happy enough to let that go. He *was* tired.

"Web-series," replied Harrigan. "Calls himself Al the Astrologer. He lives in Nurse Emily's block, that's how I came across it. I just have it on in the background sometimes. I'll turn it off."

"You're watching a web-series?"

"Many things have changed during Lockdown. How did you sleep?"

"Well," replied Elsa. "You have a comfortable bed."

"It's a lot more comfortable with you in it."

Elsa grinned. "You big softie."

"Coffee?"

"Thanks."

The coffee maker had been a Christmas present from Don. Harrigan seldom used it when he was home alone but Elsa consumed coffee as if it was jet fuel, and it was sensible to always have a pot going.

"I've been thinking."

"About…?" Elsa enquired, leaning against the kitchen counter.

"What we do next."

"I was hoping breakfast."

Harrigan shrugged. "I haven't got much in but I can run to cereal and toast (jam is an option), and if you fancied an egg then hang the expense."

"Egg on toast then."

"I think I'll join you." Harrigan reached for the frying pan, wondering how easy this would be with one arm. "But that's not what I was talking about."

"I know."

They kept the 'shop talk' to a minimum till they were seated with coffee and fried egg on toast before them.

"Would you have preferred scrambled? Didn't think to ask."

"Fried is good."

They began to eat.

"I want to keep investigating the Golem," said Harrigan.

Elsa swallowed. "It broke your arm already."

"I can't just leave it out there."

"You told me about it."

"Yes, but…"

"Harrigan, if a member of the public reported a crime to the police, would you then encourage them to go all vigilante? Or would you suggest that they leave it to the professionals?"

"But I *am* the police," Harrigan objected. He might not be official any more but cut him in two and you'd find a thin blue line running right through him.

"The police aren't the professionals in this case," Elsa pointed out. "We are. Universal. Leave it to us. Rest up." She tapped the plaster on his arm with her knife. "Let your bones knit before giving it the opportunity to break some more. This is not your problem."

It felt as if it was. Nurse Emily had come to him and asked for help. He'd been feeling pitifully useless and it had been a chance to shed that feeling and *do* something. Maybe he wasn't best placed to do something but he had been asked and that mattered. At least to him.

"Think of your grandkids," Elsa added, seeing the indecision in his eyes.

Harrigan winced. "Don't play that card. You can't keep doing that."

"Sure I can."

"Then I can do it too," pointed out Harrigan. "They'd miss you as much as me if something happened. You're as much a grandparent to them as I am."

The look on Elsa's face was quite different now. "Am I?"

Harrigan gave an awkward shrug. "Well... as far as I'm concerned you are. And as far as they're concerned too, I reckon. How do you feel about that?"

Elsa considered for a moment. "Touched. And terrified. I had a 'boyfriend'," the air quotes again, "and suddenly I have a family."

Harrigan gave her a nervous smile. "I think this is the relationship milestone for old people; not '*Will you move in with me?*' but '*Will you have grandchildren with me?*'."

Elsa worried a toast crust with her knife. "They're pretty great kids."

"Yeah. Hard to believe they're related to me."

"Very." She took a swig of coffee. "Well that's going to be in my head next time I run down an alley after a vampire."

"Sorry."

"I'm not quitting."

"I wouldn't ask you to." He knew how much a job like that could mean to a person, how it could come to define you (in a good way), and how useless you could feel after you let it go.

"But... Yeah. How about that?" Elsa paused. "I think I like it."

"That's a relief."

Elsa finished eating and looked at her watch. "I have a meeting, then I have to go Schreck hunting."

"During the day?"

"Best time. It's harder to spot when it's awake and aware."

"You think it's around here?"

She pulled a face. "I think it's in London. Best place for it. Lots of food, lots of places to hide. *Where* in London... We've got a

185

couple of possible leads, but..." She shook her head. "The truth is it could come into the country via a millionaire's private jet or stowing away in the hold of a cargo ship. It's all the same to a Schreck. People are people."

Harrigan looked away, suddenly getting some semblance of what his family must have felt seeing him off to work every morning all those years ago. "Just be careful, alright. If you find this thing then..." he couldn't finish the sentence.

But Elsa just set her jaw grimly. "That's a problem I'd like to have."

Thursday (The day something followed Emily to McDowall House)
("Now, I know what I said yesterday about Pluto, but don't let's forget Uranus is rising. Dark planets. And what I have been saying? Change is coming. For some it's already here.")

They breakfasted together again the following morning, then, after Elsa had gone out, Harrigan wrote an email to Will asking for an emergency shop, as he was suddenly cooking for two. He then deleted it because Will would bring the shopping around and see the plaster cast and then Harrigan would have to lie, which he didn't want to do. It was getting easier to secure delivery slots at supermarkets now; he would try that instead.

Yesterday, Harrigan had spent some time composing a text to Emily. He wanted to put her mind at rest, so that when her quarantine ended she would not immediately risk her life by going after the Golem again. The trouble was that the truth was not as restful as he would have liked.

He plumped for vague honesty: '*Have reported Golem to the appropriate authorities. The one outside M. House is not the same one you saw. Nothing to worry about. Best, Harrigan.*'

This prompted a quick reply: '*There are appropriate authorities?*'

A fair question, but Universal was not his secret to share, so he answered '*Apparently so*', and hoped that was enough. It seemed to be, as he got no further messages.

186

For the rest of the day, he had mostly pottered. He had not considered himself to have yet reached the pottering time of life, but those activities not already precluded by Lockdown were precluded by his arm, and so he pottered, feeling as if he had surrendered to old age. He was not one hundred percent sure how one was supposed to potter, but he had done so by addressing those jobs about the place which he had been putting off because he had something better to do. Then he *planned* dinner, something which normally entailed looking in the fridge and checking the '*use by*' dates. Actual planning meant that when Elsa returned they had been able to sit down to a nice meal together. He had asked about her day, even though her despondency spoke for itself, and she had confirmed that the Schreck remained elusive. He had not asked what Universal was doing about the Golem.

Today, having no more tolerance for pottering, Harrigan sat down at his laptop and examined maps of the area around McDowall House.

That was only place to start looking for the Golem, but its spot had been usurped by Henrik's Golem #2 (soon to be replaced by #3). So where would the original go? It wouldn't go far because of its close ties to the block. It would find somewhere else to stand that kept it close to home. That made sense. The problem was that if a second Golem had shown up on a street corner then it would have excited interest. People would assume that Henrik had expanded his artistic vision, it would be in the news or at least on social media. And there was nothing.

The maps revealed an endless number of places in which a golem could hide during the day; side roads, alleyways, those little cuts between houses where people kept bins or bikes – any of them could hide it, and Harrigan was itching to look for himself and ask around amongst the residents. As a detective he had always believed that ninety percent of crime-solving was shoe leather, and while his success rate suggested that the other ten percent was pretty important too, he remained convinced of that.

But, even if he had been able to go and have a snoop around (without upsetting Elsa), it was unlikely he would have obtained any answers to his questions. While Harrigan had not been the greatest detective, he had always looked the part and still did. There was something 'policeman' about him; in how he held himself and in his gait. He looked to be always on the verge of bending his knees and saying *'Evenin' all. What's goin' on 'ere then?'*. It was not a look that played well in areas like that surrounding McDowall House.

The trouble was that those places where a Golem might hide were also the sorts of places in which clandestine crime thrived. They were where you went to buy drugs or take a look at that stolen DVD player, they were where threats were made and assaults occurred. They were the sorts of places where the police suspected everyone, whether they were guilty or not, because of where they lived, how they looked and, yes, sometimes because of the colour of their skin. As a result of which, they were also the sorts of places where everyone hated the police. The unjustified suspicion drove people into crime and crime justified the suspicion. It was a vicious circle.

No wonder the Golem had a grudge against the police; these were its people.

Harrigan snapped his laptop shut. The truth was that he didn't need to go look for himself; if it was there then someone would have seen it, and that would have made its way online.

Why had no one seen it?

"No luck?" Harrigan asked Elsa as she entered that evening.

"What tipped you off?"

"The way you didn't cartwheel through the door shouting 'Yippee!'."

Elsa couldn't help smiling but she was obviously frustrated. "We're putting together a list of suspicious places where the death toll is spiking. But it's just a list of anywhere people are in unavoidably close proximity; every warehouse, factory, block of flats, bus depots, nursing homes – Holy God, the nursing homes." She rubbed her temples. "It's miserable and hateful and probably for nothing because the Schreck doesn't binge feed, it knows how to stay hidden. The 'spike' we're looking for is so tiny that we have next to no chance of spotting it in amongst... everything else."

188

Harrigan gave her a moment, then spoke again. "What about the Golem?"

"We'll get to it."

If death by Schreck was hard to spot, then death by golem would be impossible to miss, and so far there had been no such reports, so the Schreck remained the priority. But Harrigan didn't like the idea of waiting until the deaths started. Prevention was better than cure, and there was a potential killer out there.

But one look at Elsa told him not to push.

Friday (The day of Emily and Paul's date)
("Change comes in all shapes and forms, my friends. For some it is temporary and for others permanent. For Yvette McCulloch, the final change came last night, courtesy of this damn virus. She lived a few floors down from me. I can't say I knew her but she was a listener as well as a neighbour.")

What was odd, Harrigan considered, returning to his map after Elsa had left for the day, was that the Golem *had* to be hiding somewhere; that was the only explanation. But it seemed very out of character. This was a creature that had bulldozed its way into shops, that had no qualms about revealing itself to Nurse Emily and which had attacked a him in a manner that could hardly be called 'clandestine'. In normal times it would have been spotted on day one, only the Lockdown had kept it relatively secret. Why was it suddenly keeping a low profile?

And yet it had to be.

He wondered about calling Nurse Emily, who had a greater insight into its behaviour than he did. But she didn't need to know that the genie which she had, to some extent, let out of its bottle, was still at large. Harrigan had no wish to make her feel guilty. After all, who knew what the Golem might have done if Emily had not got involved? It might have kept on stealing flour and toilet paper or it might have escalated its actions of its own accord. It was impossible to say definitively what influence she had had on it.

Harrigan paused in his train of thought. What if it had

acquired a new 'owner'? Someone who might have encouraged this secrecy? That could be good news but it could also be a double-edged sword. Even Emily, who had only wanted to use it for good, had led to the damn thing putting a policeman in hospital. What if it fell into the wrong hands?

Saturday
("I know that you, my loyal friends and viewers, tune in from all over the world to hear the prescient wisdom of Al the Astrologer, but I like to keep things local too. Yesterday in the tower block I call home we lost Yvette McCulloch. Last night she was joined by Cadence Burns. McDowall House is having a bad run of it, and I only hope it's at an end.")

Though the Golem had to be hiding by day, there was no reason to assume it was not still active by night, Harrigan reasoned. And, presumably, in the vicinity of McDowall House. The best thing he could do, therefore, was spend another night out on the streets in that area. The thing had little to no subtlety, its footfalls could be heard from streets away. If he was out there, then he would find it.

At which point the Golem would likely think '*There's that policeman I almost killed, time to finish the job*'. But was his personal safety a good enough reason not to look?

That evening Elsa returned home as usual and fell back onto the sofa in a brooding attitude. "It's a needle in a haystack. A needle in a haystack that keeps killing people. Where do you start? Even if we could be sure how it came into the country – which we can't – there's no saying where it went from there. London is one big buffet table to this thing. Normally with vampires you follow the deaths (it's not ideal but it's the only way). Normal vampires drain their victims completely – that's a medical anomaly so it stands out. The Schreck doesn't drain them, its bite kills in its own way. It doesn't show up in a run-of-the-mill post-mortem. And right now, post-mortems aren't sweating the details when all signs suggest Covid. We're trying to get into the morgues so we can double-check bodies for the tell-tale signs but…" She thumped the arm of the sofa.

"Damn this is depressing work!"

Harrigan got her a drink and sat beside her. He waited for some of the frustrated anger to drain from her before speaking.

"I'm going out tonight."

Elsa frowned. "Night on the tiles?"

"Night on the streets. I'm going to look for the Golem."

Elsa sighed irritably. "Harrigan, I told you, you need to leave this to Universal…"

"And you'll get right on it?"

Elsa looked sharply at him as if she had a cutting response, but her eyes dropped as she seemed to think better of it.

"I'm not criticising," Harrigan hastened to add. "You guys are doing your thing and you've got your priorities right. And I've been on your end; *'Why aren't you doing more to find my stolen stereo?'* Cos three people got assaulted last night, that's why. Police priorities get people mad all the time, but there's a reason and the same's true for you. The Golem has the potential to kill but it may not. The Schreck doesn't do anything but. If you weren't all hands on deck to find it then that would be wrong. You've got your hands full, you're not going to look for the Golem. So let me."

Elsa threw up her hands. "Let you? You're a grown man, Harrigan. If you want to, I can't stop you. But I'm telling you not to. It's not safe. Obviously." Her gaze went to his arm.

"I'll be careful. And," Harrigan gave a little shrug, "I'd really rather you were cool with this."

"Do I need to break out the grandkids argument again?"

"I wish you wouldn't." Harrigan had spent much of the day going back and forth on this. "There's a potential killer out there. No one is looking for it, and the only thing keeping me from looking is the possible risk to me. What would you do in my place?"

Elsa made a face that might have been almost a grudging smile. "I'd sooner you do as I say, not as I do."

"I just want to help."

It would be a lie to say that Harrigan was not a bundle of nerves returning to the corner near McDowall House where he had spent a sleepless night that had ended in broken bones and near-drowning. The silhouette of the Golem standing before him brought it all back, and the first thing he did was go up to the thing and check it over. There was no number '2' carefully hidden amongst its symbolic decoration, but it knuckles were intact. That made this number 3. Henrik worked fast.

So, to paraphrase Obi Wan Kenobi, this was not the Golem he was looking for, but, assuming his theory was correct, that Golem would be about somewhere, probably 'shopping' for the residents of the block.

For the next few hours, Harrigan traipsed around those streets with shops, hoping to catch the Golem in the act, ears always pricked for the regular thumping footsteps that had announced its approach at their last meeting. Every hour he swung past McDowall House itself, on the basis that this was where the Golem would bring its shopping.

But there was neither sign nor sound.

Was that not odd? If it wasn't here then where was it? If it was so dedicated to those 'Truths' inside it, then why had it ceased to follow them?

Since Emily had dumped the Golem outside the city, its behaviour seemed to have become erratic. It had returned (he could vouch for that first-hand), but how had it known the way back? How had it not been seen? And why was it no longer performing its regular activities? There was a missing piece in the puzzle.

In the early hours of the morning, Harrigan visited McDowall House one last time. He was just in time to see the stretcher being carried out to the ambulance. The body was covered from head to foot.

Chapter 20 – Cleaning House

At the same time that Clive Harrigan was beginning his night on the streets around McDowall House, sixteen floors above him, Maxie Feld was arriving home.

Maxie never wore a mask. The people who did were sheep and he would not be one of them. Masks were for suckers, they did more them harm than good. He had seen a video about it on YouTube.

Which made it all the more annoying that he had picked up a cough which he couldn't seem to shake. It was just a cough – Maxie was sure of that. He'd had coughs before the pandemic and there was no reason this one should be any different from those coughs.

As the lift doors opened he checked the corridor up and down for people. In a block the size of McDowall House you couldn't possibly know all of your neighbours, and in a country like England you certainly didn't *get to know* them, that would be overfamiliar, but Maxie was still cautious of being found out. He was not supposed to be living here.

The corridor was empty, and Maxie trotted along to his door and let himself in.

"I'm back."

Perhaps to prove to himself that he was not sick, Maxie had called Lizzie the other night and she had stayed over.

"You have a good day?" asked the blonde girl, who did not look as if she had moved from the futon since he had left that morning.

Maxie did not answer.

"Max?"

On his way home he had been thinking about polite ways to tell Lizzie to leave (although Lizzie was a club dancer, so used to people being rude to her), but now he was here and she was already in bed and… and he needed something to get the taste of today out of his mind.

The chain of events had started twelve days ago, with the appearance of the Golem under the railway bridge. Or perhaps a few days after that, when Maxie had made the decision to go back for it and bring it to the city. Driving back with the Golem in the rear of the truck, he wondered if he was doing the right thing. But if he didn't bring it back then there was no way his Boss would believe him – he needed to see it. Plus, if the police found it then he couldn't guarantee that it wouldn't… well, it wouldn't *talk*, but it might identify them somehow. Besides all that, the thing was useful, if you could find the right words to instruct it then it could do the work of ten men and it didn't need paying.

It was only once he had begun the drive that Maxie realised he didn't know what he was going to do with the thing when they arrived. Though the Golem was biddable, Maxie had a hunch that if he tried to lock it up (they had plenty of places in which people could be locked up), it would simply walk through the door. He could tell it to stay put, and it might for a while, but if it got another idea in its head then that was that. The damn thing could probably walk through walls if it wanted to.

He was almost back when he had a brainwave.

"Look, I don't know if Golems can catch the virus or transmit it, but I'm not taking any chances. You need to quarantine for a bit." He was deliberately vague about the length of time.

Truth be told, although it seemed unlikely that an airborne virus could be caught by something that did not breathe, he felt safer for having it quarantine. Technically it was as susceptible to infection as a garden gnome, but why take chances? Either way, it was a damn fine excuse and, to Maxie's relief, the Golem seemed to buy it. It was all about the words you used; if you could convince the thing that it could defeat Covid by smashing itself to pieces, then all you would have to do was hand it the hammer.

The people traffickers worked out of a row of shuttered shop fronts – common enough even before the pandemic hit the High Street. They hid in plain sight, not in central London but in a residential area, and conveniently just around the corner from McDowall House, where Maxie was currently crashing. Beneath the shops, the Edwardian cellars had been converted to holding cells, one filled with illegal entrants into this country (the 'cargo' of the second truck), another with the Golem, standing perfectly still through the days of its quarantine, waiting.

Then, one night, five days after the Golem had strode into Maxie's world, Booth came running in.

"There's someone out there watching."

Maxie spat irritably. "Watching? Watching what? The stars? The bats? You?"

Booth shook his head. "I don't know. All I know is there's someone round the corner from McDowall House with a pair of binoculars."

Lockdown had brought the crazies out of the woodwork, so you got all sorts out and about by night – this didn't have to be someone watching them.

"Watch him back," said Maxie, trying to ignore the pinch of anxiety at the back of his brain. "Follow him if he goes anywhere."

It was the middle of the night and there was not currently anything at street level that would give away their presence. They had to be cautious, but could afford to investigate further without panicking.

That time was not long in coming. An hour or so later, Booth returned.

"He's police."

"How do you know?"

"I followed him when he went for coffee," Booth related. "He flashed a warrant card."

Maxie stood quietly, listening to his own breathing and trying to block out the rising roar in his head. A policeman in plain clothes, carrying binoculars, was stationed unnervingly close to the building where they were housing illegal immigrants to be sold into servitude.

"Right."

Maxie had grown up around criminals. It wasn't his parents' fault, they had tried to keep him out of that life, but when it surrounded you then it was natural to grow into that world, and Maxie hadn't been strong enough to go against the grain. It was an adolescence that had left him with very definite feelings about what you did when policemen were around.

"Maxie?" pressed Booth.

"We'll move the cargo."

"What; with him up there watching?"

"No," Maxie sighed, shaking his head. "We wait until he's gone, then get them out as quick as we can. I don't know what he's seen – I don't think we've shown him shit – but if police are around then we move."

Booth nodded. "To McDowall?"

"For now." The unused basement of McDowall House was their immediate fallback position in case of emergency, because why would anyone look there? It wasn't a long-term solution, but it was good for few nights while a new place was secured.

"What about…" Booth's face briefly assumed the constipated expression it took on when he spoke about the Golem. "…It."

Maxie paused in thought before speaking. "It'll have to come with. If the police *do* show up then I don't think it'd hesitate to finger us if someone asked the right question. It's not a grass, it just doesn't get it."

Booth nodded. "So… put it in with the cargo? There's only one basement at McDowall."

Maxie smirked. "That should keep them quiet."

With Booth running back upstairs to keep an eye on the policeman, Maxie briefed the rest of the gang, and they got ready to shift the cargo up to the waiting truck as soon as Booth gave them the all-clear. It was only a thirty second drive but taking the cargo out across the plaza was not an option; they might be seen, they might make a break for it. It would be bad enough taking them through the block's entrance hall, but there was only one door to the basement and in the dead of night the hall ought to be empty.

Because it seemed to listen to him the most, Maxie himself went to fetch the Golem.

"Your quarantine's up. You're all clear. Come with me." He didn't want to give it more specific instructions yet, not until he was sure what he wanted of the thing.

In hindsight, he would rather wish that he had played that differently.

Upstairs, George was hunched next to Booth, peering through a crack in the boarded-up window.

"What's going on?" asked Maxie, the Golem thumping up the steps behind him.

Booth looked back. "Our policeman is on the move."

The change in the Golem was instantaneous, its slow steps suddenly becoming quick, determined strides as it crossed the room, pulling open the door and heading out into the night.

"What are you…? Where are you going?"

Maxie started after the thing but Booth grabbed him and dragged him back.

"Don't go out there shouting. You want to tell the whole street we're here? At least that thing keeps its mouth shut."

Maxie stared frustratedly after the Golem. "Well what if the filth sees it?"

Booth pulled a face that could almost have been a smile. "Oh I think he's going to see it. Look at the way that thing's moving." He shook his head. "Reckon it doesn't like pigs."

Maxie relented – it wasn't as if he could stop the thing. "Come on. We've got work to do."

The transfer went quickly and smoothly. By this point of their confinement, the cargo of immigrants were blankly and silently compliant, all defiance starved out of them. In the early hours of the morning, Maxie and Booth left McDowall House.

As they did so, they caught sight of an approaching figure.

"What the hell?" murmured Maxie.

The Golem was covered in mud, its clay body caked from toes to neck, only its head free.

"I reckon there's a policeman with a pair of binoculars at the bottom of a hole somewhere," grinned Booth.

Maxie didn't smile. A dead policeman – even a missing one – meant more attention. One more thing to tell his Boss, and he had enough to tell already.

"Oh." Booth pointed. "Now what's it going to do?"

The Golem had come face to face with its doppelganger, the replacement golem erected a few days ago after the original had gone AWOL, and which the council was pretending was the same one.

"Punch his lights out!" called George.

Perhaps that thought was going through the Golem's head. Then again, Maxie reminded himself, *no* thoughts went through its head. It did not think, it simply followed its 'Truths'. It was easy to forget that. When it stared at you, it was hard to believe that there was nothing going on behind those penetrating eyes.

Did it recognise itself in the statue standing before it? Or did it have no sense of self and was simply confused by finding someone else in its spot? Where was it supposed to stand now?

"Get it downstairs, before someone sees it," snarled Maxie. "And get some of that crap off it." He had an idea.

The problem with using the block as a halfway house for the cargo was that people lived there, and while the basement was well-insulated, noise might filter up and alert someone to their presence.

"See this here?" Maxie addressed the rows of sad, thin faces, staring at him in the subdued light of the basement, and indicated the Golem. "He's in charge. Anyone tries to leave, anyone makes any noise and BAM! You don't want to see what he can do."

Few of them, perhaps none of them, understood a word he said, and he neither spoke nor understood their language (he wasn't a hundred percent sure where all they came from). But the Golem, by its mere presence, spoke a language that needed no words.

"Do not let any of them leave," Maxie spoke to the Golem. "You know what they are? Illegal immigrants. They shouldn't be out there. Do not let *anyone* leave this basement unless I tell you say otherwise."

He was guessing at what was in the Golem's head, but diatribes against immigration were so common that it would be a miracle if there weren't a few 'Truths' in there that he could use to his advantage. The Golem would keep them here, and keep them quiet.

A few days later, new accommodation was arranged for the cargo, and both they and their warder were moved out of McDowall House. Now the Golem was freed up from guard duty, Maxie could introduce it to his Boss, and give an anxious and overdue report on all that had occurred in recent weeks.

The meeting was tense for Maxie but it seemed to go alright – the problems had not been his fault and he had handled them. Afterwards he only recalled the edited highlights:

"If a policeman went missing on assignment I think we'd have heard about it by now," his Boss had pointed out.

So perhaps the Golem had not killed him.

Once he had gotten used to it, Maxie's Boss accepted the Golem's existence with surprising ease.

"And it does what you tell it?"

"Not exactly," Maxie had replied, carefully. "Sometimes. Although, I sometimes think it does what it wants and it just happens that's sometimes the same as what I ask it."

On the subject of it doing what it wanted, Maxie had to admit that, now its 'quarantine' was over, the Golem was taking to the streets by night and there was nothing they could do to stop it. But his Boss's concerns seemed more focussed on other recent events.

"Have the police found the truck yet?"

"No." Maxie had checked.

His Boss's eyes narrowed. "Then how are they onto us?"

A handful of phone calls assembled Booth, George, Bill and the rest of the gang, and they arrived in the basement of the new building where Maxie was waiting for them, the Golem standing behind him, close to the door.

"What's that thing doing out?" Booth was always nervous of the Golem.

"It does as its told," replied Maxie.

Booth made a face. "So far."

"What's up?" asked George.

"I met with the Boss," said Maxie. His mouth was very dry, and he suddenly felt awkward around these men, whom he had hired and all of whom he knew well.

"Are we getting a pay rise?" asked Bill, and there was a murmur of polite titters.

"He's got some concerns." Maxie stopped the laughter. "He asked me…" He reached into his pocket and drew out the letter (*'Read it word for word, Maxie. Word for word.'*). "He asked me to read this."

"We're getting a written warning?" Sullivan rolled his eyes. "Should have stayed at MacDonald's."

Maxie cleared this throat. The page before him blurred and he blinked back unaccustomed anxiety, trying to focus. Maxie had done things he was not proud of. And he was proud of some things he should not have done. But this was… More than anything, it was weird. He didn't know what was going to happen next.

" 'As I am sure you are all aware'," he began to read the letter, his voice throaty and his delivery unnaturally stilted, " 'there has been a security breach.' "

He could sense the nervousness in the room, but there was strength in numbers and Maxie didn't seem to be carrying a weapon.

" 'I do not for a minute think that any of you is a grass. Maxie knows what he is doing and he would not have hired anyone who would go to the police.' "

That seemed to allay fears somewhat.

" 'That said; they found out somehow, so maybe there have been some loose lips.' " Maxie swallowed scratchily, then kept reading. " 'Maybe you mentioned something to a friend over a drink, and gossip spreads. However it happened, it happened. I am not pointing fingers, but obviously a change has to be made. I do not think any 'punishment' is required… *per se*,' " he wasn't sure what that meant but '*word for word*' had been the instruction, " 'but it is time to clean house and move on.' "

The ripples of nervousness were building again.

" 'You are all smart enough to realise, and have been in this business long enough to know, that this is not just a matter of a handshake, a gold watch and good luck in your future endeavours.' "

The men were starting to move now, realising what was

200

going on and not wanting to be here when it did, their fight and flight instinct kicking in.

" 'The bottom line is'," Maxie read on, eyes fixed to the page, not thinking about what he was saying but just saying it and be damned, " 'you brought illegal immigrants into the country. They brought Covid with them. And as long as you are alive then you will continue to do so.' "

The Golem was moving before Maxie had got to the end of the sentence, blocking the door. There had been a bunch of trigger words in there and any one could have roused it to action.

The gang scattered about the room, all of them trying to get to the exit and all hoping that the Golem would be too busy with the others to notice them – no loyalty amongst desperate men.

Scurrying like a rat, Booth tried to get around it. He probably didn't even see the Golem's arm move, even to Maxie it was little more than a blur, whipping out to the side, the clay monster's fist catching Booth under the chin so hard that it was unclear if jaw or neck broke first. He wouldn't have felt a thing, dead before he hit the floor.

George broke to the other side, hoping the Golem was not yet done with Booth, but the creature's other hand shot out, grabbing him by the skull and slamming him against the wall. Maxie's stomach lurched as George's head burst like a watermelon against the white-washed plaster.

Bill and Sullivan both ran at the same time, each counting on it going for the other. But the Golem caught Bill a glancing blow with its left hand, stunning him, then grabbed Sullivan in its right, hurling him across the room, screaming as he went. The scream was cut off as he hit the wall with a sound like a bag of wet twigs. He slumped the floor, his breath coming in bubbling whines. The Golem turned back to Bill, too dazed to see the fist falling like it was playing one potato, two potato. More blood, more grey matter, no more Bill.

Durham was the last of them (*And the youngest*, Maxie's mind added). He cowered by the wall as if he was trying to push himself through it.

"No, no, no, NO!"

He scrambled and flailed desperately as the Golem grabbed him. Its hands closed over his skull as Durham shrieked. Maxie looked away, although the sound was almost as bad, the young man's scream imploding in a crack and a squelch.

Sullivan was still technically alive and the Golem now turned back to him. Its foot descended like a piston, Sullivan's head putting up as much resistance as a jelly.

It occurred to Maxie that he had known Sullivan almost ten years.

He looked around the gory carnage of the room, his brain swimming. He'd seen death before, that was part of the business. But this… It had been too clean. Too easy. Too detached. Something about that sickened him.

The Golem stood, still as before, its job done.

Maxie wanted to go outside and throw up, but there had been more, and he was more determined than ever to follow his Boss's instructions to the letter.

"All this needs cleaning up," he parroted the words as he had been told them. "Cleanliness saves live; hands, face, space. I'll show you what to do with the bodies. Clean yourself up too."

He turned away as the Golem began work, and, without thinking, coughed into his sleeve.

He heard the Golem turn, and realised the mistake he had made.

"No…" It bore down on him. "It's not Covid! It's just a cough!" The clay hand reached for his throat. "I live in the block! I live in McDowall house!" Maxie shrieked and the Golem came to an uncertain halt.

For a few moments it was frozen, one arm out towards Maxie, who stood shaking, choking on his own bile and aware that he desperately needed to cough but couldn't allow himself to do so.

After what seemed like an age, the Golem moved again, calmly going back to cleaning, apparently deciding that its loyalty to the block outweighed its instructions to eliminate the virus.

That had been earlier this evening. Tomorrow Maxie would put together a new crew. For now he needed sleep, but every time he closed his eyes he saw the blood, heard the screams, and the Golem's face bore down on him once more.

Fortunately, Lizzie was there and he still felt the need to prove that he wasn't as sick as he felt.

"You've still got that cough," said Lizzie.

"It's nothing," said Maxie, as he undressed.

"I'm just saying, maybe you can get tested or…"

Maxie slapped her, and Lizzie shut up.

"That's better." He slapped her again, to be sure.

Half an hour later they were both asleep. Neither woke when something entered the room. It did so silently and with purpose, sniffing the air then making straight for Maxie, ignoring Lizzie as if she was not there.

The sound of Lizzie's screams in the early hours of the morning, alerted the block to its third death in as many days.

Chapter 21 – The Hunters (Part 2)

Sunday (The morning after Maxie died)
("Another loss to mourn, people; one Maxie Feld. Once this damn virus takes hold it runs through a place, taking no prisoners. I cannot see the stars.")

After his long night on the streets, Harrigan rose late, missing Elsa. A hasty word with the paramedics he had seen last night had given him few details but the tentative cause of death for the man on the stretcher was Covid, which would not be the case if the deceased had been killed by a golem.

The poor man hadn't even gone to hospital. That was becoming more common; people were scared of hospitals because they might catch Covid, but also because they were afraid of being told that they had it. As long as you didn't know, then it remained just a cough.

As he breakfasted, Harrigan took stock. Last night had not achieved the results he had expected but it had left him sure of one thing; between Emily dumping it and it attacking him, *something* had happened to the Golem, which had changed its behaviour.

Which at least it gave him a place to start.

Elsa was not using her car today and Harrigan located the keys in what he thought of as her non-work bag, which contained things like hairbrushes rather than wooden stakes. He headed out.

When she had first called (ten days ago, though it felt longer) Nurse Emily had given him a reasonable idea of where she had left the Golem that night. It was a long drive, even through the reduced Lockdown traffic, so it was early afternoon when Harrigan arrived in the scrubland on the fringes of the city, and immediately set out to find the spot, hunting through rusting hulks of abandoned railwayana, and tripping over wooden sleepers hidden beneath the nettles and long grass.

It wasn't a difficult hunt. The Golem's heavy feet left a clear trail, flattening the vegetation and leaving deep imprints in the ground. Where there were large banks of brambles that any normal person would walk around, the Golem had ploughed straight through, leaving a wake of broken stems. You did not need to be a Native American tracker to follow the trail of a golem, it stopped for nothing.

That was when Harrigan happened on the police tape.

"People traffickers?" Elsa frowned.

"Bastards!" Harrigan chopped an onion with ferocity. "They just left them to die! Fifteen people! Starving and suffocating in the back of a truck. You believe that?"

Elsa looked oddly thoughtful. "Do you think the Golem had anything to do with it?"

Harrigan shook his head. "I wondered, but I can't see how. It might have been there days later or days before. Its tracks vanished in amongst all the police activity. Anyway, the people in the truck weren't pummelled to death. 'Natural causes'. If you call it natural to shut up your fellow human beings with no water, no food, no air! Rats had started to eat them for God's sake! Bastard son of a …!" He had cut his finger. You should not chop onions while in a temper and a plaster cast.

"How do you know these details?" Elsa always spotted the little things.

"Officer in charge used to work in Cambridge," muttered Harrigan, as he headed for the bathroom to find a plaster for his bleeding finger. "Nice guy. Always destined for big things."

"Do they know when the truck arrived in this country?"

"Couple of weeks ago," Harrigan called back as he fumbled in the bathroom cabinet. "Why?"

He got no answer, and as he went back into the kitchen he found Elsa staring into middle distance while a pot boiled over on the hob.

"Elsa?" Harrigan turned down the heat.

"How well do you know this guy from Cambridge?"

"Well enough. We got along." Harrigan hadn't always hit it off with the fast-trackers, who looked at him as if he was an anchor holding them back, but Doug Kildare had been one of the few with whom he had been friends.

"Well enough that he might do you a favour?"

"What sort of favour?" asked Harrigan, still not sure where this was going.

Elsa looked at him, and her green eyes seemed brighter than they had for days. "Fifteen dead people, recently arrived from the continent? I need to see the bodies."

Monday
("I'm going to keep doing this, reading their names whether I knew them or not. I know they're a handful among thousands, but they were my neighbours. Last night it was Abdul-Hafez – I'm sorry, I don't know if that's his full name.")

It was a day of frustration and phone calls as Harrigan tried to get in touch with the busy Inspector Kildare, who (not unreasonably) had better things to do than answer unsolicited messages from an old acquaintance. Harrigan sat with the phone to his ear and his head in his hand listening to tinny hold music until he got to speak to the next assistant standing between him and Kildare, before being put back on hold again.

It took all day. Another day gone.

Tuesday
("I have to add Noel Parker to the list. I've put together a website to commemorate them. It's not much but... I guess it's something. They're in the stars now.")

Doug Kildare looked through the small round window in the door of the morgue as Elsa, in full personal protective gear, pored over one of the corpses. He turned back to Harrigan.

"You've got a good one there, Harrigan. Odd but good."

Harrigan nodded; he was well aware. "Thanks for letting us in."

Kildare gave a '*screw it*' shrug. "It's a long way from protocol, but frankly I'd welcome another pair of eyes on this. What is she? Special Branch?"

"Very special," said Harrigan, as deadpan as he could.

"Didn't see any ID," Kildare noted. "And Special Branch don't usually have to call in favours to look at a body."

Harrigan opened his mouth, fully intending to lie his ass off, but Kildare held up his hands.

"Don't bother. I don't care. We can use all the help we can get. Doesn't add up. Doesn't add up at all."

Harrigan frowned. "Seems pretty clear cut. This sort of thing happens, doesn't it?"

"Oh yeah," said Kildare, grimly. "Standard practice amongst these scum. If you hit a problem then you don't kill the poor sods in the back, you ditch the truck and leave them locked in. Less of a fuss, *and* that's manslaughter not murder: '*I meant to come back for them, your Honour*'." He shook his head. "If that doesn't make you sick then nothing will."

"So what doesn't add up?"

"The door," said Kildare. "They'd been rear-ended. Nothing major. Might even have been self-inflicted to get the truck out the mud. But it bust up the rear door. Wouldn't shut properly. When it was found there was just a bit of wood keeping it closed. If the people inside had tried, they could have got it open."

"Yeah," Harrigan acknowledged. "But they knew the traffickers were outside."

"So they sat there and died?" Kildare raised an eyebrow. "In that situation, would you sit still? Or would you rush the doors and chance it?" He sighed. "We're missing something. And if your wife…"

"Girlfriend."

"If she can see something we've missed, then bring it on."

Harrigan looked through the window. It was not often that he got to see Elsa at work. They had met through work of course and he had been instantly struck by her drive, always pushing onto the next thing. Here she was quiet, studying the remains of a young woman who had hoped to start a new life in the UK, but beneath the surface Harrigan could still sense that drive. If she had found a lead that might take her to the Schreck, then he expected to see sparks.

She finished up and came out to join them, sanitising her hands using a dispenser on the wall.

"Who found them? You?"

Kildare shook his head. "Couple out for a walk. Bit cagey – I think they were walking the edge of the restrictions, but…"

"I need to speak to them."

Kildare sucked at his teeth. "I've pushed regulations just letting you in. I can't give you the names of members of the public without the proper paperwork. I can show you their statements…"

"You won't have asked the right questions," Elsa pushed. "This is important."

"I'm sorry."

Even behind the mask and face guard, Elsa's frustration was clear. "Can you tell me what time they left the site?"

"Not exactly."

"Had the sun set?"

"I think so. Is it…?"

"It's important. Would they have been the first to leave?"

"I suppose so. We were still working the scene."

Elsa nodded and was silent for a moment, considering this. "Alright. Let me see the statements. Please."

Kildare nodded. "Come this way."

They passed a cleaner as they went back upstairs, dark-skinned and diligently wiping a banister. Harrigan wondered where he had come from. Born here or born there. Legal or illegal. You never asked, you seldom wondered, you just accepted that a vast number of menial jobs were done by an imported workforce who half the country didn't want here but would miss if they weren't. What had he run away from? What had he been through to get here? What had those eyes seen? The risks people took just so they could end up a cleaner, or end up behind the door with the small, round window.

In his office, Kildare went to his desk and handed Elsa a file. "You can take these with you. These are persons of interest – the usual suspects we round up when stuff like this happens. All of them have previous in people trafficking." He shrugged. "I don't know who you work for but if any of these names come up on your system…"

"You'll be the first to know," nodded Elsa, flicking through the mugshots.

Presumably she was used to lying about this sort of thing, but Harrigan could not help feeling guilty, knowing how little help they were likely to be.

"It's not them we want really," admitted Kildare, "it's the higher ups. The money. But you never get a sniff of them."

Elsa nodded again. "The statements from the pair who found them?"

Kildare handed over another file and Elsa began to read, her eyes racing quickly but intently over the text.

Turning to Harrigan, Kildare pointed to a picture on the wall, one of many crime scene photos. "There. What do you think? Would that bit of wood stop you if you were starving to death?"

But Harrigan's eyes were on another picture. He felt as if his brain had just exploded. There in the background, standing beside a man who was being interviewed, was Nurse Emily Jennings.

"You're sure?" Elsa asked.

"Hundred percent," said Harrigan.

Elsa got out her phone as she spoke. "At least eight of those refugees were killed by the Schreck. It was there, in that truck. The question is where it went next." Her fingers glided swiftly across the phone screen until she found what she was looking for. "McDowall House was added to our list of suspicious places yesterday. They've had a death every night for the last five days. All sudden. None of them even made it to hospital." She thought for a moment. "Do you have Nurse Emily's phone number?"

"Yes."

"Call her. Don't mention the truck. I just need to know if McDowall House has a basement."

Harrigan rang Nurse Emily, who gave a puzzled affirmative that McDowall House did indeed have a basement but it wasn't used much.

"Is this about… you know?" she asked.

She meant the Golem. "No. At least…" Harrigan paused. Was it? It was a massive coincidence if these things weren't linked somehow. "I don't think so. Leave it with me."

"Leave it with…?"

"Bye." Harrigan hung up and turned to Elsa. "Is this to do with the Golem? Or is it all the Schreck?"

Elsa shook her head. "I don't know. I don't like coincidences, but I don't see… There's something we're missing."

Harrigan felt that there was *a lot* he was missing. "Are you going to tell me what you're thinking?"

"Walk and talk." She continued to scroll through her phone as she strode briskly back towards the car, Harrigan jogging to keep up. "Here's how I see it; bullet points. The Schreck came over here with a group of refugees. Ideal for it – food to travel with. They were met by the traffickers, who bundled them into a truck. The Schreck went with them. Then something happened to derail their plans and, for whatever reason, the traffickers decided to ditch the refugees."

"Covid?" suggested Harrigan. It was the *de jour* derailer of plans.

"Quite possibly; the Schreck wouldn't have gone with them unless a few were infected. So the bastard traffickers sealed the refugees in the back of the truck and the Schreck with them." She shook her head. "Hell of a way to die. I hope they didn't see it coming. Although being sealed in, in the darkness, knowing there's something in there with you wouldn't have been much better."

Harrigan frowned; that made Kildare's conundrum still more puzzling. "Why didn't they try to get out?"

"Can't answer that," admitted Elsa, before continuing with her bullet points. "So the Schreck is alright for a while; it has victims to feed on, but when they're gone it's stuck in the middle of nowhere starving. Nobody's coming by – that's why the traffickers use that area. Then; stroke of luck: someone turns up."

"Nurse Emily. And whoever she was out walking with."

"Followed by the police. Now there are people, with cars, so the Schreck can hitch a lift to the city. Chances are it stows away with the first person to leave; Emily or her friend. Based on what's happening at McDowall House, I think we can assume it was in Emily's car, and that it's been killing a person a night ever since. All it needs is a dark place to spend the day. A basement would be ideal."

Harrigan glanced at the skyline; Kildare had not been available till late afternoon and evening was now encroaching. "I need to warn Emily."

As they arrived back at the car, he reached for his phone, but Elsa's hand shot out to stop him.

"What is it?"

Her eyes were on her phone screen, face grim. "That astrologer you like has set up a web page commemorating the dead in McDowall House. Check out the third name down."

Harrigan took the phone. Al had done a nice job, but he didn't have pictures for all of the dead, including the one Elsa had been interested in. All there was, was a name; Maxie Feld.

"Who's...?"

"Look." Elsa thrust a piece of paper in front of Harrigan's eyes. It was one of the mugshots from the file Kildare had given her of known people traffickers: Maxie Feld, of no fixed abode.

Muddled thoughts and reactions criss-crossed Harrigan's mind, bumping into each other and generally getting into one another's way. "What does it even mean?"

Elsa turned a hard stare on him. "It means that, until a few days ago, a known people trafficker lived in the same block as one of the people who found that truck. Which is another extraordinary coincidence." She grimaced. "Harrigan, I have to ask; are you sure Nurse Emily's not involved? In the trafficking I mean."

"I'm sure." Harrigan was.

Elsa nodded. "Then her friend may be."

Chapter 22 – The Basement

"Has McDowall House got a basement?" Emily frowned at Harrigan's question. "Yeah. Doesn't get used much but, yeah. Is this about... you know?" What did the Golem have to do with the basement?

"No," Harrigan replied, quickly. Though he added. "At least... I don't think so." Sounding a lot less certain. "Leave it with me."

"Leave it with...?"

"Bye." He hung up before Emily could quiz him further.

"What's that about the basement?"

Emily looked up to where Paul stood in the doorway of her kitchen, a glass of wine in his hand, his eyes on her.

"Who knows?" Emily tried to wave it off. There were things you talked about on a second date and things that you did not. One of the things that you did not was living statues. She would rather that Paul did not think she was crazy. "Just a guy I know (he's a policeman actually) wanted some information about the block. I wouldn't be surprised if they were bringing in extra restrictions. Even quarantining the place."

The four days since their first date had not been good ones for McDowall House. Mrs McCulloch's death seemed to have started a landslide; there had been one every night since. None of the victims had displayed particularly serious symptoms beforehand, all of them had died so suddenly that they did not even have the opportunity to go to hospital, and there was rising concern that this was some new and more aggressive form of Covid.

Emily was cagey about stuff like that; 'facts' that seemed to be spread exclusively on the internet and had no clinical basis. Five people was a tragedy, but still a comparatively small number. She thought it more likely that people in McDowall House didn't like doctors and so kept quiet about symptoms that they should have taken to hospital. Lydia and Masud were not the only ones who didn't want to pop their heads above the parapet and draw attention to themselves. Plus, there was still a large part of society that believed you didn't really get sick until a doctor confirmed it.

All that said, the deaths were only too real and she had thought seriously about cancelling her date tonight. That would have been smart. Right now she wasn't even convinced that Paul was enjoying it.

"I dread to think what the basement would have to do with that." He sat down beside her.

"I'm sure they won't do anything before checking with you." Emily tried to move on from the subject.

But Paul grimaced. "I think they probably would. It's not like I'm the owner – it's a corporation." He drummed his fingers on Emily's coffee table. "It would be the height of bad manners for me to make a call now, wouldn't it? During our second date. That would be unforgivable, yes?"

"Pretty close," said Emily. "But I already took a call, so..."

Paul gave her an apologetic smile. "I'm so sorry. Me and business. Probably best you know now, before it's too late. It *is* my worst fault, so at least there aren't any other surprises waiting."

He stood, patting his pockets as he did so, then looked guiltily at Emily.

"That is my *worst* fault, but another fault to which I should admit is my carelessness with my phone. Not as bad a fault, but inconvenient right now."

"You want to use my phone?"

"I'll pay for the call."

Emily handed her phone across with a smile. "Have this one on me."

"Thank you, thank you, thank you."

He took the phone, heading into the kitchen as he dialled. Emily tried not to listen in on the conversation, and checked her reflection in the mirror on the wall. Still good – good enough; hair straightened specially, dress doing its job, make-up making her look marginally less like the walking dead than she had in recent weeks. And yet...

The phone call from Harrigan hadn't helped but, overall, tonight was a bit flat compared to their first date. That was the

213

problem with starting on a high; it was hard to recreate. Weirdly, being socially distant had made them seem closer, it had provided that extra bit of magic that made the spark leap the two metre gap between them. Now they were 'bubbled' together and could be actually, factually, physically close without breaking any rules, and it felt like there was a distance. The spark no longer had to make the effort and so it hadn't bothered to show up.

She still liked him, but…

No. Emily shook off the doubts. She was being stupid. Give the guy a chance. Even if tonight went poorly that was still one poor date against one great one, so she would owe him a third to break the tie. He was a nice man and they did not come along every day.

Paul strode back in, looking worried. "They've been trying to call me for the last hour. Bloody phone."

"Problems?"

"You could say that." He looked genuinely nervous, which was an odd thing to say about the super-confident, always in control Paul.

Emily smiled. "You have to go, don't you?"

Paul looked desperate. "Do you mind? I mean… I'm sure you *mind*. I hope you mind. I'd actually be a little offended if you didn't mind. What I mean is, despite minding, are you willing to excuse me while I go see if I can hold my business interests together with both hands?"

Emily laughed. Even when he was having a bad night Paul was still effortlessly charming. "Go. This'll keep."

"Yes." Paul nodded, then paused. "The food will keep or…"

"It'll all keep."

Paul looked in two minds for a moment. "This has not gone as I intended." He looked at Emily. "I will make it up to you."

"I shall insist upon it."

There was a beat, a moment between them when, in normal times, a kiss might have suggested itself and perhaps even occurred. But not now, not here in McDowall House.

"I'll call you tomorrow."

"Okay. Goodnight. Hope you can save your business."

Once he was gone, Emily felt flustered and irritable. Should they have gone ahead with the date at all? Probably not. They weren't breaching regulations, because people who lived alone were allowed company, but... Much as she liked Paul and much as he talked a big game about following the rules, she had a hunch that the businessman in him could not keep away from the office, and perhaps he was overegging his own rule-abidingness because he knew she was a nurse. '*It's one rule for them and one rule for us, Princess,*' her Dad was fond of reminding her, and Paul was undoubtedly '*Them*'. Maybe it was as well to put off any more close contact until... Well that was the sentence which no one could currently finish.

She drained her wine glass, then picked up Paul's; waste not, want not. She stopped, the glass hovering before her lips. Better to play it safe. Damn virus, making her waste good wine.

Paul's wine went down the sink and Emily went to pour herself another.

Maybe she should call her parents and see how they were doing. How long had it been?

Then she realised that Paul had walked out with her phone. "Damn."

He had probably pocketed it without even thinking, as one does with a phone. That also prevented her from calling Harrigan back, which was irritating because that had seemed like an unfinished conversation. Why was he asking about the basement?

The night after her first date with Paul (the thought of it still made her smile involuntarily), Emily had finally followed through on her intention to spend a night outside, watching the Golem.

It did nothing.

She owed Harrigan an apology for some of the things she had been thinking. He had said that this was not the same one and, since it did not move, she was happy to believe him.

So where was her Golem? Was it still out there? If so, where? The mystery gifts left outside people's doors had stopped after she dumped it in the wilderness, then had returned briefly and then stopped again. The night before her quarantine ended (when it had delivered Robert's bleach and, apparently, some cats) had been the Guardian Angel's last appearance. People were getting tetchy over where their free stuff had gone. Why had it stopped? Also, where had the new golem come from? What was the deal there? Many questions.

What had the basement got to do with any of it?

She changed out of her date night dress (red – red was her colour and she leaned into it), and put on tracksuit bottoms and a white vest top.

Surely, the only reason that Harrigan would get in touch would be something to do with the Golem. So why ask about the basement if it wasn't to do with the Golem?

Maybe she should tidy up. She had tidied before Paul arrived but that had mostly involved shoving stuff into the broom cupboard in the kitchen. A proper tidy was overdue and she had nothing else to do tonight, having finished watching *Tiger King* using Jill's Netflix account.

What would the Golem be doing in the basement anyway? Had it been there all this time? That would explain why it wasn't around anymore but why would it stop there? Doors certainly weren't an obstacle to it.

Emily leant on the back of her sofa, closed her eyes and tried to centre herself. In her head, her Dad's voice reminded her that '*People who do nothing get nothing done*', while her Grandpa countered with, '*It's none of your business*'. They both made good points, but right now she'd rather they both shut up.

Of course, if it was to do with the Golem then it *was* her business.

Then again, the basement was always locked.

Wasn't it? It wasn't as if she'd ever had reason to check.

Emily opened her eyes to stare at the mirror on the wall opposite. She'd found it in a charity shop and had liked its weathered driftwood frame. She met her own gaze in the age-silvered glass.

"Well we both know I'm going to check."

It was bound to be locked, so she was just going to check the door and come back up again. Then it would be out of her head for the evening.

Emily pulled on her plimsoles and made for the door.

The stairs felt safer than the lift these days, especially with McDowall House's new status as Covid Central. In the enclosed space of the lift you imagined that you were breathing in infected air. The stairs might not that be that much better but every little helped.

She arrived in the barely lit entrance hall. The light was on a timer, operating on the perplexing basis that it was not needed by night, and so provided only a faint glow. To her right was the basement door. She walked past it practically every day of her life and never really thought about it; now it seemed to take on a deathly significance.

Maybe Harrigan had been trying to protect her, and had lied about the Golem. Maybe it was dangerous and being contained behind that door.

In which case the door would be locked.

She had started this thing (sort of. She had been there early on and had some sort of influence on the Golem which hadn't ended well), she wanted to see it finished. The Golem was frightening, but she had seen worse; she had been in the Covid wards, she had been in the back of that truck. A walking statue held no fear for her.

The handle turned in Emily's hand and she felt her stomach clutch in on itself as the door swung inwards. Unlocked.

She went through the door, determined but quiet with it; a person could be just as determined on tip-toes. The blank, concrete steps led down a narrow stairwell, smelling faintly of mould and bleach, to the door at the bottom. No sound came from beyond.

This door was sure to be locked.

It wasn't.

Emily breathed in the darkness as she entered the basement, her heart accelerating. She groped for a light switch and found one to the left of the door.

The strip lights snapped into life on a ceiling encrusted with fantasy maps of black mould. There were six but only three worked, one of them flickering erratically while the others buzzed with the effort of producing the limited orange light they managed to summon up.

A sound from the darkened far end of the room made Emily start, catching her breath.

She peered into the gloom. It wasn't down here. There were many words that could be used to describe the Golem but 'inconspicuous' was not one of them.

That was a relief really. It was only just occurring to her that the last time she had seen the thing was when she abandoned it in a ditch. Did golems hold a grudge?

But there was no sign. Nothing down here but some pipes, boxes of electricity and a lot of mould. Odd really. In London this was practically prime real estate. Odd that it should be almost empty.

But not completely.

The shadowy lump on the floor by the wall did not interest Emily at first, and she was about to leave when the flickering light made a particularly stern attempt at staying lit, and revealed it more clearly.

Emily's heart jumped into her throat. With slow steps, she made her way across the dusty floor, suddenly scenting distinctly human smells she had not noticed till now, and not pleasant ones.

Reaching the lump, she stooped to pick it up, bringing it into better light. As she did so, a sense memory took her screaming back to the interior of the truck; she could smell that rank odour, even taste it at the back of her throat, she could see...

She could see...

The woollen blanket in her hands was not exactly the same as the one that she had glimpsed on the floor of the truck, wrapped about a shape that had once been a person, but it was close enough to know that it was from the same source. Charitable organisations and individuals donated care packages to the camps in France where refugees made an uncomfortable home for as long as they had to. The one she had seen in the truck looked as if it had been crocheted by some kindly French woman, wanting to do her bit no matter how small that bit was. Didn't everyone?

The blanket she now held was its twin. Not an identical twin, but similar enough to know that they came from the same place, probably crocheted by the same blue-veined hands.

For a moment, Emily's mind was numb to the possibilities, then it reeled with them, different explanations gathering momentum as they combined uncomfortably with those human smells she had started to notice. People had been kept down here.

A sound from behind made her turn; footsteps on the stairs and a voice speaking.

"It needs to be cleaned quickly. The police could be here any…" Paul came to a frozen halt mid-sentence as he entered to find Emily, standing in the middle of the basement.   Behind him, stood the Golem.

Chapter 23 – The Golem's Master

One Week Earlier

"When you say 'watching'?" Maxie's Boss held up a finger. "Watching Booth? Watching the building? Watching what?"

Maxie swallowed, suddenly very aware of his palms sweating, as they always did when he was alone with his Boss. Paul Haworth was a different kind of criminal to those that Maxie knew, and not a kind with which he was comfortable. He hadn't grown up to it, he had chosen it. He hadn't needed the money, he had seen an opportunity. And he was a Boss. Bosses were the same no matter what line of work you were in.

"All Booth knew was the guy had binoculars and was outside."

"And it was Booth who established that he was a policeman?"

"Saw the warrant card when he went for coffee."

Haworth nodded slowly. "This Booth; good man?"

Haworth had never met Booth, nor any of the gang, and had no interest in doing so. As much as possible he avoided getting his hands dirty, and employed people like Maxie to keep them clean. He was new to this business; recognising that Britain's fast-approaching divorce from mainland Europe would threaten his supply of cheap foreign labour, he had moved into people trafficking simply to cut out the middle man, then discovered it could be a profitable little side-hustle. But Covid had turned that side-hustle into practically a cottage industry. Demand for labour was up, legal immigration was down (thanks to travel restrictions) and turnover had increased because… well, because workers kept catching the virus. Haworth treated it like any other diversification of his business interests and was well-placed to run it – he owned enough small properties that they could keep the cargo moving around, and he offered employment and housing to a handful of those they brought across, just enough that word filtered through to relatives back home or in the camps that this was a man you could trust. He was also in an excellent position to sell on the rest, because he knew other men, like himself, who needed cheap labour, liked a bargain and didn't ask questions. That last one was important; if you didn't know where they came from then you hadn't done anything wrong. Not really. Maybe you should have asked but that wasn't the same as being complicit. They were just people who needed a job and were happy to get one – you were doing these people a favour.

"I trust him," replied Maxie. It was sometimes hard to tell if Haworth approved or disapproved of what Maxie had done.

"And you decided to move the cargo into the basement of McDowall House?"

"It seemed like the thing to do." McDowall House was the nearest building owned by Haworth and it was understood to be their emergency fallback.

"It was," nodded Haworth, smiling. "I'm not mad at you Maxie. You did the right thing. It was an emergency and you moved quickly. That's initiative. I like initiative. What's troubling me is how we got into this position, but we'll circle back to that once we've dealt with…" his gaze shifted to the other 'person' in the room, who stood, silent and unmoving by the wall, "…with what happened next. It went after the policeman?"

Maxie nodded. "Hard."

"What do you mean by that?"

Maxie paused; what *did* he mean? "It looked determined. Soon as it heard the word 'police' it was off. Straight after him."

"How long was it gone?"

"Long enough for us to move the cargo into McDowall."

"Then it returned?"

"Covered in mud," Maxie confirmed. "Me and Booth went and wrangled it down to the basement of McDowall."

Haworth drummed his fingers on his desk for a few moments as he thought.

"If a policeman went missing on assignment, I think we'd have heard about it by now."

"That is odd," admitted Maxie. "Maybe it didn't kill him."

"Maybe."

Haworth got up from his desk and walked over to examine the Golem, which had been standing there like a statue throughout their conversation.

"Unbelievable. But it's amazing how quickly you believe it."

Maxie nodded fervently; he had felt the same way.

"And it does what you tell it?"

"Not exactly. Sometimes. Although, I sometimes think it does what it wants and it just happens that's sometimes the same as what I ask it."

"All supervisors feel that way from time to time," mused Haworth. "And it's been useful?" He walked around the Golem, looking it up and down with interest.

"Couldn't believe it when it picked up the truck."

Haworth nodded absently "And while a potentially dead policeman is not ideal, if we're not hearing anything, then…"

"Quiet is good?" suggested Maxie.

Haworth returned to his desk. "My feelings exactly. Quiet is good. Maintaining that quiet is now our top priority." He looked back at the Golem. "How do you get it to do things?"

"It can't think," Maxie explained. "It can only do what the words inside it tell it."

Haworth smiled. "The perfect employee. How do you know what's inside it?"

"Guesswork mostly," admitted Maxie. He was aware that he was on thin ice here, because there was another reason that the Golem looked to him, a reason which he could not admit to his Boss. "Helps if you can tie it to McDowall House."

"It's loyal to the block?"

"It *is* the block," emphasised Maxie, who had been reading some of his Grandad's old books. "In the old days, the Golem was the embodiment of the community it represented – the ghetto. This one *is* McDowall House. Their words made it, so it belongs to them."

"Is that a fact?" Haworth sounded thoughtful.

He got up from his desk and went to a safe set in the wall. He opened it and drew out some papers, flicking through them as he strolled back to the Golem. It didn't seem to bother him the way it did some people. Maxie found that slightly disconcerting.

"Hello there." Haworth addressed the Golem wearing his best smile. "We haven't been formally introduced, my name is Paul Haworth (you don't have name I understand. No worries there; not as if I'm going to mistake you for someone else). I think you'll find that I am a very important person in your life. (Is 'life' the right word? Existence? Doesn't matter.) Now, I understand that you are animated by words, that words form who you are, so I can assume that you understand words. Maybe you don't *read* exactly, or not as I would understand it (or maybe you do – what do I know? Not judging.), but somehow the meaning is there. Am I right?"

The Golem remained still.

"Hard to tell if he's rude or bored," Haworth muttered to Maxie, then back to the Golem. "I'd like you, if you would, to cast your eyes over these papers."

The Golem stayed completely static as Haworth held the pages up in front of its eyes.

"There's a lot of complex legal jargon, even I don't understand all of it, but the gist is that, though there are a certain number of shell corporations and dummy businesses and a bunch of directors (some of whom just plain don't exist, the rest of whom prefer not to know how their money is made), I, to all intents and purposes, own McDowall House."

On the word 'McDowall', the Golem's hand reached out so suddenly that Haworth started as the papers were snatched from his hand.

"Yes, yes, good. Important that you should read for yourself and gratifying that you now seem to be taking a more active interest," Haworth recovered himself. "Now, full disclosure, because I don't want you to think that I am in any way misleading you; I am not sole owner and proprietor. The block is in fact owned by a corporation. But if you look through all those documents then you can trace it all back to me. Financially it's a house of cards – these blocks don't go for peanuts. I'm a well-off man but I can't just stick hand in pocket and say, '*Here you are, give me the block*', so one business sort of lends its collateral to another, and you hope no one notices that they're all leaning on each other without any one actually having the security to do so. It's the sort of thing that can keep a man up at night. Not this man – I enjoy a full eight hours every night. There's very little point in doing this sort of thing if you spend all your time worrying about it. You've got to enjoy it."

His Boss's words mostly washed over Maxie, who was watching the Golem. It did not seem to be reading as such, but it looked at every page (or at least held them up in front of its eyes). Was this possible? It knew, somehow, that it belonged to McDowall House – Maxie was sure of that. But this? Could you tie a magic (a *religious*) creation with a contract? You had to admire Paul Haworth for trying.

The Golem's arm extended, handing the papers back to Haworth.

"Thank you." He smiled. "Now, where did we land?"

The Golem did nothing.

Maxie coughed.

The Golem moved like lightning, striding towards the source of a possible infection, its hand raised to strike.

"Stop!"

At the sound of Howarth's voice the Golem came to a halt, inches from Maxie. Did it now recognise Howarth as its owner? Or had it remembered that Maxie lived in McDowall House? Either way, Maxie's heart was racing.

"We'll call that a successful first test," mused Howarth. Then to the Golem, "It's not Covid. Just a cough. Right Maxie?"

"Right," said Maxie, with absolute certainty.

Howarth looked at him as the Golem backed away. "How close did you get to the cargo?"

"I'm fine."

"You should wear a mask."

"They do more harm than good," Maxie hurried to point out, "I saw this video…"

"And I've seen videos saying that we didn't land on the moon," Howarth replied briskly. "For every idiot theory there is one

224

video to support it. How many videos do you suppose there are that contradict that one? Why is it that a paucity of evidence is assumed to be proof of a conspiracy rather than proof that the theory is nonsense? Listen to the science, Maxie. The mask is there to protect others, not yourself. So when you go out without one then it is not bravery, it is simple selfishness. More to the point," the charm of Paul Haworth could become steel in an instant, "when you come in here without one, then it is *me* you endanger."

He reached into a desk drawer, took out two medical grade masks, put one on and tossed the other to Maxie.

"I'm sure it's just a cold, but I don't want that either."

Maxie nodded unhappily as he put the mask on. He could taste his own breath and was sure he could feel the germs, which his body was sensibly breathing out, all rushing back into him, just as the video said they would.

"Now," Howarth seated himself and drummed his fingers once more, "have the police found the truck yet?"

"No." Maxie shook his head.

"Then how are they onto us?"

Maxie said nothing. He didn't know the answer, and speculating might seem as if he was trying to shift the blame.

Howarth drummed again, and Maxie found himself focusing on the fast-moving fingers, as if they were a clock ticking out the remaining seconds of his life.

"Maybe it's time the police find that truck."

Maxie opened his mouth to speak then closed it again.

"Maxie?"

"Yes."

"You wanted to say something?"

"No."

Haworth opened his hands expansively. "Maxie, I hope I've never given you reason to think me an ogre of a boss. Ask anyone I work with and they'll tell you that I welcome communication with my employees on all levels. I'm not down there in the trenches with you so it's possible that I miss important stuff sometimes, and the only way I find out about it is if you talk to me. You need to feel that you can talk to me, Maxie. We need to be," he pointed back and forth between the two of them. "Just like that. Two minds; one thought. Tell me what's on yours, Maxie."

Maxie swallowed. "I just… The police finding out about the truck hardly seems like 'quiet'. We could drive it off someplace, set fire to it. They'd never make the connection."

Haworth smiled, leaned back and pointed at Maxie. "Good question. You're smart Maxie, it's only your attitude that holds you back. Think big; be ambitious; ask out the prettiest girl in the room. That is the secret to life. I want the police to find it because that truck points them away from McDowall House. It takes the investigation elsewhere. Stories like that get the public riled, so they will put more resources on the truck, which means less looking in my direction." He gave a little shrug. "In business, you have to get used to acceptable losses. McDowall House is a *big* investment for me and one I'm rather fond of – some cool people live there. I cannot risk *anything* linking back there and so on to me. So, when plain clothes policemen are hanging about outside with binoculars then I become nervous, and I do what I can to point them in a less personal direction. Possibly the truck will lead them to your gang – I don't deny that as a possibility – but we will address that; you and I. We're in this together – you know that, don't you Maxie?"

The way he said it made Maxie actually believe it, at least for a moment.

"I'll deal with the truck," said Howarth. "The cargo are out of McDowall?"

Maxie nodded. They had been moved into new accommodation; another cellar, still a convenient walking distance from McDowall House.

"How long were they in there?"

"Two days."

"And the Golem?"

"We moved that too..." Maxie trailed off.

"I hear a 'but' in your voice."

"It won't stay put."

The Golem had unhelpfully picked up the idea that its

quarantine was over and, though it was happy to spend its days in the cellar, they could not stop it from taking to the streets by night, going about its usual business. Locking it up just cost them a new door.

Haworth nodded. "I'll have a word to it. It will prove a useful second test. But there is now nothing to tie our little operation to McDowall House. Correct?"

"Absolutely," nodded Maxie, adding mentally, '*Unless you mean me.*'

Maxie's previous living situation had become untenable following an argument with his landlord; things had been said, feelings had been hurt, people had been evicted. Suddenly finding himself homeless, he had taken advantage of his inside knowledge of McDowall House. He had done a few jobs there for Haworth and knew of a vacant room. So he moved in. On the plus side, it was close to work, really quite comfortable and rent-free. On the down side, he was a living link between the block and the people trafficking, and if Haworth found out then the shit would hit the fan. Maxie was not entirely sure what that would look like; Haworth was always so friendly and personable. But that type was often the worst.

"Well then," said Howarth, rubbing his hands, "that leads us back to how the police got wind of us in the first place. It may be time to make some staffing changes."

"None of my boys would have talked to the police," Maxie interjected.

"Maybe not intentionally." As he spoke, Howarth opened his laptop and began typing. "But men gossip, Maxie. People talk about women gossiping but that's a reductive stereotype and I've no time for it, men are far worse. Take a few days, get the cargo moved on – Adam Khan is whining about staffing in his cold store – then I'm going to need you to deliver a message to the staff. I'll tell you what to say and you say it, *word for word.*" He looked at the Golem. "Take that with you." He scratched his head absently. "Oh, and we must get that basement cleaned at some point. There must be no sign left that the cargo was down there."

Chapter 24 – These People

For a long moment, Emily just stared at Paul across the expanse of the basement. She hoped her face was a mask of angry judgment, but knew that it probably wasn't.

Damn. She had liked him. The voice of her Dad whispered an uncalled for '*I told you so*' in her head, adding, '*You can't trust rich people, Princess*', before the voice of her Mum could shush him.

It was Paul who spoke first. "I think I know the answer to this, but, any chance I could go out and come back in again saying something else? Something less… definitive."

"No."

"Are you sure? I could act surprised to see you and… You know, you'd believe it if I did it, I'm a very good actor."

Emily shook her head.

Paul slumped. "No. No, I suppose not." He turned away, reaching past the Golem to close the door behind it. When he looked back at her, Emily had to admit that he seemed genuinely upset. "Damn. I mean… I know we're very different people – different values (as is rapidly coming into focus) – but I did think we could get past that and…" He trailed off. "Damn."

That summed it up. Emily had thought all that too.

"You know," Paul's face still had a trace of that charming, happy-go-lucky optimism that characterised him, "if you knew more about what I do – what *we* do, I should say; mustn't take sole credit, it's a team effort – if you knew more about it then perhaps you might appreciate it more. You're only considering one side of it."

"I only saw one side of it." Emily's voice was almost a growl, and she felt for a moment as if the spirits of the dead in that truck spoke through her. He had known. He had known they were in there. He had probably allowed her to get there first so she would be the one to find it. He had let her walk into that.

"What about Lydia and Masud?" Paul jumped in quickly. "You've seen that side too. Ask them if I did a good thing. There are people who thank me for what I do. I can't save everyone, Emily. I can't give a home and a job to every person that I bring here, but the few that I can, I do, and they go on to make homes and lives in this country. There are some happy families here because of me."

"Don't you think they'd give it up to get Jakeem back?"

Paul shook his head. "What happened to him – what happened to all of them – was terrible. But people die. The people in that truck had Covid. What's the difference if they die in a truck here, a camp in France, or back home wherever? They knew the risks. They died in pursuit of a dream. There are worse things."

"Like being sold into slavery?"

Paul held up a finger. "You see, that's not fair because I don't get to lecture you on slavery. Even if I was a professor who'd spent his entire life studying the subject you'd still have the last word just because of skin colour (which, by the way, isn't supposed to matter), and I'm not sure that should just *give* you the moral high-ground. Especially as what we're talking about is centuries past, it's history."

Emily glared. "It's not history if you're still doing it."

Paul scoffed. "You can't make that comparison. The people I help – they'd rather be here than there, they *want* to come here. If they have to pay for it then they will, if they have to work for it then they will. If they're willing to make those sacrifices then they must *really* want to come here and how am I the bad guy for granting their wish? Now more than ever. You think this country's made a mess of Covid you should see some of the others. People want out. And it's difficult for them – even the pro-immigration lobby don't think now is the best time for people to be hopping countries unchecked. Which leads to a labour shortage. That's what's called a gap in the market. Maybe I'm taking advantage of a bad situation but that is what good businessmen do. And in the end, everyone gets what they want; I get money, they get to come to Britain. These people are grateful to me."

Though it sometimes seemed as if the Golem was completely inhuman, Emily wondered if it was really so different. We all have words inside us that provoke a reaction. *'These people'*. It was intrinsic to Emily's sense of her own identity that she was a sometimes uncomfortable amalgam, and she had spent a lifetime avoiding the big, clear labels that put her in a box and said, '*Because you look like this, you should feel like this*'. And then, someone defined her and everyone who looked like her as '*These people*'. In fairness, well-meaning individuals used it too; at one protest or another someone would say '*We're here to support these people*', without thinking. But usually it was someone like Paul; smug, superior and casually condescending. It didn't matter that those people to whom he was referring weren't '*these people*' with whom Emily was grouped, it was the words themselves, the ability to look at ten, fifteen or a hundred people, and not see a single *person*.

"Can I take your silence as an acknowledgement that I'm right?" suggested Paul.

"Do you really think this is defensible?" Emily felt like screaming. He had been caught in a hideous crime and genuinely didn't seem to feel guilty about it.

"I think we help some people," said Paul. "We can't help them all, but it's not like you save everyone who comes into your hospital, is it? I bet there are some angry families out there who blame you and wish their loved ones never set foot in there – maybe he caught Covid there when he'd have been safe at home."

"You make money off other people's misery!"

"Don't you get paid?" Paul held up his hands. "This is silly. I don't want to compare what I do to what you do because that's an argument I am going to lose. No one has more respect for the NHS than I do and you deserve to be paid a damn sight more than you are. I'm not claiming to be any better than I am. But I don't think I'm as bad you're painting me."

Emily took this in. "No. You don't. That's what makes you worse."

Paul's face changed, as if he was only just now realising that he was not going to talk her around or charm his way out of this.

"You don't seem as surprised as I would expect by the large clay man behind me."

"We're prior acquaintances."

"Really? Small world."

"I'm surprised to see him with you. You shouldn't use him like this." When had she started calling the Golem 'him'?

Paul rolled his eyes. "It's not a 'him'. If you're going to be angry about human rights then at least stick to humans." Suddenly he seemed harder. "It likes people from this block."

"Yes." Emily wasn't sure where this was going but doubted it was somewhere good.

Paul looked down at the ground a moment. "I suppose your policeman friend will be here shortly."

"I don't know. I genuinely don't know why he asked about the basement."

"Seems like some wires may have gotten crossed."

"Yes."

"That never ends well." Paul took a phone from his pocket and looked at the screen. "Although, you do have *a lot* of missed calls from him – the policeman – so..."

"You took my phone deliberately?"

Paul sighed. "If that's the worst thing I do tonight then you should consider yourself lucky. I had a hunch he might call back, and if he had somehow found out my name then that was that. Although that seems to be that anyway." He looked up at Emily with an unexpected sadness in his eyes. "I really did like you, you know?"

Emily nodded. She believed him. It would be so nice if bad people had no feelings to hurt, if they were just Bad Guys like in movies. But that wasn't the case. Rather stupidly she actually felt guilty that she might be breaking his heart a little bit. They had only been out twice – barely that – but... there had been something there. Which meant she should probably re-examine her taste in men.

"But there's no way, is there?" Paul went on, maybe a little hope in his voice.

"No."

"No." He nodded. "Thought not. Just wanted to check. Because, much as I like you – and I do – I'm not sure I can trust you."

A cold sensation was creeping across Emily's body, making her skin prickle.

"I think…" she paused. There really was no point in lying. "I think that's probably the right instinct."

Paul nodded. He jerked a thumb towards the Golem. "It knows that I own this place. And it understands what that means. The hierarchy. I'm above it, so it believes everything I tell it. We had a problem with it going out at night, but I made up some reason for it to stay put and it did. We've been keeping it not far from here. Just in case." He turned to face the statue. "This is Emily. I understand that you two know each other. Emily lives here but I have been forced to reconsider her tenancy." His gaze turned to Emily, and she wondered if he had always looked like a sociopath and she just hadn't noticed it until now. "You're evicted."

It wasn't that simple, of course. Even in normal times you couldn't just chuck someone out without notice, and right now there was a government bar on evictions. But the Golem was probably not big on boilerplate. With time it might be made to understand, but it was more at home with large, clear concepts like eviction. Emily no longer lived here, she was no longer a resident of McDowall House, she was no longer protected in the Golem's eyes.

"She spends every day alongside people suffering from Covid," Paul went on, talking to the Golem once more. "Laudable, but very risky for everyone else in the block. I wouldn't be surprised if this new variant came from her. Kill her. Try not to make a mess, I don't know how long we've got to clean."

Emily's instincts fought between running, screaming or both, and in the end settled on staying where she was, frozen to the spot while her stomach seemed to fill with ice.

"Wait until I've gone," said Paul. He sounded sad. Somehow that made him even less human.

He turned towards the door, where the Golem still stood. "Well, I can't get out with you standing there."

The Golem did not move.

Paul frowned, and tried to go around it instead.

The Golem's arm shot out, barring his way.

Paul rounded on it angrily. "What the hell do you think you're doing?"

The Golem did not move.

Paul shoulder barged it, pitching his weight against the static solidity of the statue, succeeding in nothing but bruising his arm.

"What are you doing? Why are you doing this?"

"You had them down here, didn't you?" It was strange how fear could give you a sort of awful clarity. Suddenly Emily felt as if she could see exactly what had happened. "The refugees? You kept them locked up down here."

Paul shrugged irritably. "A handful of them spent two nights here. They had food, water, somewhere to sleep. Don't start on at me again, they were all fine."

"But you had him keep them here," said Emily, indicating the Golem. "You posted him on the door, like a guard."

"I wasn't here," Paul corrected. "I like to be a hands-on boss, but there are places where I draw the line."

"I bet there are," smiled Emily, though there was nothing to smile about. "'Hands-on' leaves fingerprints. But whoever you put in charge, whoever *was* here, I think they got him to guard the door. And I just bet they said something along the lines of '*Don't let anyone out*'." She saw Paul's face change. "And if that person knew the Golem then I guess he put it in terms the Golem would understand and respond to. Maybe he linked it to Covid – that always works. But whatever he said, the Golem heard it, and once he has an instruction in his head it's very hard to get it out again." Which meant that once it was done guarding the door, it would follow orders and kill Emily, but one thing at a time.

Paul rounded on the living statue. "It was Maxie, wasn't it? He told you? Well, you know that he's *my* employee. What I say countermands what he says!"

"Have you got that in writing?" wondered Emily.

Paul shot sharp look at her. "I don't know what you're joking about. You're as trapped as I am."

"In my case it means I get to live longer," said Emily, meeting Paul's gaze with a new and unexpected confidence. She had no idea why Harrigan had asked her about this basement, but based on current evidence maybe he *was* connected to some official investigation. Maybe the police *were* on their way and were going to storm in at any minute.

Paul glared. "Not necessarily. As long as I stay in here and stop trying to leave then I think it will go back to doing what I tell it. You're still a trespasser and I'm still in charge. And when the police show up, they'll be just in time to save me from this terrible monster that killed my girlfriend. I can sell distraught, you know. They'll believe me. They'll have a few questions about the Golem of course, but I won't know anything about that. Just a victim of circumstance. Can't you just see it?"

Emily had to admit that she could. Why did the bastards always seem to win?

'*I warned you, Princess.*'

And then it happened. The hairs rose on the back of Emily's neck and she started around, eyes flicking about the corners of room, shrouded in shadow where the low-watt strip lights did not reach.

"What now?" sneered Paul.

"Did you hear that?"

Paul scoffed. "Nice try but I didn't hear…"

His words petered out as he heard it too, a sound that Emily had heard before, like fingernails dancing across a slate blackboard. She tried to control her breathing. It was here. She could sense it. She did not know what *it* was but she could feel its eyes on her and hear its slow, stealthy movement across the room. The thing that she had caught a glimpse of in the back of that truck, that she had felt again in her car on the way home, and which had seemed to leave her when she entered McDowall House and walked across the entrance hall above them. Was this where it had ended up?

"It's just the pipes," Paul dismissed the noise, but while his words said one thing his face said another. He was scared.

"There's something down here," breathed Emily. She moved slowly, backing towards the wall, checking all around her as she went. Was this what had killed the people in that truck? Was that why they had not charged the door and run?

"Open the damn door!" Paul turned his attention back to the Golem. "I'm ordering you! It's my block, my instructions are the ones that count!"

The Golem's head turned to look at Paul, examining his frantic features with its sternly impassive gaze. As ever, Emily felt that she could read thoughts and emotions into the Golem that were probably more her than it, but right at that moment she could have sworn it looked smug.

Interestingly, Paul seemed to have the same reaction. "You bloody-minded flower pot! You know damn well Maxie didn't mean it to apply to me! You're being deliberately obstreperous and you've picked the wrong time and the wrong man!" He turned away again, fear still written across his face. "What is that smell?"

Emily looked up sharply as a scritching sound traced slowly across the ceiling towards the door.

With a sudden 'Bang!', one of the strip lights burst, scattering broken glass. Paul jumped back from the Golem, looking up at the ceiling, searching back and forth in frustrated panic.

"There's nothing there, there's nothing there, there's nothing there."

"I wonder if they said the same thing in the back of that truck?" whispered Emily.

"Shut up!"

"Do you think they saw what was coming for them?"

"There's nothing there!"

"I saw it."

Paul looked at her, pale and wild-eyed. "What? No you didn't."

"In the truck. Just before you arrived. I saw it."

And suddenly, she realised that she could see it now, as if knowing what she was looking for allowed her to recognise it. It hung from the ceiling above Paul like a giant spider, bony elbows pointed down, long fingers splayed out, somehow finding purchase on the plaster ceiling. Its head arced back at an extreme angle, almost turning back on its own spine so it could look down to the room below it. It did not even seem to notice Emily, ignoring her completely. The Golem too was of no interest – just part of the furniture. All its intent was focussed on Paul Howarth.

235

He was looking right at it, staring straight into that ghastly face that made Emily shiver. She had only seen it momentarily in the truck, and that had been enough to haunt her nightmares. Now she had a good, long look, as the creature sized up its target, the flickering strip light making shadows jumps across its body. Its skin looked dead, not just pale but with the flaccid, slackness of death, stretched across its angular skull, hollowed in the cheeks and eye sockets. The pallor was unhealthy, darker around the eyes and pockmarked on its cheeks. It had pointed ears with bristly hair sprouting from the points – the only hair on its head. Its mouth was not wide but was almost circular and always open, revealing the sharp teeth beyond, small and pointed like a rodent, like a rat. That was what it reminded Emily of the most. Either that or a cockroach; something verminous that could crawl through any gap, climb any wall, that would survive fire, flood or nuclear apocalypse, crouched in its hole. There was something loathsome about it; the face; the air of foetid death that hung about it. Even its posture, all joints and long bones folded together, was horrible to see.

Paul stared at the ceiling, following Emily's gaze. How on earth could he not see it? "What are you looking at?"

Emily didn't answer him. She couldn't. She had no idea what she was looking at, and describing it would not help.

The creature moved, getting into a more advantageous position, and while he couldn't see it, Paul could certainly hear the sound of its long, clawed fingers, sliding across the plaster.

"What the hell was that?" He moved away from the sound. "There's nothing there. You're just trying to make me nervous. Trying to string this out. Let me out!" He roared at the Golem. "You do as I say – let me out!"

The Golem did not move. Emily wondered if it could see the thing on the ceiling. It wouldn't matter either way; this creature did not exist in its 'Truths'.

"There's got to be another way out." Paul rushed away from the Golem, skirting the edges of the room, seeking the other door that he probably knew did not exist.

Emily shrank back, trying to push herself through the wall of the basement as she watched the creature on the ceiling follow him.

Her flatmate, Jill, was arachnophobic, and Emily had once asked her what was wrong with spiders. Jill had replied '*There's just something obscene about having eight legs*'. Emily had thought that was pretty funny, but now, when she saw the creature move, she suddenly understood exactly what Jill had meant. It didn't have eight legs, it was basically humanoid (though it made a mockery of the word) yet it moved in a scuttling, invertebrate fashion that made her skin crawl.

As Paul came to a stop at the far end of the room, eyeing an air vent with a misplaced optimism born of desperation, the thing stopped above him. Its mouth opened wider.

"Paul…"

"Shut up, I'm thinking!"

The creature's body drew in, again reminding her of a spider about to pounce.

"Paul!"

The thing launched itself at Paul. A hunter that had found its prey.

He saw it then. As it landed on him, hands gripping his shoulders, feet planted on his torso, he saw it, its hideous face only inches from his own. He saw it, and his scream echoed about the basement.

Acting more on instinct than conscious thought, Emily ran towards them. She wouldn't have called herself any braver than the next person but sometimes your body made these decisions for you. She cannoned into them, the creature losing its grip on Paul and falling to the floor.

Screaming hysterically, Paul shoved Emily out of the way, knocking her head against the wall. He ran back across the room, full tilt towards the door, smacking into the immovable block of the Golem, banging his fists against it.

"Let me out! Let me out! You can't keep me in here, you've got to let me out! Please!"

The Golem did nothing. It did not even look at him.

Still dazed, Emily could only watch as the creature recovered itself, hissing angrily – it might be pissed at her, but its target remained unchanged. At high speed it scuttled around the wall of the basement, its eyes never leaving Paul as he frantically attacked the Golem, screaming at it, begging it, beating his hands bloody against its clay.

But the Golem just stood.

As he looked back over his shoulder, Emily got a look at Paul's face. His eyes were wide, the pupils no more than pin-pricks. His skin was white, his mouth open with a thin line of drool trailing from it as he panted, hyperventilating in blind fear, trembling uncontrollably.

"You're not there. You don't exist. This is a dream."

Looking at his face and listening to him babble, Emily thought it possible that the shock had made him lose his mind.

Perhaps there was some mercy in that. Perhaps more than he deserved.

The creature on the wall sprang, this time taking the screaming Paul to the floor. Squatting on his chest, it clasped his head in both hands, its long fingers proving unexpectedly strong, keeping him still as its head bent inexorably forward.

Emily closed her eyes and turned away, but she could not block out Paul's shrieks, as the creature claimed its first meal of the night.

The Schreck more commonly attacked when people were asleep, but if a suitable victim entered its lair then that was another question. Maxie had had the relative comfort of never knowing, never seeing what had come to take him in the night, a comfort that his Boss did not have as he died screaming in fear. Perhaps it would also have given Maxie some comfort to know that his distaste for masks, which had killed him, had also doomed his Boss, to whom he had passed the virus. Killing your boss is the dream of every employee.

Chapter 25 – The Golem of McDowall House

To Emily, hunched on the floor of the basement, back to the wall, head aching where she had hit it, eyes tightly shut and hands over her ears (which made little difference), the screams seemed to go on for a very long time.

When they finally stopped, she dared to open her eyes and look across the room to where the creature still squatted, bent over Paul, and as she pried her hands away from her ears she heard a regular '*gluck, gluck, gluck*' as it drank. Emily had to supress the urge to hurl.

The room was a static tableaux; Emily by the wall, hugging her knees; the creature with the corpse of Paul; and by the door, the Golem, solid, still, silent.

Though her body fought against it, Emily kept her eyes on the creature. The sight was horrifying and would live in her nightmares for years to come, but if she took her eyes off it then she might not have those 'years to come'.

Was she next?

The thing had definitely been more interested in Paul than her - it had given her barely more attention than it gave the Golem. But now that Paul was dead would it be looking for another meal? And if it was between Emily and the Golem then there really was only one choice. Whatever this thing was, it did not look as if it ate clay.

There was a dull thud, as the creature let Paul's head drop to the floor. He had been dead some little time now but Emily still winced at the sound of his skull on the bare concrete. An hour ago he had been a boyfriend about whom she had been cautiously hopeful, then he had been her prospective killer, and now she pitied him. He had done terrible things and caused misery to many innocent people, but did he deserve a death like that? Did anyone?

The creature looked up, flinching against the flickering light. It was looking at her.

An involuntary gulp of guttural terror escaped Emily as it seemed for an instant as if the creature was starting towards her. But it was just leaning forward, craning its head to sniff in her direction.

One sniff was apparently enough. It turned disinterestedly away from Emily.

A little insane part of Emily thought; *What the hell do I smell like that that thing is repulsed?* But relief won out; she could breathe again and the pounding of blood in her ears eased. She wanted to cry and throw up at the same time, but settled for dissolving into a limp heap by the wall. She hadn't realised the tension with which she had been holding herself and now her whole body ached as if she was coming off a twelve-hour shift.

But, relieved though she was, there was still plenty to worry about.

Her eyes never left the creature as it slunk away from Paul and stood up. On two legs, and not crawling across a ceiling, it could almost pass for human. You had to ignore its face, but if it raised the collar of the shabby, non-descript coat it wore, and maybe put on a hat, then you might pass it over in a crowd. The creature approached the door, still guarded by the Golem, and went through it.

How it did that, Emily could not be one hundred percent sure. Getting past the Golem presented little difficulty; the creature was skinny and seemed able to become more so, compressing its body to insinuate itself through the gap between the statue and the exit, while the Golem ignored it completely as if it did not exist. But the door did not open. The thing did not walk through it, like a ghost, but seemed to find a crack through which to pass. Which was insane, it was far too big.

But it was not the most insane thing to happen to Emily in the last month. It was not even the most insane thing to happen to her in the last hour. Plus, she didn't really care how it had gone, the important thing was that it *had* gone. Relief and anxiety did battle inside Emily; that it was gone was great, but where was it going now?

Five deaths in the block in the last five days. Six if you counted Paul. And those deaths had started when this thing arrived – or at least that was how Emily saw it. They had all been put down to Covid, but it seemed more than a coincidence that… Emily frowned.

Was that why it had ignored her? She'd already had the virus?

Didn't matter. There were people in the block still at risk. So far it had only killed one person per night, but that guaranteed nothing; it might see Paul as a mere *hors d'oeuvre*.

She had to stop it.

On jelly legs, and with her head still spinning a little, Emily stood and stumbled across the room to face the Golem. As she did so, it occurred to her that it ought to be killing her – Paul had given it a clear instruction.

But he had also said '*Wait until I've gone*', and he now wasn't going anywhere. At least not without help.

"You have to let me out! That thing is going to kill people."

The Golem did nothing.

"It's going to kill people who live here. In the block. I have to stop it."

If there was a reaction then it was so minute as to make no difference. Perhaps her words had given the Golem something to think about, but it had received unambiguous orders to keep people down here, orders which had come from someone who lived in the block, which Emily no longer did in its eyes.

A thought struck Emily.

"I don't belong here. I've been evicted."

The Golem's head moved to look at her.

"So I shouldn't be in the building. I need to leave. I'm not from here."

The right words. It was all about finding the right words. The Golem had been told by the block's owner that she was evicted, and its head was filled with angry ranting about '*people who aren't from here*'. Some of those people looked like Emily, and maybe that was a factor too. It was hard to tell. The Golem knew that '*Black Lives Matter*' (perhaps that was another reason it hadn't killed her), it also knew that they should all '*...go back where they came from*'. That was the problem with the Golem; it believed what it was told depending on how it was told it, and the voice of the people can be very dangerous indeed when they are fed misinformation.

Whatever the reason, the Golem stood aside.

"Thank you." Emily had been raised to be polite.

As she grabbed the door handle and opened the door she kept waiting to feel that massive, heavy hand on her shoulder stopping her. But the Golem did not change its mind, its world was painted in black and white.

Charging up the stairs, Emily's body chemistry continued to do battle with itself until she barely knew what she was doing. The relief of getting out of the basement alive was extraordinary, but she was doing so specifically to go after the creature. Her brain didn't know whether to be happy or terrified and so was sending conflicting messages to other bits of her body, making her lightheaded and dopey.

Reaching the top of the stairs, she cannoned out of the door into the hall, breathing in what felt like sweet, fresh air, at least compared to the basement. She had noticed that, although the thing (whatever the hell it was) was capable of moving very fast when it needed to, it did not *always* move fast, and had certainly seemed more sluggish after feeding, as if it was glutted with Paul's blood. Which meant that it might not yet have gone too far.

Jogging across the entrance hall to the stairs, Emily could feel her heart rate increasing again, thumping in her chest like a snare drum, while her rapid breathing strained through a dry throat. What the hell was she doing? Best not to stop and think about it. It was like working the wards; you had to keep going because if you stopped to think about the situation then you would simply drop.

Uneasily she peered into the stairwell that led up to the first landing. There was nothing on the stairs, but she had seen enough of the creature to check the ceiling as well.

At first she saw nothing by the dimmed lights, but then, as she stared harder, a shadow moved. There it was, on the underside of the next flight, crawling up the incline of the ceiling. It was just reaching the top, navigating the corner.

Don't stop to think. Just act.

Emily dashed up the stairs. At the top, she jumped, her fingers catching the creature's trouser leg, the material oddly cold and clammy as if the garment itself had died. Its leg came free as she

242

tugged, but the creature remained glued to the ceiling. She could not tell how it was able to cling there, when there was nothing for it to hold onto, but it clearly wasn't going anywhere. Viciously it kicked down at her, but Emily hung on like grim death and yanked again.

From around the lip of the ceiling the creature's head suddenly ducked back into view, looking down sharply to see what was going on. Its wide eyes focussed on Emily, and its mouth opened in a low, breathy snarl. She might not be food, but that didn't mean it wouldn't kill her.

With its other leg the creature lashed out, catching Emily in the face and sending her spilling back down the stairs. For a few steps she managed to maintain her balance but then lost her footing, tumbling down, the sharp edges of the stone steps catching her, till her bruised body landed at the bottom.

But there was no time to recover. Emily kept rolling, keeping her distance, landing on her backside, facing the stairs, instantly alert. By the soft light of the energy saving bulbs, she saw the creature drop from the ceiling, landing in a crab position at the top of the stairs, regarding her with its head upside down. Still in that position, it descended the stairs, walking on its fingers and toes, back arched, stopping a few steps from the bottom to twist around onto all fours, long fingers curled over the edges of the steps, elbows raised and head low in the attack posture she had seen earlier when it stalked Paul.

"Oh shit."

Emily scooted back away from the thing on her backside. She wanted to look about for a weapon but did not dare take her eyes off her attacker. Besides, there was not usually weaponry lying about the entrance hall of McDowall House.

When the thing moved it did so with the sudden speed and scuttling gait of a tarantula, mouth open, eyes on its target. Emily made a desperate burbling sound as she scrambled away until her back hit the wall.

The creature stopped, looking at her as Emily pushed herself upright, her eyes never leaving the thing on the floor, a shadow come to life.

It darted forward again and Emily rushed backwards, following the wall, till she was cowering in the corner.

The thing didn't follow her, it had just feinted towards her once, enough to scare her and make her run. Now it stood up, unfolding its thin body into a humanoid shape. One last deadly glare shot at Emily, then it turned and stalked back to the stairs with long, silent strides. That had been a warning, enough to tell her that it had no interest in killing her but would not hesitate to do so if she persisted in following it.

Hunched against the wall, shaking, hyperventilating and close to tears, Emily wasn't sure what she could do now.

But she had to go after it. If she didn't then someone else was going to die tonight. *Better them than you*, some part of her brain said, *Cos if you go after it then you are going to die.* That was true, and good advice, because once she was killed the thing would continue, she wouldn't have saved anyone. What good did it do to get herself killed? But that wasn't how stuff like this worked. She heard her Dad's voice in her head, '*If you don't stand up, then who will?*'

When the patients had started to come, in the early days before anyone knew anything about Covid, the doctors and nurses hadn't backed away and refused to treat this unknown and deadly virus. They had stepped up, like they always did. Because that was how it worked; you did the job in front of you, even if you knew that there would be consequences. For some of her colleagues in the NHS, those consequences had been fatal, but they had gone down fighting.

"Hey!" Emily yelled at the creature. "I'm not done with you yet!"

The creature ignored her; clearly it *was* done with her. It reached the stairs, mounting the wall, going smoothly from humanoid to insectoid, folding its body into the darkness, a consummate hunter.

"Look at me when I'm talking to you!" Emily strode towards the stairwell. Her legs weren't quite as brave as her mouth but they did as they were told, even if they shook a bit. Her Dad had always

244

impressed upon her the importance of '*Standing Up To Power*'. He had meant the government, the police, even the military if necessary; stand up for what you believe and be counted. Emily wasn't sure if the thing crawling up the wall of the stairwell counted as 'Power', but she hoped her Dad might have been proud to see her standing up for what she believed. Even if what she believed was as basic as; not letting anyone else die. As for being counted... Well there was just the one of her, but that would have to do.

"Stop right there!"

As Emily reached the base of the stairs, yelling what was probably a pretty futile command, the creature's head snapped back to meet her gaze, its apparently boneless neck allowing it to look her full-on while its body was pointed the other way. It hissed at her. Another warning. This one final.

Though each individual breath now seemed like a battle, Emily stood her ground. "Don't make me come up there."

The creature looked back to the front. It had nothing to fear from her. It continued up the wall.

Emily drew in breath, and started up the stairs.

But she was only able to climb one step before she was suddenly and roughly pushed aside, hard enough to bounce her off the wall.

It was a measure of how intently focussed on the creature Emily had been that she had not noticed the Golem's heavy-footed approach until it thrust her out of its way. The Golem was on a mission and, as ever, nothing stood between it and the accomplishment of a goal, certainly not someone who did not even live here anymore.

To this point, it was fair to say that the thing on the wall had not put a foot wrong. As a predator it was peerless, easily overcoming the limited resistance of its human prey. What it saw when it looked at the Golem was hard to say. If Emily had to guess, she would have said that the creature saw the world like a snake, in coloured patterns of heat. The Golem, presumably, produced no heat, so to the creature it looked like a piece of furniture that moved around. It was not prey, so it was not interesting. At worst it was an object to climb over. That was where the creature made its first error.

The Golem's hand shot out, grabbing the creature by the scruff of the neck and hurling it back across the entrance hall to smack against the glass doors and drop to the floor. It was up again instantly, shaking its head in surprise; it had not expected that, but now it knew the score.

What the Golem saw when it looked at the creature was equally uncertain, but again, if Emily had to guess, she would have said; an interloper. Letting this creature out of the basement was one thing, but letting it up into the block? That was something else. Who knew which of the Golem's 'Truths' had come good and identified the thing as the threat that it was, but as long as the creature remained in McDowall House, the Golem was its enemy.

The clay man strode across the entrance hall towards the doors where the thing stood, snarling. As the Golem approached, the creature sprang straight up, landing flat on the ceiling. It scurried swiftly across the room, straight over the Golem's head, making for the staircase and the prey that lay beyond.

But it didn't get far. Though it had all the grace of a bulldozer in ballet shoes, the Golem was not ungainly, it never missed a step, even when moving its hefty bulk at speed. It turned fast now, back to the stairwell, reaching up to snatch the creature from the ceiling and hurl it once more across the room.

This time the creature was ready, twisting in mid-air so it landed on the doors like a gecko on a wall, keeping its eyes on the Golem, those eyes now filled with anger.

This time it tried to go around the Golem, sticking to the wall, but the Golem was wise to that, thrusting out a hand as it went past, grabbing it by the arm with the intention of flinging it at the doors again. But the creature too was learning, and before the Golem could throw it, it had scrabbled along the Golem's arm, winding its sinuous body about the clay man. It might have been thin, and it might look as if it had been buried for a few years, but the creature had a wiry strength and a grip like steel, as well as being as quick as a greased weasel. The Golem aimed blows at it but the creature dodged and ducked, so the Golem ended up hitting itself.

The blank face registered no frustration, but Emily read confusion into its impassive features as it pummelled itself in the head, so the room resounded with the teeth-on-edge sound of ceramic against ceramic.

The creature was clearly smart enough to know that it could not bite this massive attacker, so instead, head downwards, it looped a long leg about the Golem's neck to try and strangle it. This gave the Golem the chance to grab it and wrench it free, though the leg stayed about its throat, trying to squeeze away breath that wasn't there. Holding the creature by its lapels in one hand, the Golem used the other to pry the leg away from its neck, then attempted to hurl the creature again. But again it slid free, tangling itself in the pottery arms, its ability to compress itself through small gaps making it hard for the Golem to keep a grip on it long enough to punch the thing.

With a triumphant hiss, the creature slipped through the Golem's hands, leaping to the floor. As soon as its hands touched the ground it rebounded back again, planting both feet in the Golem's chest, knocking the clay man backwards, sending it to the floor with a resonant '*DUNG*' that sounded as if it might crack open.

Again the creature darted for the stairwell, but again the Golem's hand shot out, grabbing it as it passed where the Golem lay. On the floor they tussled; one brute strength and immoveable determination, the other quick and sinewy, driven by the need to feed. It seemed impossible that the Golem could lose, it was so much bigger, so much stronger and surprisingly quick, but it could not hold the creature for long. Worse still, the creature had noticed the Golem's weakness when it hit the deck. Now, every chance it got, it was grabbing the clay man's head or hand, bouncing them off the tiled floor with that unanticipated strength, each bounce marked by more cracking noises. Clay dust began to hover in the air about the Golem as it dragged itself back to its feet, the creature still wound about it.

Emily suddenly realised that there was a chance the Golem could lose. But what could she do? If the Golem couldn't deal with this thing then she certainly couldn't.

The Golem tore the creature from its body and positioned

itself at the base of the stairs, seeming to say (like Gandalf in *The Lord of the Rings*) 'You shall not pass!'. The creature leapt up to the ceiling again, springing away at the last moment as the Golem made a grab for it, landing on the wall and scuttling up the stairway. Moments later it was back in the entrance hall as the Golem again laid hands on it.

The speed with which the creature evaded the Golem brought a memory to Emily's mind. It was one she that had tried hard to forget, from when she was in the back of the truck. The creature had been right in front of her, but had vanished as soon as she turned her torch on it. All the people who had died in the block had done so at night, and down in the basement it had broken one of the strip lights.

The lights of the entrance hall might be in 'energy save' mode right now, but the switch to change that was there beside her.

Emily flicked the switch.

The creature issued a high-pitched whine, springing off the Golem mid-fight, desperately hunting for darkness. Emily backed away as it came in her direction, but she was the least of its concerns right now. It was making for the basement door and the comforting darkness that lay beyond, but before it could reach it, the Golem's arm blocked the way. Frantically, the creature tried to get around, but the Golem shoved it away, back into the wall, the impact shaking even the resilient creature. It moved just in time to avoid the Golem's fist coming towards it like a sledgehammer. Instead, the fist hit the fire alarm, breaking the glass.

Emily covered her ears as the deafening alarm bell jangled noisily, then gasped as the sprinklers went on, spraying the entrance hall with cold water.

Finally managing to grab the creature by its coat, the Golem dragged it through the main doors and out into the night, leaving wet footprints in its wake.

Emily hesitated for a moment, then followed them out.

Outside, the two implausible creatures had separated again, the Golem positioning itself in front of the doors of McDowall House; a guardsman on duty – nothing would get past. The creature, relieved to be back in the dark of night but tormented by the knowledge of the prey that lay within the building, stalked frustratedly up and down in front of the block, edging closer with each pass, readying itself for its next move.

At this point, Emily wondered if this was still about food or if it simply did not want to be beaten by the Golem. Neither creature seemed to have much in the way of human emotions and yet she could not help reading those emotions into them – it was what humans did.

The creature darted forward, but the Golem was there to block its way and it backed down, retreating to the penumbra of shadow about the light that shone from the door of McDowall House. Another try, this time going low, through the guardian's legs if it could, but the Golem was there again and the creature narrowly avoided being stamped on. One more last ditch attempt; the creature scuttled up the wall. If it reached a window it could get in that way (windows presumably offering as little resistance as closed doors). The Golem moved like lightning, jumping up after it and grabbing the creature's heel at the outstretch of its reach. It landed with a fragile crash, bringing the creature with it and smacking it into the concrete of the plaza.

The furious creature rebounded on the Golem, trying to get past it by frontal attack, twisting its body about the clay man which strained against it like Laocoon and his sons attacked by sea serpents. But the creature could try all it wanted, The Golem of McDowall House was going nowhere, it would not let this trespasser in.

Emily watched in awestruck wonder. She still did not know, and perhaps could never understand, what specifically it was that was driving the Golem at this moment. It was not impossible that some child in the block had asked to be protected against monsters. It was equally likely that the Golem had identified the creature as an immigrant, someone '*not from here*', and was reacting to an ugly Britain First mentality inside it. But Emily liked to think, rightly or wrongly, that somehow all those bits of paper with their disparate, discordant or downright disagreeing statements had come together to form a primitive neural network – call it a mind – and that the Golem had learned to think. It had recognised a danger to the block, and had acted against it. Once more it was the Guardian Angel of McDowall House, the block's hero.

As it hit the ground again, the creature hissed and spat, shooting a hate-filled glance back at the Golem. It seemed defiant, but enough was enough. Straightening up, it loped off into the night.

The Golem had won.

Chapter 26 – Giving Chase

"Emily – Nurse Jennings – this is Harrigan. Again. Don't know why I'm leaving another message because if you had the damn phone with you, you'd have either answered or heard any of the others I've left. But, on the off-chance; Get Out. Get out of the flat, out of the block. It is not safe, there is something in there. I'll explain when I see you. Or possibly not, it's a little hard to explain. I'm on my way now. Also, the man who was with you when you found that truck (don't ask me how I know about that); do not trust him."

That covered the bases, but it was the fifth such message that Harrigan had left. With a bit of luck, Nurse Emily had got the first one and had already left of the flat, perhaps leaving her phone behind in her haste. That was perfectly plausible and yet Harrigan rejected the explanation; that would be too easy.

Now he was racing across London in the direction of McDowall House to warn Nurse Emily in person. The sun had already set, the Schreck was already active. There was a chance that he was already too late to stop another death.

How long would it take Elsa to get a Universal party together? '*Give me half an hour,*' she had said. That sounded pretty quick, given that her fellow agents were spread across the capital, but a lot could happen in half an hour. Harrigan had walked onto crime scenes and wondered at the carnage that could be wrought in a matter of moments, let alone half an hour.

Elsa had taken her car; that was only practical since she was the one with the team who could actually take care of the Schreck (Harrigan was just an item on its food chain), so he was braving the tube network for the first time since Lockdown had come in. What would Don and Will say about that? They wouldn't be happy, but neither was Harrigan. Frankly, he hadn't much liked the breathing in on London Underground even before the pandemic, now all his fears about respirating something nasty had become real. But it was the fastest way across town and it was much quieter than it had been, as people had finally got the message that the place was a petri dish for Covid transmission. Harrigan still felt as if every breath he took was potentially his last, but he always felt that way on the tube. Besides, he had bigger things to worry about.

Out of the tube he was onto a bus (far more people than he was comfortable with and far too many of them treating mask-wearing as optional) – why did Emily have to live so far away? That was when he got his phone out again to leave yet more messages. The eyes of the other passengers started to twitch in his direction as he left one panicked, desperate voicemail after another. It was amazing what people could say with just their eyes, and masks actually accentuated that ability because it was all you had to look at. Right now those eyes were saying, *'Why is the bus always filled with crazy people?'*. On the bright side, being thought of as crazy was a much more effective method of social distancing than mere risk of infection. It was better than coughing.

When the bus came to a stop, Harrigan was already at the door, pacing like a champion racehorse waiting for the off. The door opened and he sprang forth, hitting his stride immediately, shedding his mask and stuffing it into his pocket so he could breathe more easily in the marathon ahead of him.

By the end of the road he was straining for breath, his legs were aching, his broken arm was throbbing in its cast and he had developed a stitch in his side. He was no longer a young man, and even in his prime had not exactly been Mo Farrah. But he kept running. It was possible that brisk walking would have been a better, more sustainable use of his limited energy but he kept running because this was an emergency, time was of the essence, lives were at stake, and in those situations one ran. One ran as fast as one bloody well could.

With his breaths coming in wheezing gulps that sounded like a ruptured bagpipe, a red mist descended before Harrigan's eyes and fogged up his mind. He couldn't think straight, he couldn't see straight, all he could do was run (although he couldn't do that straight either). It occurred to him, in that oblique way that things will when you are trying not to think about the pain your body is in, that he only really ran when chasing or being chased. Most recently he had run from the Golem (not far from here in fact), which hadn't gone brilliantly but could have gone worse. Before that, he had probably not run – not *really* run – since the night in Cambridge when he had chased down an invisible serial killer, who had ended up pushing him off a bridge into a frozen river. Again, hadn't gone brilliantly but it could have gone worse; he hadn't died and it had been Elsa who had saved him. The resulting relationship had been worth the near-death experience. How would this run end?

Rounding the last corner and heading down the final straight, Harrigan resisted the majority verdict of his body that he could, and should, slow down now. Up ahead of him he could see Golem #3, and in his mind it seemed to be holding up a chequered flag ready to wave him home. McDowall House loomed behind it, pin-pricks of light in its upper windows, and a spill of light coming from the main doors, in which…

"Oh shit," was what Harrigan would have said if he had had the breath to do so.

There were two figures silhouetted in that light.

Or one…?

No; two.

One of the figures Harrigan recognised immediately; the massive proportions and heavy yet quick movements were unmistakable. It was the Golem, which he had last seen powering after him on the mud flats of the Thames. But it was the other figure, though he had never seen it before and it had not chased him almost to his death, that slowed his pace, tied his stomach in knots and sent a cold shiver across his skin. It was lean and dark against the light from the hallway, its long, thin limbs making it look like a figure from a Lowry painting, except that L. S. Lowry never drew a face like this. What was it that Elsa had said? '*Like Edvard Munch had a bad LSD trip*'. That was it. That was what he was looking at. It was the Schreck.

When Harrigan had first seen the creature, it was locked in combat with the Golem and he could see it clearly. But when the Golem flung it away, the Schreck seemed resist being seen, and Harrigan felt his eyes watering as he struggled to keep the thing in focus and in front of him. That confirmed his identification.

The Schreck charged again. It did not seem to be trying to kill the Golem (was that even possible?), but was trying to get past it to enter the block. Harrigan had seen some strange things during his time on the force, but nothing to match this. It looked as if the Golem could have snapped the Schreck in half, but the creature was almost bonelessly limber, twisting and writhing from the statue's grip.

As he got closer, and his breathing started to sound less like a cross between a runaway train and a punctured accordion, Harrigan noticed two more things. Firstly, a fire alarm was going off somewhere. Secondly, there was another figure outside the block, hanging back to the side of the doorway. It was Nurse Emily.

Harrigan wondered if he ought to shout 'Hello', or if that would be ridiculous in the circumstances.

The Golem hurled the Schreck to the ground once more, and this time the creature seemed to have had enough. McDowall House had been convenient, but this was London, bloated with infection, and it would not have to look hard to find another suitable victim or another place to hole up. It raised its head, drawing in the viral scents, seeking the strongest. Then it started off into the night, away from the block, walking at a brisk pace with long, spidery strides, following its nose.

For a moment, Harrigan's attention was torn between the Golem and Nurse Emily, and the departing Schreck, his eyes fumbling to find the creature that was already blending into the night. That was what made up his mind; they had been very lucky to run this menace to ground once, if it got back out there into the city then it would find another block, another rock to crawl under, another community of helpless victims on which to prey, and they would not get so lucky again.

Leaving Nurse Emily and the Golem, Harrigan forced his unwilling body into activity once more, running after the Schreck as it stole through the slumbering streets.

Harsh things had been said about districts like this by the media and the government, or at least harsh things had been implied. Compliance with the regulations would be low, people would not do as they were told or understand what was at stake, they would fail to protect their friends and families and so infection rates and death rates would rise, and it would be the fault of a certain sort of people. That had been wrong. Of course there were idiots here ('Covidiots' as they had quickly been dubbed) as there were everywhere, but no more here than anywhere else. People cared, they were careful, they did the right thing, and they stayed at home.

The emptiness of pandemic-hit London stretched out before Harrigan, that oppressive silence laid down across the streets. Curtains did not twitch, lights went out early, as if the city felt that merely staying indoors was not enough and was trying to hibernate its way through the crisis. Though it made London feel like another world, right now Harrigan was grateful for it. In amongst people, the Schreck could have disappeared – they would not see it and it could vanish in the narrow spaces between their bodies. But in this ghost town, he could make it out, because it was the only thing moving.

Not that it was easy! Elsa had been right; you had to be looking for it to see it. You had to know what you were looking for and where to look, and even then you might miss it. It was hard to explain; it was not camouflaged like a chameleon, nor was it actually invisible. It was more like the shy, plain girl at a party; there, but so easily passed over. It was an effort to see the Schreck, as mentally tiring as the running was physically tiring.

The Schreck itself did not run, but it kept up a brisk pace that the exhausted Harrigan struggled to match, its steps long and swift. It had the quality of a snake on the hunt, slithering with purpose through its natural habitat. There was no doubt that that was what this was; a city full of people was where the Schreck was most at home, and Harrigan wondered how long this one had stalked the cities of Europe (or beyond?).

As he jogged after the pestilential vampire, Harrigan got out his phone and called Elsa.

"Are you at the block?" she answered sharply, all business.

"No," Harrigan puffed. "Was there… Saw the… Saw the lot! Golem *and* Schreck… Fighting…"

"Fighting?"

"Golem… keeping it out… drove it off."

"Drove it off?" Harrigan could hear the anxiety in Elsa's voice, fearing that she might have lost this thing that she had chased across the continent.

"Following…" Harrigan gasped. After his all-out run earlier, just jogging to keep up with the swift and stealthy movements of the Schreck was an effort, especially while simultaneously conducting a phone conversation *and* keeping the damn thing in sight. He felt that if he took his eyes off the Schreck for a second, if he so much as blinked, he would never find it again.

"Stay with it!" Elsa emphasised. "We'll be with you soon. Don't lose it. And be careful." It could have sounded like an afterthought, but Harrigan recognised the concern of a girlfriend cracking through the professionalism of Elsa the Universal agent. This was why she tried to keep the two sides of her life separate; when they met it could be brutal.

"Will do," said Harrigan. "Both."

"We'll be there shortly," Elsa reassured. "I can track you on my phone."

"You can?" But she was already gone.

Harrigan struggled to find his pocket as he shoved the phone back and, for a second, took his eyes of the street. As he looked back, panic surged through him: it was gone! There was no sign of the Schreck.

Calm down, focus, it was there and it can't have gone far.

He stared at where he had last seen it, just a moment ago, focusing his mind, *believing* that the creature was there.

Perhaps it was that belief, perhaps it was the movement of the creature that gave it away, but Harrigan's heart slowed a bit as his eyes found the Schreck again, where it hugged the shadows. The street along which it now moved was lined with shops, not just closed because it was night but because none of them qualified as essential retail. They were hairdressers and nail salons, a betting shop, one boarded-up that looked as if it had gone out of business even before Lockdown hit. From doorway to doorway the Schreck stole, finding the darkness within the night, the shadow inside the shadow, and then becoming the deeper shadow within that.

To anyone who looked, who knew to look, who chose to see it, the face was what you saw first, the ghostly death's head almost seeming to float through the darkness; staring eyes, bared teeth, ghoulish skin. It was a nightmare come to life, so horrific that the human mind rejected it; it could not exist, it had crawled out of the primeval inherited memories of humanity, the thing that lurked in the caves of our ancestors, the tapping on the wall, the wind in the night, the shadows from the fires around which people sat and told stories that sought to explain the mystery of death. And so the Schreck had grown up with us, before anyone thought to put a name to it. It hung at the fringes of human existence, feeding on those who slipped away and creating a legend of its own, indistinguishable from death itself.

And now it was being chased by Clive Harrigan.

That was not a story Hollywood was optioning any time soon; the short and embarrassing struggle between an ancestral evil as old as humanity and a retired policeman in his early sixties. (Although if Hollywood did come looking then Harrigan felt it was the part that Tom Cruise was born to play.)

Until now, the Schreck's movement had been constant, but suddenly it paused a beat, its head raising a fraction, tasting the air, before moving on again.

Nervously Harrigan held back. So far the creature had shown no interest in him, nor even acknowledged his existence (which felt like a cheap and accurate Covid test – if he'd been infected then the Schreck would have at least sniffed at him), it had its own priorities and Harrigan did not pose a threat. It was also still reeling from its fight with the Golem and was probably anxious to move on. Now though, it was recovering its senses and… Had it only just noticed Harrigan? He might not represent food or a threat, but that did not mean that the Schreck liked being followed. Harrigan watched its head, waiting for it to turn and look at him.

If it knew it was being trailed, was there a chance that it might try to get away? If it picked up the pace then Harrigan would struggle to follow.

What a loathsome thing it was.

There was an anger brewing in Harrigan, wiping out both exhaustion and fear. This thing had killed and killed, and here it was stealing on to its next victim. It didn't look so tough.

The Schreck started to move faster. Following a scent trail? Or planning to give Harrigan the slip?

He couldn't let it escape, and suddenly that felt like a real possibility. Look at it; so skinny it would snap like a twig. Its hideous face looked as fragile as porcelain. One swift punch and down it would go. Harrigan might not have been in the best shape, but he had been in plenty of fights and knew how to handle himself. He had taken down fit, strong men half his age by knowing *how* to fight. This would be no different. He could take it with one hand behind his back (which was good because he had one arm in plaster).

And *that* would help.

For months he had been varying shades of useless, but now he could *do* something. An opportunity had been handed to him to make a measurable difference, to save actual lives.

All of a sudden, attacking the Schreck was not a matter of last resort, it was something that Harrigan *had* to do. He was not keeping an eye on this thing until Universal arrived, he was a hunter pursuing his prey.

The Schreck was definitely going faster now, loping along the street. It had identified its next victim and they lay in this direction. Someone else was going to die tonight if Harrigan didn't step in.

Now.

Headlights flared up ahead of him, coming out of nowhere.

The Schreck, reacted as if it had been burnt, scurrying back, using the shadows, disappearing into its background as never before.

Harrigan started forwards. The damn car had panicked the creature, it was now or never and there was only him.

But suddenly, there wasn't only him. As he ran towards the Schreck, three people jumped out of the car, heading in the same direction. Others passed him, carrying torches with bright, powerful beams, keeping the Schreck always in sight, always in the light, pushing it back, hunting it down.

Harrigan skidded to a halt, momentarily confused. "What the…?"

A hand on his shoulder. He turned to find Elsa.

"Are you alright?"

"Yes!" Harrigan shouted, the adrenalin inside him needing some outlet. "But the…"

"It's okay, they've got it. Let them do their job."

"But…" Harrigan looked desperately back over his shoulder. *He* was the hunter, this was *his* collar.

Elsa laid a hand on his arm. "We got it because of you, Harrigan. But let the professionals handle it."

Harrigan breathed. And it was fine. He was here with Elsa, Emily was safe, the block was safe, his family were safe, and the Schreck was being chased down by people who knew how to kill it (an important piece of information to which Harrigan was not privy). Sometimes in life, the most important thing you could do was to recognise when someone else was the right person for the job. And all too often in the wretchedness of 2020, the best thing you could do was step back, stay at home, save lives. Be a hero by not being a hero.

"You got it," he said.

"Team effort," shrugged Elsa.

"You don't want to be with them?"

Elsa shook her head. "The result's all that matters. Come on. There's still a Golem we've got to decide what to do with."

It was a busy night.

Chapter 27 – The Hero

The alarm still jangled in the background as Emily watched the creature stealing off into the night. It was probably wrong to let it go, though she was not sure that she could do a damn thing to stop it. To her immense relief, and some surprise, she saw a man running after it whom she recognised as Clive Harrigan.

There seemed to be more to Harrigan than retired policeman. Had he known about the creature? Was that why he had asked about the basement?

Lots of questions. But right now, the overwhelming emotion remained relief. They had won. The Golem had won.

It – *he* – was now standing guard in case the creature returned. She could see the lines of cracks here and there on the terracotta surface. It was missing two fingers from its left hand and the helmet of its hair had been chipped in several places. There was more damage here and there where it had been repeatedly slammed into the walls or floor. A tough fight but it still stood, and Emily found herself wondering if a good potter could patch it up. It deserved that, didn't it?

Her relationship with the Golem had, to use the cliché, been a rollercoaster one. She had seen its dark side but now she had seen the best of it. It had saved actual lives tonight. It had that capacity, if it was used correctly, if it did not become the tool of bad men.

She walked over to the statue, where it stood, staring out into the night.

"Thank you. I don't know if you understand what you've done, but thank you."

The Golem did not look at her. It did not look for thanks, it simply did what it did.

Suddenly it looked out to its right, and then it was on the move again, striding with determined steps towards the replacement golem that stood in its spot. The Golem came to a halt in front of its doppelganger and, for perhaps thirty seconds, it simply stared.

Perhaps it was making up its mind what to do next because then, without warning, it moved again, its left arm whirling out, smashing the head of its twin in an explosion of clay dust. The violence of the blow made Emily catch her breath, and the Golem was not done yet. With balled up fists it pounded chunks out of the statue's torso, then picked up the disembodied legs and hurled them to the ground, shattering them, not angrily, but with an unemotional violence that was so much more disconcerting than anger. Finally, it stood over the largest surviving piece of the doppelganger's head, from which one blank eye still stared, and drove its foot down into it, crushing it to powder.

The Golem resumed its usurped spot. It had earned this place, proving itself the true and only guardian of the block.

Now what? Emily wondered. Did she tell other people about it? They were bound to notice at some point. Lockdown would not be forever, people were already venturing out more as the restrictions began to bite. Sooner or later, someone *was* going to notice a walking statue.

She wandered back towards the block, thinking over the problem while the fire alarm continued to ring. That alarm was roundly hated throughout McDowall House for its frequent false alarms, which was why, so far, no one had left the building. If it kept going then, grudgingly, people would start to filter out, just in case there was an actual fire this time. At which point they might notice that the Golem was standing surrounded by the shattered debris of its twin. They were unlikely to believe Emily if she tried to explain how it had happened, but if it moved then…

Emily stopped, staring at the ground, a wave of nausea suddenly passing over her.

By the door were the wet footprints the Golem had left as it strode out after setting off the sprinkler system. She had not previously noticed the level of detail that artist, Henrik, had gone to with every aspect of its costume. Even though it was designed to stand in the same spot forever, he had given its shoes distinctive treads like training shoes. Or like car tyres.

That was what Emily had mistaken those marks for when she had seen them last, sunk into the mud of the disused railway tunnel. The Golem had been there. It had stood directly behind the doors of the truck. And suddenly, Emily could see it all, as if it she had been there to watch it unfold.

Chapter 28 – What it Did Then

Keep Covid out of this country.

"You'd best get over here," called Bill, standing by the back of the truck. "There's a problem with the cargo."

Leaving the Golem, Maxie walked over to the recently freed truck. He could hear the voices of the 'cargo' from within, getting more and more frantic.

"Can't you keep them quiet? What's going on?"

Bill shot a sidelong glance into truck's crowded interior and spoke in an undertone. "Couple of them are coughing."

Unconsciously, they all shuffled back a bit.

"Coughing?" There were different kinds of coughing, after all...

"A lot," stressed Bill. "Sounds nasty."

Maxie shook his head. They had orders to fill, people were waiting. The reason that people trafficking was such a lucrative business was that it paid at both ends; people paid to get into Britain and people in Britain paid for first dibs on cheap labour who were willing to live in a basement (they were going to live in a basement whether they were willing to or not, but them actually being willing was a plus). But the pandemic had changed things. The camps on the continent were crowded and unsanitary, and if you sold your clients infected merchandise which then infected the rest of their workforce, then those clients would be unhappy. And this was a business in which unhappy clients did not mean legal action, it meant large men with blunt objects. Sometimes sharp ones.

"What about the other truck?"

"All quiet."

Maxie nodded. That was something; half a cargo was better than none at all. Still... "Get them straight into a cell when we get back. We'll quarantine them."

Bill nodded. "What about this lot?"

Maxie eyed the coughing truck. "They can't go any further."

"Then what?" asked Bill, sharply. "The door won't close."

There were things you did and things you didn't. These were all men who were happy to sell their fellow human beings, but killing was something else; they weren't murderers. In cases like this (because from time to time shit happened), sealing people in a locked truck was an acceptable middle ground, because those people died by natural causes. That technicality allowed them all to live with it, largely because they didn't have to be there to watch it happen.

"I don't care, how it's done," Maxie snarled.

"Then you do it."

Maxie grabbed Bill by the lapels. "I give the orders. Understood? And... Get back in there!"

One of the truck's occupants had decided to make a bid for freedom and rushed the door, trying to barge past Maxie. For a few moments they were face to face and Maxie felt the man's breath on his skin like a burn.

Bill came to his aid, shoving the man back inside and jamming the door closed again as best he could.

"That's going to keep happening. And if they get out there'll be hell to pay."

Maxie didn't need to be reminded of that.

"You can't jam the doors any better?" Anything that gave them that little bit of distance from the event.

"You want to try?" asked Bill. "And then you'll be happy to just walk away?"

They didn't carry fire arms – the Boss was clear on that; if you carried them then it was asking for trouble. They could set fire to the truck, but that might attract attention, and with the busted door the cargo would surely try to make a run for it, at which point Maxie or one of the gang would have to take the direct action they had wanted to avoid. Plus, if they all made a break for it at the same moment then it would be hard to stop them all.

"Look, if they've got Covid then..."

Throughout this exchange, the Golem had been standing motionless some small distance away, it now came to life, striding towards them, moving with the force of a continent. The people inside, who had been massing at the door, now rushed back into the comparative safety of the truck, yelling for help. But no one would hear them out here.

At first, Maxie had thought the Golem was going to kill them all, but it just closed the doors, and held them. In its mind (*If you could call it a mind*, Maxie added to himself) it was holding back the tide of the virus. It did not see people, or if it did they did not matter. So it held the doors closed. Even if Maxie had wanted to stop it, he didn't think he could have. They were infected, and the Golem seemed to see it as its personal mission to stop infection.

"Do we stay?" asked Booth.

Maxie swallowed. "I don't think we need to. Seems to know what it's doing."

To be successful as a people trafficker, you had to stop thinking of them as people. They were cargo. But, even for someone as hardened as Maxie, that was hard to maintain when they were weeping and screaming for help.

It did not seem to bother the Golem. It heard their cries, it listened to their pleas, but it did not move from the doors. It did not even flinch.

That, Maxie thought afterwards, was the most frightening thing about it. Not the daunting strength or its terrifyingly blank face; the fact that it could hear all that, and not react.

The second truck left with its human cargo, and Maxie drove home. There was still time to get some sleep, but he would not be sleeping tonight. He would check back in a day or so, to make sure the job was done.

At the truck, the Golem remained in position, solid and unmoving, as if it had been built on this spot to fulfil this purpose. Inside, the people realised that they had to do something if they ever wanted to get out. They rushed the doors, all together, throwing their combined weight against them, but that was of no consequence to the Golem. They tried to squeeze out past the warped metal at the top of the door, but the Golem batted them back with a swat from one massive hand. Above all, they begged.

If anyone had been there who understood the languages

being spoken, then, in amongst the cries for help, the begging and pleading, they would have heard people saying, "There's something in here with us!"

It took days. The cries died long before the people did. But the Golem stayed, unmoving, hands on the truck doors, until there was no sound from within. It had stopped Covid. It had followed the 'Truths' in its head.

Chapter 29 – The Villain

That was why the refugees had stayed inside, why they hadn't been able to force that broken door. The Golem had stood there to block their way, to hold the doors closed with its indomitable strength. They had Covid. They were a risk. And the Golem had only one reaction in that situation. It kept them in. It had not known what horrifying creature was in there with them, but it wouldn't have made a difference.

Emily had to remind herself to breathe as she turned back to look at the 'Guardian Angel'. The solid, static figure looked quite different to her now. It had killed those people, or as good as. It could be an instrument of good – she knew it could – but it could equally be one of evil, and while it did partly depend on who was standing behind it, pulling the strings, the bottom line was that it did not know the difference, and that was something it would never be able to learn. There was no good and evil to the Golem, there were only the words in its head; a chorus of shouting, dragging it this way and that, demanding of it, telling it what to do in an unnuanced roar, insisting they were right and that there was no grey area, no middle ground.

The Golem was the voice of the people, but that voice needs to be filtered by basic humanity. Humans understand that the slogans they shout, the headlines they read, the angry posts they hurl into the void of social media, are to be taken with a grain of salt. They are a call to action, not a guide to life. The Golem made no such distinction.

"What the hell's going on?"

"I thought they had that damn alarm fixed."

The residents of McDowall House were now emerging through the doors. It had probably started with heads poking out, '*Is this real?*' '*I don't know. There's no fire in mine,*' and so on, until they started to filter down in dribs and drabs, because no one wanted to be the one who went first (that person was an alarmist), trying to maintain social distancing and probably failing to a great extent.

"There was… I don't know." Minutes ago, Emily had been

unsure what she could say about the Golem, but after seeing that footprint, after realising what it meant, 'unsure' did not even begin. She was cut adrift. It had protected them from the creature, and had risked its own existence to do so. But the footprint spoke volumes. And she could not guarantee that something like that would not happen again. All it needed was for someone to whisper a few lies in its ear, and the Golem was a monster.

In that respect too, it reflected the masses, the people, the mob.

As she fended off questions from the other residents (this was another reason you didn't want to be the first one out), she saw, in amongst the growing crowd, Lydia and Masud. Lydia was holding a baby in her arms, trying to shield its mouth – Covid wasn't supposed to affect the young but you didn't trust that sort of statistic when you were a first-time mother, nervous of everything.

That baby would never know its uncle.

"They didn't die of Covid." Emily muttered so quietly that only a few people even noticed she was talking.

"What?" Robert was closest to her.

"What did you say?"

"Did you set off the fire alarm?"

"They didn't die of Covid." When it came to talking in front of lots of people, Emily was decidedly not her father's daughter, but her head was up now and her voice raised. "Mrs McCulloch and the others in the last few days. It wasn't Covid. Something else killed them."

"Emily, are you okay?" asked Camilla.

"I'm fine. You have to listen." They would never believe her, and the Golem wasn't a trained seal that would do tricks on cue.

"You've been working too hard," Camilla chided gently.

"You're bound to be stressed," nodded Eric.

"I saw it coming," agreed Al the Astrologer, who never missed an opportunity.

"Did you set off the alarm?" Camilla went on. "No one here will blame you. We all know what you do every day and we appreciate it."

They would never believe her.

In Camilla's arms was little Ursula, her gaze fixed on the Golem. She pointed. "He wouldn't eat my apple pie."

And suddenly, Emily knew what she had to do.

She coughed.

The crowd immediately stepped back, as if they had been choreographed for the Covid quick-step, but none of them moved as fast as the Golem, and when it moved then the crowd, which had been backing away, kept backing, now faster in panic. Cries of disbelief and shock went up, and people tripped over themselves trying to get away as the clay man bore down on Emily. There were some at the back who laughed it off as a trick, a practical joke, a man in a suit, but the ones closest, those who got a good look; they *believed*. As ever, something about the Golem left no room for doubt.

As for Emily, she stood her ground as the Golem pounded towards her, its deep eyes boring into her. She was its target. She had coughed. She had been evicted from the block and so no longer enjoyed that protection.

"You see!" Emily yelled. She had their attention now.

As the Golem charged she hurried away from the block, and the Golem put itself between her and the people of McDowall House, once more assuming its role as protector.

"You see!" Emily repeated. "I don't know what it is or why the council put it here." Stress the council, make it seem as if this was 'official', 'governmental', something put here to spy on *you*. Maybe they were part of a pilot project and soon there would be one of these things on every street corner. McDowall House was filled with people who, for one reason or another, lived in fear of the 'official'. "I don't what it's supposed to be for, but it killed Mrs McCulloch. It killed Noel on third and Abdul-Hafez, and that guy on the sixteenth floor (who I think was squatting, but still)." She zeroed in on Lydia and Masud in the crowd. "It killed Jakeem."

Maybe she shouldn't have gone that far, but it mattered to Emily that she said one true thing. If she was going to condemn the Golem, then let it be for something it had actually done.

From somewhere towards the back of the group, the first half-brick sailed over the heads of the crowd. It was the sort of thing that could have ended badly, but it was a magnificent shot, catching the Golem on the side of its head, knocking a chunk out of its hairpiece.

The statue turned, looking for the source of the attack, looking to see if it posed a threat to the block. As it did so, it met a sea of angry faces, the faces of those it had protected, those it had served, now turned to hatred. They did not know that this was their Angel, they did not have any proof that Emily was telling the truth, but that didn't matter; it was the scary '*other*'. It had no place here. Another brick flew over from the back, this one less well-aimed, smashing on the ground to the Golem's left. It did not move.

People were actively searching now, looking for stuff to throw. A few discarded beer cans made little impact, but there were also chunks of broken concrete that found their target and widened the cracks in the Golem's exterior, caused by its earlier fight. Parents with children hastened to get them inside, out of the hitting zone, because it is seldom in life that vandalism is given an ethical pass and people were clearly determined to make the most of it. This was a year in which the opportunity to hit something was not one that you wasted. You couldn't throw bricks at Covid, but this would do.

Having been behind the Golem when the bricks started to fly, Emily was in very much the wrong place as more and wilder shots started coming, and she hurried back towards the block. As soon as she was into the Golem's field of vision, she saw the head move towards her, the eyes picking her out. A rock slammed into its face, chipping its chin, but it did not even flinch. It had not forgotten about her; she had coughed, she had been evicted, she was a threat to the block.

Emily backed up again, away from where the projectiles were landing but nowhere near the doors to McDowall House. If she started towards those doors then the Golem would be after her, regardless of how many bricks were hurled at it.

The crowd had thinned, but that was partly was because people had gone to fetch more effective weapons. As he lived on the first floor, Masud was one of the first to return. He was a taciturn man, at least towards Emily, but you never really knew that much about your neighbours; who they were behind closed doors. The Golem had robbed him of a brother, and he showed no sign of fear as he strode towards it, a hammer in his hand. He was already winding up as he approached and as soon as he was in striking distance he swung. The Golem's head did not turn as the hammer hit, but dust flew and a crack spread across its face, like a scar on its cheek.

It did not look at Masud. It did not make any attempt to defend itself.

And Masud was not the only man to own a hammer, a mallet, a heavy saucepan, a spade. The doors opened, swung shut and opened again, each time admitting someone with a new makeshift weapon. The saucepan cracked into the back of the Golem's head, a lump hammer broke its nose while repeated blows from a mallet widened the cracks in its shoulder. Now the spade was jabbed into its head, the blade gouging a cleft into the already damaged clay. This being Britain, a nation built around the ability to queue, a sort of rough order developed, people taking turns with their weapon, so that everyone had a go.

A cheer went up as Masud swung again and the Golem's right forearm shattered, shards dropping to the ground. The Golem raised what was left of its arm, regarding the stump dispassionately, perhaps wondering how it would carry flour and toilet paper now.

A cry of shock and panic erupted from the wreckers as the Golem suddenly moved. Its steps were slow now, as if it was having to hold itself together from the inside, but it still kept one eye on Emily as it limped away.

"We've got it on the run!"

As the crowd swelled with more people (those on the upper floors who had had a long walk to fetch a hammer), confidence grew again. To them, the Golem was on the run. To Emily, it was trying to preserve itself, because it could not protect the block if it was destroyed.

One by one, people darted in, delivering a glancing blow then dodging back in case of retaliation. But as they continued, and as the Golem stumbled on, it became increasingly obvious that no retaliation was coming. The blows came faster, heavier, more targeted. The spade swung again and again, hacking at the Golem's ankle until it was too weak to take the weight of its own body and shattered, bringing the Golem to its knees. Another cheer went up from the group. Now they encircled it, weapons rising and falling furiously, breaking its legs so only its head and torso remained.

Still the Golem dragged itself on. Its left arm went at the shoulder, a saucepan finally stove in the back of it head, and it toppled down onto its chest. Still it crawled on, using the stump of its right arm as a crutch. Until…

It stopped.

It had reached its spot, the place where it had been set up to stand, to guard the block, to be a symbol of the people who lived within, the people who now surrounded it. This was the only place that the Golem could call home.

The fact that it stopped seemed to disconcert its attackers. It meant that they had not driven it away, they had just followed it to where it was going. Perhaps there was also something… *unnerving* about the fact that it behaved like an animal in distress, retreating to its lair.

With difficulty, the Golem managed to push itself upright on the broken remnants of its hips. Normally it would have stopped moving once it reached this point, but it had to keep adjusting to maintain its precarious balance, rocking left and right, back and forth.

Above it stood Masud, and it seemed right to Emily that the man taking this responsibility should be one who had suffered a genuine loss at the Golem's hands.

Did the Golem look up to see him? At that last moment, did it want to look him in the face? Or ask for mercy? Or perhaps it was just trying to keep its balance.

Masud's hammer fell, and the Golem's face exploded in a cloud of dust and shards of clay. The torso fell backwards. The mood of jubilance amongst the wreckers had now been replaced by

272

something more solemn, but they fell to their task never the less, the hammers rising and falling until there was nothing left.

Emily watched. She didn't want to, but she had to. She was the only one who knew the whole truth, the only one who could watch and understand that this was horrible, but *had* to happen.

Amongst the clay dust that floated on the night breeze were scattered scraps of paper, mostly torn so only a few hand written words remained: '*I want...*', '*I wish...*', '*Please...*', '*...protect...*', '*...Covid...*'.

She stooped to pick up one complete slip that had somehow survived.

I'd like to be safe walking home at night.

How did you get from there to here?
Emily started to cry.

Epilogue – A Whisper in the Chorus

"Hello, astrology fans and welcome back to another episode of Your Stars, with Al the astrologer, that's me! Didn't I tell you? Didn't I say? Something was coming, I said. Change was a-coming, I said. Closer to home than I thought – I don't even know who *owns* my home any more. Events and revelations last night have left the future of McDowall House uncertain. But, hell, we're all getting use to that."

By morning, none of it had happened.

The ramblings of a rooftop astrologer were as close to a media frenzy as it got, and Harrigan had been impressed by the way in which Elsa's Universal colleagues had moved in, smoothing things over, giving explanations and, in the nicest possible way, suggesting that, since council property had been destroyed, maybe it was best to keep it quiet. It moved, you say? Are you sure about that, sir? Because statues don't move, so if it did then you want to be very careful of what you're admitting to.

It didn't move because it couldn't have, and everyone more or less accepted that. Harrigan thought back to the Schreck; invisible unless you looked for it, unless you could force your mind to accept the impossible. It was a great survival strategy, because the human brain lied to itself even better than humans lied to each other. Living in the world was a hell of a lot easier if you didn't think about it.

Harrigan put the phone down.

"Kildare?" asked Elsa.

"They've managed to track down all the people in the second truck."

"That's good."

Harrigan nodded. "Who knows what'll happen to them now, but I reckon it's better than what would have."

"Any questions about how Paul Haworth died?"

Harrigan shrugged. "Picked up Covid from somewhere. There's a nasty strain of it in McDowall House apparently."

"Not anymore."

"Now they know who was in charge," Harrigan went on, "there'll be more arrests. May even get some of the other money men. Though they will all, no doubt, deny knowledge – shocked to learn where their staff were coming from."

"It's amazing what you fail to learn if you don't ask." Elsa was silent a moment before speaking again. "Did he say anything about the man Emily was looking for?"

"Jakeem." Harrigan shook his head. "He would seem to have been on the first truck."

Unconsciously they moved closer to each other in the bed, neither knowing what to say when discussing someone else's tragedy.

"How's the arm?"

"It aches," admitted Harrigan. "Think I rattled it about a bit last night. My bones'll probably knit funny now."

"You should get it checked."

"Yeah, but… hospitals right now. I don't like to give them anything else to do."

Elsa nodded.

"Do you mind if I point something out?" asked Harrigan.

"Go ahead."

"You just took out a demonic creature that has eaten its way across Europe, and not for the first time. If you wanted to go back to Spanish flu or the Black Death or…" those were the only 'celebrity' pandemics he could think of, "then the number of people it killed is in the hundreds. Maybe more. You're not exactly jumping for joy about it."

"No," admitted Elsa. "It usually feels different."

"It's age. Don't fight it."

Elsa half-smiled and shook her head. "No, it's… When a mission comes to an end, you've taken down a monster and the world is a better place for it. The Schreck is dead, but the world…" She shook her head. "I don't know if I've made a lick of difference."

Harrigan started to put an arm around her, then realised that in plaster it was not such a comforting gesture. "Look, some of the people that thing would have killed are going to die anyway, but they'll live longer now. And that's life. We're all running out that clock, making the best of every moment." He smiled wanly. "I'm not a man in the first flush of youth, and if I'd died in a river in Cambridge then it would have been less sad than if some teenager with their whole life ahead of them had gone in. But I'm still pretty damn glad to be alive, and I think I'm making the most of it. Just look at what I would have missed out on." He went to stroke the hair from Elsa's face, but ended up clonking her on the forehead with his plaster. "Damn thing. If I'd died that night, then I would never have made peace with my boys, I'd never have even met my grandchildren. If I die tomorrow then I'll be glad to have had that opportunity, but I'm hoping to live a little longer and see how many more moments I can get out of it. Every time you save a life, Elsa, whether you're saving it for a few years or a few weeks, then you give people more moments like that. Moments they wouldn't give up for anything. I can't think of anything better."

Elsa considered this. "You're very good at that."

"Thanks."

The point, Harrigan hoped, could be extrapolated. Maybe he wasn't out there saving lives. Maybe he wasn't the one who chased monsters to the finish. But as long as you did *something*, as long as when someone asked for help you said 'Yes', then you were still 'helping'. You were still useful.

Harrigan's phone blipped and he reached it off the bedside table to check the message.

"Oh sod it, I forgot what day it was. It's Will. Video call with Grandad later."

Elsa nodded. "I'll get out of your way."

"Don't be ridiculous. They'll want to see you too."

For someone who was relatively at ease with chasing down highly evolved vampires or invisible men, Elsa looked almost dazed when presented with the idea that a pair of small children were anxious to see her. She breathed in.

"Okay. Tell them…. Tell them Grandma will be there too."

He was lying in bed, but Harrigan felt as if he was walking on air.

"We've got a bit of time."

They settled back in bed.

"We did alright, didn't we?" said Elsa, after a while. And it seemed as if she was really asking.

"I think you did amazingly," replied Harrigan.

"It's never enough."

Harrigan sighed. "You may have to accept that. These days, the monster chasers aren't the only heroes out there."

Nurse Emily Jennings put on her uniform. A day off was probably called for but it always was these days. She was tired, but wasn't everyone? You kept going no matter what happened, no matter what you saw, because if you didn't then who did?

The images still haunted her, even now, though she was awake. The thing had been hideous, but it was the death of the Golem that told on her subconscious.

Was 'death' even the right word? Probably not, but it was the one she would use.

Had she done the right thing? She'd gone back and forth on that, torturing herself with might have beens.

She could guess what her Dad would say, but he hadn't been there and she had. It had been her decision and she had made it.

Words could be dangerous, and without a conscience to guide them they could be outright lethal.

On the breakfast news, artist, Henrik, was giving his appraisal of the destruction of the Golem and what it meant for culture in modern British society. He had been given a major new commission and was talking enthusiastically about how his proposed Covid Memorial would heal the nation, once it was all over. In a few weeks.

On her phone was a message from Harrigan, asking how she was doing. They had not really spoken last night, though he had made sure she was alright before the woman he was with (tiny and with lots of curly red hair) had whisked Emily off to explain how this was going to work. There was no embargo on her, she could say what she pleased and tell anyone she liked, but she was advised against it because no one would believe her.

That was fine with Emily. She didn't want to tell anyone. She still felt guilty.

Imagine if it had marched on the Houses of Parliament at the head of a protest – what a day that would have been. It was filled with the voices of the people and had the capacity to make those voices heard in a way that could not be ignored. And she had silenced it.

The problem, Emily considered, with the voice of the people, was that when they all shouted at once you only heard the loudest. The voice of the people drowned out the voice of the person. Maybe the person didn't matter as much as The People, but, then again, when you came right down to it, maybe it was all that mattered. All those individual voices.

You couldn't help everyone. In Emily's estimation you were lucky if you managed to help *anyone*, so that was a good place to start.

She put her NHS lanyard around her neck, popped a much-read copy of Terry Pratchett's *Interesting Times* into her bag, and headed for the door. Doing *something* was better than doing nothing. And *doing* something was better than talking about it. If every person shouting about how things ought to be, stopped shouting and did one real thing then maybe…

She would rather be a barely discernible whisper in a harmonious chorus, than shouting above the crowd.

The streets were growing less empty now, but that was not necessarily a good thing. Masked key workers headed to their prescribed jobs, trying not to get in each other's way. Shuttered shops sat sullen and idle as people peered from their windows, wondering how much longer it could last or if this was how the world now looked.

You had to do something, even if it was only going to work.

On the bus, Emily put in her ear buds and called up YouTube on her phone.

"…with the effect that's having on Mars. And of course with Mercury in opposition to Neptune that can only mean one thing, people; Change! That's right, change is coming, and you can call me a sentimental fool, but when I see the arc of the moon, then I think it looks damn good. You hear that? Change for the better. And you know it's true because your old pal, Al the Astrologer says so."

The End.

About the Author

Robin Bailes lives in Cambridge and has been writing in one capacity or another for the last twenty years. Outside of these books, his fondest achievement is the 6-part comedy/drama web-series Coping, which you can find on YouTube (if you look hard enough). Robin's interest in old films began with a book about Lon Chaney that belonged to his Grandpa, which led to a lifelong passion for cinema, particularly the horror movies of the 1920s and 30s. That passion has also led Robin to volunteer at London's Cinema Museum (where he can be found serving coffee at most silent film screenings) and to the creation of weekly web-series Dark Corners…
@robinbailes

Dark Corners

Co-created by Robin Bailes and Graham Trelfer, Dark Corners Reviews began as a bad movie review show on YouTube and has grown into a sprawling collection of videos celebrating the best and worst of cult cinema. With bad movie reviews every Tuesday, streaming movie reviews every Friday, and monthly specials about classic films and franchises, the show has a loyal following of movie fans from all over the world, people who share a love of cinema and a sense of humour. The success of Dark Corners directly gave rise to The Universal Library…
@DarkCorners3

The Universal Library

The idea of a series of books featuring characters from horror's golden age initially came when the movies themselves were being re-booted, and while those reboots have now gone in a very different direction, the books remain a tongue-in-cheek, but respectful, take on the classics. Hopefully the series meets with the approval of horror fans, film fans and neophytes alike.

Facebook – The Universal Library

Printed in Great Britain
by Amazon